D0387572

Dallas Public Library
950 Main Street
Dallas, OR 97338

the
BEAUTIFUL
DREAM *of* LIFE

the
BEAUTIFUL
DREAM *of* LIFE

A NOVEL

DOMINGO ZAPATA

GALLERY BOOKS

new york   london   toronto   sydney   new delhi

2/17

G

Gallery Books
An Imprint of Simon & Schuster, Inc.
1230 Avenue of the Americas
New York, NY 10020

This book is a work of fiction. Any references to historical events, real people, or real places are used fictitiously. Other names, characters, places, and events are products of the author's imagination, and any resemblance to actual events or places or persons, living or dead, is entirely coincidental.

Copyright © 2017 by Domingo Zapata

All rights reserved, including the right to reproduce this book or portions thereof in any form whatsoever. For information, address Gallery Books Subsidiary Rights Department, 1230 Avenue of the Americas, New York, NY 10020.

First Gallery Books hardcover edition July 2017

GALLERY BOOKS and colophon are registered trademarks of Simon & Schuster, Inc.

For information about special discounts for bulk purchases, please contact Simon & Schuster Special Sales at 1-866-506-1949 or business@simonandschuster.com.

The Simon & Schuster Speakers Bureau can bring authors to your live event. For more information or to book an event, contact the Simon & Schuster Speakers Bureau at 1-866-248-3049 or visit our website at www.simonspeakers.com.

Interior design by Jaime Putorti

Manufactured in the United States of America

10 9 8 7 6 5 4 3 2 1

Library of Congress Cataloging-in-Publication Data is available.

ISBN 978-1-5011-2925-4
ISBN 978-1-5011-2926-1 (ebook)

To my children, the light of my life:
Domingo Jr. and Paul

Dallas Public Library
950 Main Street
Dallas, OR 97338

The king dreams he is a king,
And in this delusive way
Lives and rules with sovereign sway;
All the cheers that round him ring,
Born of air, on air take wing.
And in ashes (mournful fate!)
Death dissolves his pride and state:
Who would wish a crown to take,
Seeing that he must awake
In the dream beyond death's gate? . . .
'Tis a dream that I in sadness
Here am bound, the scorn of fate;
'Twas a dream that once a state
I enjoyed of light and gladness.
What is life? 'Tis but a madness.
What is life? A thing that seems,
A mirage that falsely gleams,
Phantom joy, delusive rest,
Since is life a dream at best,
And even dreams themselves are dreams.

—Pedro Calderón de la Barca, *Life Is a Dream,* 1635
(Translated by Edward Fitzgerald)

the
BEAUTIFUL
DREAM *of* LIFE

PROLOGUE

In dreams, everything is possible." I heard it in a whisper reminiscent of my mother's voice, as I lay in that exquisite state between a fractured floating sleep and a sobered reality. I had been out on the town the previous night, tossing back considerable quantities of Scotch as I made the rounds, not an uncommon occurrence for me. In fact, I did it almost every night, if you must know—and I do want you to know. I will tell you the truth; I won't sugarcoat my wild nights and club-hopping and extracurricular pursuits and "biological exploits" and painful wake-ups.

"In dreams, everything is possible."

My mother had first told me this old saying when I was a small child longing to be an artist. I didn't understand whether she meant "If you *believe* in your dreams, *anything* is possible," or "*In your dreams, everything* is possible."

As an aspiring artist, I was attracted to the abstract meaning of it, to the infinite possibilities that a dream has to offer—a mental landscape that is limitless in your imagination, where anything can and will happen during deep sleep.

In reality this was the way I conceived my works of art and the way I became an artist: a dream was like a nocturnal canvas, emanating from my soul and dwelling in the profound recesses of my mind, where, on a nightly basis, I devised and revised it, brushstroked and finessed it, until it was ready to be put to paint and color in the physical world—or not.

HEARING MY MOTHER'S VOICE in my head took me back to my childhood in Mallorca, where I first learned to paint. My most prized possession at the time was a little red box; I still have it. Back then, the little red box was my personal coin safe: it held my meager wages from summer employment, the fruits of labors including the imperfect washing of cars, uneven lawn mowing, and other hastily performed odd jobs. I was saving my money, for what I can't remember. Probably to buy something for Luisa with the long black hair. That sounds right. Any beautiful girl—with hair of any length—who I was convinced needed my gifts, sounds right.

My father suggested that I, Rodrigo Concepción, his precocious and hyperactive child, should open my own savings account at our local bank. Skeptical of anyone handling my hard-earned wages, I of course had questions for him.

"Will they keep these same dollars for me and not let anyone else touch them? This ten, this twenty, all these ones, and change—will they give this money back to me?"

When my father explained to me that the bank would not return the very same physical stack of bills and coins, but others totaling the same amount, I became very upset.

"But I don't want other dollars. Why won't they give me back exactly what I give them? That's not fair. And, Dad?"

"Yes, Rodrigo?"

"Will they keep my red box?"

This was my introduction to one of the ways of the world. But it was also an introduction to the way I saw the world: from a different angle.

It wasn't that I was miserly or carrying a torch for societal fairness, it was that I didn't want to be taken advantage of. In the case of the little red box and its contents, I suspected that someone might be pulling a fast one on me.

THESE WERE SOME of the splintered thoughts I had on a November morning in Manhattan, when I woke up with yet another metal spike pounding away at my skull, after yet another night on the town. I had been an artist for a long time now, and had achieved some success, even fame, but something intangible was missing from my life, and I had been out in search of more. What I had found so far was more alcohol, more drugs, more women. I guess that made my life, if nothing else, a tad exhilarating, if not shameful as well. But that is for others to decide.

"In dreams, everything is possible." Even the beautiful dream of life. Then I had such a dream, and I held on to it for dear life, even while I was on the verge of falling into the abyss.

And now, as I promised, I will tell you what happened.

part one

MY WORLD

1

SOHO DAZE

f you had peered through my window and observed my life, you might not have thought there was much to inspire pity. I lived in a SoHo loft with sixteen-foot-high tin ceilings and a smattering of murals left on the walls from the artists who'd worked and lived there before me. It was a privileged existence; even I can't deny it.

"Morning, sir."

On that day Alfonso, my butler, was right on time with my survival kit: black coffee, Advil, a joint, and omega-3 fish oil tabs served on a silver tray.

"Morning, Alfonso. My paper?"

He withdrew it from beneath his wing and extended it. "Yes, sir. Crispy, as you like it."

He maneuvered over to the windows facing Wooster Street and opened the shades on the dark and shadowed room. He left the windows raised slightly, allowing the chill of the morning air to pass through. It was always soothing to feel that first fresh gust of the day sweeping from one end of the loft to the other.

Alfonso was Italian, with slicked-back hair, a furrowed brow, and a slender yet athletic frame. He had trained to be a butler, and his presence was something of an incongruity with the artist loft apartment. I must say the artist in me appreciated his traditional trappings, even though I was a painter of contemporary urban art. I enjoyed the contrast, juxtaposing the classic with the nouveau. Even Alfonso himself could be considered an installation conceived and positioned in that regard. Prop or hired necessity, the man was competent, dutiful, and well apprised that my bedroom constituted a judgment-free zone.

As the parting gesture to our morning ritual, Alfonso twisted on my bath, and the brass fixtures shrieked as he adjusted them to the perfect temperature. When he left the bedroom, he was as silent as the cool breeze he had let in. I downed my dose, detached and disassociated myself from all things bed, and plopped with little grace into the tub for the big soak.

In the bath I would try to reconstruct my dreams from the night before. I had always dreamed extensively every night, but lately I often had a difficult time remembering them. Maybe it was my own mind protecting me from myself, rejecting these unsettling nocturnal visions and surreal, eerie fantasies. I had had no blow to the head and never suffered from hallucinations or endured any type of psychotic break, but as an artist, when the dreams came, I had to follow them. I felt their presence lurking in my subconscious, haunting me.

While I lay back and tried to recall these elusive phantasms, Rafaela pitter-patted into the adjacent bedroom. Rafaela was more a friend than an employee, and though she was in her late thirties, you'd never know she was no longer the gorgeous twentysomething Colombian model of yesteryear. Her skin was olive, tight, and smooth, her face refined and sculpted, with mesmerizing blue eyes that were all her own. Her South American beauty lit up the loft. I was attracted to beautiful art, destinations, landscapes, and unforgettable faces, and I confess Rafaela's *belleza* had indeed been a factor in her hiring. More important than her beauty, however, was her competence: Rafaela kept my overwhelming daily agenda of appointments and committments straight for me. The demands on my time were way more than I could have managed on my own.

She also kept me in line. She was a cherished confidante and semi-pro life coach. I had fame, money, and beautiful women throwing themselves at me like I was some sort of god. But Rafaela didn't "yes" me; rather, she told it as she saw it, a bottom-line type that I desperately needed to help keep my life on track. And man, was it nice to look at her during her no-nonsense lectures. Any lecture. Any time.

"Rafaela, *amor!*" I bellowed in desperate Spanish-American-bullshitter slang.

She was used to my high-velocity hollow charm and said nothing. Carrying her clipboard, she sidled before me barefoot, wearing yoga pants and a stretch top with nipple pops. She took one look at me in the tub and began to reassemble the ponytail mechanism corralling her thick dirty-blond mane.

"You look like shit, Rodrigo," she said through gritted teeth as she clamped the tortoiseshell hair fastener in place.

"I feel vulnerable," I spun offhandedly.

She laughed that one off, as she should have. "And you stink of alcohol. You're still drunk."

"Perhaps. But look at me. I'm here all stripped. And insecure. And unsure. Of myself. And everyone around me."

"Bah!" she volleyed.

"Including you." I smiled then.

"You missed your calling. You should have been an actor."

"And to further my weakness, I'm naked in front of you."

"I prefer to call it sexual harassment. On your part. But I'll let it slide. Today," she added.

"Will you turn on the music, please?"

She snapped on the bathroom stereo, and a wicked AC/DC number made the house tremble.

"So, did you get *biological* last night?" she asked, using my own language against me.

"You know, Rafaela, you're like an old wife. The dreaded ball and chain. The one that *I don't get to fuck!*"

"Come on, Rodrigo, you probably fucked the entire city last night."

I sighed and lit up the joint that was the most essential part of my survival kit tray. Marijuana was crucial to my existence. I was hasty. I was manic. I had the metabolism of four hummingbirds, and I zoomed along at bottle-rocket speed. The morning treatment of weed helped calm me and keep me in bounds.

Did I have a problem? Of course. A few. But, I kept telling myself, the main one I suffered from was of the hyperkinetic variety. That was the real challenge: to slow down. Everything else I indulged in was a sedative or numbing agent to counter it.

This was my mood weather pattern on a daily basis: a bit breezy and abstract in the morning, with a touch of clouds that burned off by the midday sunshine, beholden to and in anticipation of a clear and crisp night that, with any luck, may involve moonlight. Or not.

I pushed aside any stray thought that might upset this delicate balance and remind me that my current lifestyle could result in situations with a strong potential to make me miserable. Maybe even freak me out.

"Your suitcase is ready."

"For what?"

"You have a plane to catch." She eyeballed her clipboard and spun down the volume on the stereo. "Time to get dressed."

"Don't turn it off! That's the best part!"

"You don't have time! Tex is picking you up in twenty minutes!"

Rafaela went over the healthy options. "I'll lay out your vitamins. Did you take your omegas?" She did look out for me, and I loved her caring, maternal side.

"Yes, *amor*," I said sweetly. "You're coming, aren't you? Art Basel won't be the same without you."

"Later flight."

"Promise?"

"I always come. You know that. Otherwise who would be there to hold your hand once you landed?"

"I *am* an actor, you know. And it's all an act. I play helpless so you'll stay close to me."

"I know that, too."

"So that one day, maybe—"

"Enough! Get ready!"

Like a child obeying his mother, I got out of the tub, took my vitamins, and dressed. I was ready to go downstairs and meet Tex.

2

THE TECH COWBOY

I n the bright morning sunshine, a diamond-black Rolls-Royce Celestial Phantom pulled up on Wooster Street and hummed down to an idle. Michael, the driver, wore the traditional black-and-white garb of a chauffeur and doubled as Tex's bodyguard. He got out—all seven feet of him—popped open an umbrella, and opened the rear passenger door. Tex emerged in his white suit, obscene yellow sunglasses, and signature red hair. His father had made big money in the oil business, and Tex used some of the spillover funds right after graduating from Texas Tech to found and cash in on several startup Internet companies and smartphone applications. Given the family money, plus what he'd earned on his own, Tex was worth a good billion dollars at this point, and he was a better-than-an-acquaintance friend of mine, for good reason. Tex had bought a fair number of my pieces over the years and always paid top dollar.

I'd met him at a SoHo gallery art opening, and this self-anointed "King of Fun" had shown me immediately how he'd earned his nickname. We became partners in crime, going out carousing and chasing girls, enjoying generally debauched excursions together to St. Tropez, St. Barts, Ibiza, and other saturated hot spots. Tex had a Gulfstream V, and he traveled well and heartily, and in that regard he was easy to spend time with.

For all of his twenty-first-century tech success and modern know-how, however, you could never take the backwoods Texas upbringing out of him. Having never been schooled in the finer things, he shamelessly lacked class, etiquette, and sophistication. He wore tacky clothes and bought tacky toys. This redneck geek was American nouveau riche at its finest—he did everything over the top. Hence the extravagant arrival.

The fact that I was Rodrigo Concepción, an artist and famous for it, made me attractive to Tex. That was clear. Our friendship had to be based on more than merely pursuing ladies after midnight. The truth was, had there been no commercial element to our union, we probably wouldn't have been friends. Tex would fly all over the globe in his GV to throw down bids at art fairs and fancy auction houses, party like a rock star on a nightly basis, and brag about it. He was savvy enough to recognize that if he bought art and became a known commodity in the art world, it would give his personal profile a boost in the direction of being perceived as cultured.

I followed Alfonso and my packed rolling bag out the front door. Tex was there to greet us on the front walk, standing under the umbrella held by Michael. We squeezed each other with a warm locker-room hug.

"Come on, Tex, it's beautiful out!" I derided him, nodding at the umbrella. Tex had a strong aversion to the sun and would never let it touch his skin if he could avoid it. "You could use a little sunlight."

"I hate the fuckin' sun." Tex was also a germophobe and always afraid of getting sick, which I found odd for a Texan. It may have been the most interesting quirk about him.

"Might be good for you."

"Cocaine and pussy are good for me. You can have the sun."

"Just be careful you don't get burned . . ."

"Amen," he allowed. We piled into the vast rear interior of the Rolls, and our voyage to Teterboro Airport was under way. Tex immediately made us a couple of Scotch and Cokes with spring-break-bartender fervor.

"You know this was the last car trip John F. Kennedy Jr. ever took," Tex semi-boasted.

"How upbeat of you. Cheers to better luck." We tapped lowballs, and as I sipped on mine, Tex downed his in one haul and poured another.

He reached for his glowing laptop on the side table and placed it before us, then proceeded to fly through about fifty young fashion-model portfolios, mostly naked shots.

"They'll all be in Miami," he stated. "And check this out—" He flipped to a picture on his iPhone.

"Another Picasso?"

"Damn straight, just bought it."

"How much?"

"Thirteen million. What do you think?"

I hesitated and distilled out the envy that was weighing down my voice. "I think you have one of the best collections money can buy."

I wasn't envious of Picasso or the prices his work commanded. It was that Tex could have three squares a day surrounded by some of the world's greatest art treasures—and they were just accessories to him. Of course, then I thought of other wealthy collectors I knew. Were they really any different? It is, was, and always has been about *show*—acquiring and having as many treasures as possible.

Having presented his new acquisition for maximum-impress effect, Tex fiddled with the overhead command center, and some explosive music from a rock band called 4AM took over in a deafening thumpa-thon. At eleven in the morning. In the midst of my hangover.

"Tiësto for breakfast?" I remarked, referring to the Dutch DJ who had promoted the band and made them famous.

"This is their performance live from Rio, 2012. Does it get any better?"

"Yes. If we had Molly."

"If?" Tex sent right back with a mischievous grin. And with that, he withdrew from his white jacket a baggie filled with white baby capsules. We laughed evily.

"Later," I suggested. Tex stashed them away in silent agreement.

Right then I experienced a downtick, a rapid shift in feeling. I had experienced it occasionally for years, but recently, it had been occurring more often, without warning, and it threw me into an unpredictable state of mind quite unlike that of my usual self; also, I seemed to have no control over its coming or going or how I felt during or afterward. It was the dreaded disconnect, one of the things I didn't like to think about, that always made me feel like someone else was living my life for me, and I was watching it all happen helplessly from above.

3

THE RAVEN

No one knew his real name or why he was called The Raven. Where he came from was anyone's guess, and no one particularly cared. He simply appeared, and he was the type of jackass you loved to hate unless he was on your team; then he was a welcome, indispensable guest. The Raven was a provider. A procurer. His commodity: women. Beautiful women. The young, impressionable ones. The mid-twenties, more seasoned ones. The older, somewhat wiser ones who were hanging around a little too long, still in search of a scene and the hip place to be. When it came to inviting and corralling these international beauties—models, mostly, the most glamorous twenty-first-century commodity—The Raven was a genius.

You can groan, complain, and roll your eyes at the word "model," but at the end of the day their impact is immediate: they can incite the envy of women and men in seconds, and suck the oxygen from a room in minutes. It all begins and ends with one definite asset—beauty.

The Raven's personality was not electric, but it was effective. He tossed off enough macho, enough cool, and enough of a sense of humor to get beautiful models to like him. Or to feel comfortable with him, which was all that was needed, really. If you asked him, he'd say he was in PR. But he was really the fool of the court of any sufficiently affluent and important person who was in need of his services.

In actuality, The Raven was creepy, a little sweaty, and had a noticeable belly. He was rather disgusting in that he lived like a rock star without a nickel in his pocket. He was a dolce vita disaster who always hung with the biggest names, boarded the biggest boats, frequented the most beautiful houses, rode in the most expensive cars, drank the best wine, consumed the best drugs, sat at the best tables. He was always broke and borrowing, but this total shipwreck of a guy had one talent, and that talent was finding the greatest girls in the world and getting them to simply . . . come along. The deal was he'd get a hundred dollars per girl.

The Raven stepped into the cabin of Tex's GV, which was parked on the Teterboro tarmac, and he did not disappoint. Although they were half an hour late in arriving, the models had indeed come along, and they kept on coming, up the stairs and through the doorway, ten in total.

"Sorry I'm late. We had to wait for Amber," The Raven stated in a scolding tone, and pushed his ornate black-and-gold D&G shields partway down his nose, the better to eyeball the girl in question. In this arena, beauty needed to be tamed, and The Raven was a maestro. "Don't ever do that again."

"I'm sorry," the drop-dead-beautiful brunette with the most perfectly shaped hornet-stung lips said meekly.

For the entire flight from New York to Miami, the jet was transformed into an EDM rave complete with disco lights, bottle service, coke, and Molly. The girls were dancing, jumping, making out with everyone and one another. I remember three pairs of breasts lined up before me in the bathroom as I performed some form of Charmin squeeze test crossed with a Himalayan alpine climb. There may have been some fellatio involved, too, when one pair dropped suddenly out of sight.

"Hey, Rodrigo, you got that five hundred?" The Raven asked just then.

"What five hundred?"

"Need to borrow it for my phone bill."

"Did you ask me for it?"

"Tried texting, but my phone didn't work. Dude, my phone is off—"

"So be it," I think I said. I sometimes said that. But I may have said instead, "Sure, no problem." In the circumstances, I really wasn't paying that much attention to what I was saying. And despite the attention of the models, I was still in a strange mood.

But later on, when I tried to recall the events of the trip, this was the only spoken exchange I could remember from the plane. And it hadn't even been with one of the unbelievably beautiful models; it had been with The Raven.

4

TOWER SWEET

A glaze seemed to be covering my eyeballs. I became aware that I was in bed in an immense room. Across the immaculate white expanse of the room, I could make out the unmistakable curves of a woman's beautiful backside in the bathroom. At first I wondered if I was dreaming. I must have slept through much of the afternoon, and when I tried to recap the day's activities after the hazy plane trip, I could not remember anything that would have inspired this gorgeous rear-end cameo. All was quiet until: "Rodrigo, time to get ready . . ."

I opened my eyes and Rafaela was looking down at me, her hair wet.

"I used your shower. I hope you don't mind."

I was still too groggy.

"My room wasn't ready yet. The previous guests wouldn't leave, and there weren't any other rooms. Place is packed."

"You have a beautiful ass."

"What? You were watching me?"

"I think so. I knew it would be, too."

"Be what?"

"Perfect."

I rolled over and groaned into the pillow. The groan was a release of angst brought on by my present headache, frustration at never being able to touch Rafaela, and wondering what the hell had happened on that plane ride.

I ordered OWC and showered quickly. The One While Changing feature was a courtesy perk for those inhabiting tower suites at the Soho Beach House, Miami's outpost of the exclusive London club. A bartender came to your room and served you while you got dressed or engaged in whatever activity you had in mind. I needed to equilibrate myself, and a dry martini was the appropriate hair of the dog.

The suite was enormous—an entire floor, one giant room with a bathroom. There were leather club chairs, a freestanding bathtub, fainting couches, Cuban tile floors, and oceanfront views. It was London-between-the-wars meets Havana-before-the-revolution. In lieu of a minibar was a maxibar, a gorgeous art deco reproduction stocked with lemons and limes, an impressive array of crystal stemware, and a silver cocktail shaker. I counted thirteen liquor bottles. And the act of counting made my head start to grieve again. Make no mistake, Art Basel was the international art world's excuse to have a party, and the Soho House was *the* place to be. And if you had a suite, so very much the better.

Rafaela and I debated a quick dip in the plunge pool on 8, but realized we didn't have time. We needed to get to the marina.

After the early-evening cocktail, in true fiesta fashion Rafaela and I found ourselves speeding across the waterway in Tex's lemon-colored Cigarette boat with the name *Viagra* emblazoned on either side in electric blue. Pfizer normally paid for the advertising, but Tex welcomed the Viagra logo free of charge. We were on our way to an exclusive charity dinner and auction on Hibiscus Island. Michael was there, too, and thankfully, he'd left the umbrella behind. But I was happy he was with us, because I was certain we'd need his talents as a body defender soon enough.

The kickoff event was being held at Avi Scheiner-Ross's notoriously overdone house, which was less infamous than the owner himself. Many things had been said about this Israeli who had made Miami his home: rumors concerning everything from guns, to planes, to drugs. And that type of sinister ambience was perfect for the sit-down dinner for forty, held in the luscious garden, where the cream of the art world's buyers and sellers convened—stars and starlets, and of course billionaire collectors, too. The party was a private viewing of artworks by assorted contemporary artists, and it served as a preview for the big show at the Convention Center the following day. To get things rolling and to raise money for a local Miami cause, a representative from Christie's was to auction ten pieces before the doors were opened to the after-dinner crowd.

I greeted everyone, most of whom I knew, and although I'm generally considered a gregarious and genial guy, it wasn't long before I became sufficiently bored and emotionally detached to want to get away from the crowd. Was it some kind of lingering effect from the downtick I had experienced earlier in the day, in Tex's limo? I didn't know. I pulled up a seat for Rafaela so she could sit next to me, and I didn't give a damn if anyone got upset.

"Are you okay?" she asked thoughtfully. She even patted my thigh.

I just looked at her. The answer was a resounding "no," but I chose to remain silent. I was already tired of the talk, the stroking, the bullshit, and the bullshitters. And the auction hadn't even started.

About halfway through a performance by African-American men in diapers wielding swords and ladies on stilts, I got up to find Tex, who seemed to have vanished. No doubt he was rifling rails in a bathroom somewhere, and I was soon on a mission to join him. As I passed through gaudy rooms adorned by Avi's collection of ancient Samurai swords, I felt a sudden rush of indigestion and I began to sweat. I crept up the stairs slowly, holding on to the banister, only to come upon another display I wasn't likely to forget soon.

The party's host, who had been absent from and oblivious to the festivities below, was whipping a naked woman chained to the wall. She had bright ruby lips and a Catwoman mask. The dominator was wearing a black leather Speedo and face mask. The woman craned her head slightly and looked at me, and I could see the most curious expression in her eyes and on the part of her face not covered by the mask—a certain sadness pushing through her seeming attempt at kink and submission. Had it been the me of yesteryear, the righteous, caring man of conviction and defender of Good, I would have released her. I moved on quickly, although the host did twist back and see me.

"I'm sorry you had to see that," he said deceptively, then laughed uproariously. And he resumed his activities without closing the door.

As I looked back over my shoulder in astonishment at the scene playing out, I rammed right into none other than Tex himself, who had found a pretty blond partner with whom to go extracurricular.

"What do you think of the art?" he said, all jittered up.

"Who cares?" I said, deadpan.

"Here," he said, and jammed a packet into my palm. "It's all yours."

I thanked him and proceeded to find the nearest party corner. I was not really worried about anyone witnessing my intake, largely because of the medieval Olympics going on nearby. It made my indulgence seem rather tame in comparison. Any discretion at this point was overkill.

When I returned to the table, Rafaela was gone, and the waiters were presenting dessert. As I looked around, I had the conscious feeling of a frenzy being whipped up. I could feel the energy, and there was noise coming from outside the house. Certainly, the after-dinner throng of scenesters, wannabes, and hobnobbing hopefuls had col-

lected outside, trying to get in. I took it all in and sniffled several times.

An aggressive hand assaulted my shoulder. "Hey, where's The Raven?" It was Tex again, and I just shrugged. The Raven, who hadn't been invited to the exclusive dinner, had planned to arrive for the party afterward. Tex moved on to table-hop. He was running on bathroom inspiration, and from this jacked-up perspective, he felt comfortable enough to assault the famous crowd.

"There you are," a half-panicked voice said in my ear. Without turning around, I knew it was Jazzy. She was a pal, too, and we'd been fucking around for a couple years. Her eyes were buzzing and she looked disheveled, with her long, wavy black hair twisted in an awkward low knot. "I've been looking all over for you."

"Here I am."

Exasperated, she plopped herself down in the seat next to me. "This party sucks." Jazzy, a singer, was a constant target of the press and the paparazzi, and a lot of it had to do with her own publicity-generating antics. She was part African American and gifted with a gorgeous face and café au lait skin, like a modern Beverly Johnson. She was a mess, really, a victim of the prototypical torture that often accompanied her half-white, half-black lineage. On top of that she was a pop singer, a profession that offered a perfect storm of psychological pressure on an already troubled psyche. She rope-swung through unfulfilling romances and relationships, and she'd been in and out of rehab for drugs and alcohol. She was not supposed to be out or be seen out, especially in a way-public scene as explosive as Art Basel.

"How are you, babes? Are you hungry?" I said.

She looked at me like the thought of food hadn't been enticing to her in several years. As we looked around, we could see the party growing in numbers, more and more people shooting past us to the open bar.

"I barely got onto the island. There's a total traffic jam of cars trying to get in, cars getting blocked from leaving. There are so many cops out there. I saw The Raven, too."

"What was he doing?"

"Trying to get in, but he was getting pushed around by the crowd."

I overheard someone saying the auction had raised fifteen million dollars.

Just then I could feel the weight of something. Danger, perhaps. It seemed the place was getting out of control, transforming into some sort of Caligula-style free-for-all. Pushing, drinking, clamoring, laughing, yelling, and it was getting deeply primal very fast.

"Let's escape," I suggested just as Jazzy said, "Let's get the fuck out of here." We both knew that much.

I took Jazzy by the arm, and we dashed toward the entrance past a brace of cops who seemed determined to shut the party down. As we slipped past the hordes desperate to get in the front gate, I heard The Raven's unmistakable voice frantically calling my name, but I didn't want to deal, so I pretended not to hear him. Then I heard him groan like he was getting sideswiped. I looked back and saw a cop giving him a hard time and roughing him up a bit. The Raven could "cop an attitude," too, as his years of dolce vita access made him feel, act, and talk superior to the masses—police included.

Jazzy and I quickly realized there was no way we'd get a cab in such a cluster-fuck mess. "How did *you* get here?" she asked, looking around for a way out.

Of course: I had come over on Tex's boat. As Jazzy and I spun around and carved our way through the rapidly increasing crowd to go in the direction of the private dock, I had the feeling of becoming unglued from everything around me. I wondered if it was a cocaine-infused reaction to the swirling crowd.

Finally, we made it to the *Viagra*. I thanked the skipper for taking

us on board and instructed him to go back to the party to get Tex and his entourage after he dropped us off.

"He already left. They went to the club, but he told me to get you. They're waiting for you at The Rock."

"Oh," I said. "Thanks."

Soon we were charging back across the waterways. I could see the choke of cars and the sea of brake lights on the mainland, all lined up trying to get onto Hibiscus Island.

We hailed a cab and instructed the driver to take us to The Rock. As soon as I had a moment to myself, looking out at the beautiful sweep of lights emanating from downtown Miami, Jazzy's lips landed on mine, and we made out the rest of the way. I stuck a decent but polite finger beneath her skirt and let it swim in her pussy for a while to make us both feel like we were actually having a great time. Perhaps we were. It didn't really matter one way or the other.

And then I thought about the face of the woman with the Catwoman mask and bright red lips. The woman the host had been whipping. I wondered what she thought of the art.

WE PULLED UP BEFORE The Rock Lounge at the Mina Hotel, and I shoved the cabdriver some cash. As we emerged, the paparazzi went nuts, and Jazzy shielded her face with a scarf while I just looked down.

"*Hey, Rodrigo, who you with?*"

"Not tonight, guys . . . not in the mood . . ."

"*Not in the mood? It's fucking Art Basel!*"

"*Who are you with?*"

"*Who you meeting?*"

The flock of paparazzi followed us right up to the velvet ropes.

"*Hey, Rodrigo, who's inside, anyone famous?*"

"I'm beautiful, famous, and have more money than Santa Claus. Who else needs to be here?"

Julio, the doorman, got a kick out of that one and smiled as he ushered us in. The joint was jumping to some house grooves. I saw Tex there, doing his "shopping for tables" thing. His MO was never to make a reservation at the hottest places, and then to show up with ten people, an entourage to exclude you from any possible table consideration. He'd walk around, spot a good table, and say something along the lines of "Good evening, ladies and gentlemen, my name is Tex, and I am the King of Fun." Then he would show them the cover of some recent financial periodical with his picture on it, *Fortune* or *Forbes* or the *WSJ,* that he always carried folded up in his suit-coat pocket. "I started at the bottom, but now, well, here we are. I apologize, I forgot to book a table, but I would love to offer you a nice sum for yours, say, forty thousand dollars? Sorry, ladies, I don't mean to be rude, I've been travelin' a lot, and I just want to have a great night with my friends. Of course, my offer is to this fine gentleman for his table, but all you ladies, the beautiful angels of the world that you are, are more than welcome to stay."

Once the guys picked their jaws up off the floor, they would snatch the bank check made out to cash and magically disappear. The young ladies were usually all too happy to stay. And at that price, the guys didn't really mind. I found the routine somewhat funny, as crass as it was.

"Hi, Rodrigo." The shapely young maître d' greeted me with a total-body embrace that told me I could have a table or anything else I wanted. I had her number but hadn't been around to give her a call yet. But she was worth the time. As she held on to me, I could see the row of annoyed faces impatiently waiting for her attention and service.

"Thank you, darling. I'm with Tex tonight. Don't need a table." And I said, out of earshot of Jazzy, "But your company is always appreciated."

"I'll come by," she said slyly.

The Rock was one of South Beach's celebrity-friendly boîtes. It was smaller and cozier than a lot of the other Miami clubs and had great DJs who made it a dance party. It was always filled with hot girls and models and various movie and rock stars.

After successfully negotiating yet another table takeover, Tex waved at us, and we joined him and his posse of newfound honeys, several gals he had piled onto the *Viagra* who weren't going to call it a night after that kind of ride. The rest of the girls had decided to stay on after the table had been literally bought off their escorts. Tex was already fueling their palms with his pocket powders as we sat down.

Mario, the portly owner, came up and comped a bottle for the table, which was gracious. But any time I appeared, he would hit me up for some reciprocal artwork. I could always feel it coming, too.

"Say, Rodrigo, when you going to do that drawing for me?"

"Mario, dear boy, I don't really feel like getting into the restaurant business tonight. Some other time."

Tex heard the irritation in my voice and broke up laughing, and the others caught on and laughed, too. At least they made it look like they'd understood what I meant. It was a riff off the old Picasso urban legend. Mario just walked off without saying anything.

The energy was at full tilt. The multicolored lights transformed the room into a surreal dream. I looked at Jazzy, sitting next to me, and she was crying. The lights made her makeup look like rainbows smudged with black paths where her tears were trailing down her cheeks.

"You okay?" I asked as quietly as I could.

She just held her head low and shook. I looked up and saw a bunch of people eyeballing her. It wasn't the time or place to ask why she was crying; these people didn't need to hear any answer that might cause trouble for her if the press got hold of it.

"Let's get out of here," I said.

We left Tex and his entourage to finish the place off, and took a taxi to the next club, an Art Basel pop-up of a New York club, housed at a local hotel.

I knew the owners from New York, and they'd informed me about the secret entrance. We were slotted at one of the best tables, and I took in the scene with a detached amusement. There were more movie stars and star athletes, and the Cristal was immediately popped and flowing. It soon turned into a splashing champagne extravaganza, and everyone was getting soaked.

I had a tableful of beautiful girls not even thinking of going home any time soon. And then it happened. As I spent some significant club time at other tables catching up with some acquaintances, I noticed Jazzy stand up at our table, slam down her drink, and run off.

"Where did she go?" I asked our waiter.

"She was mouthing off about your leaving her at the table and seemed pretty pissed. Think she went to the bathroom."

That didn't sound good, given Jazzy's history and her long list of late-night weaknesses. But by then I was more concerned about the fact that she was trying to cramp my style than that she was indulging in her usual theatrics. I wondered, *What the fuck am I doing here with her, anyway, when she's acting like this?*

I decided to make a bold move in the hope of salvaging the rest of my night. At the next booth over, I eyeballed two models who seemed to be good friends.

"Hey, you and you. Come with me," I commanded.

"What?" said one.

"Now?" said the other.

They looked at each other and shrugged with smiles that seemed to appreciate my directness, after what had probably been an evening full of shy and awkward marauders hounding them but lacking the cojones to tell them what to do or where to go. All they needed was a plan.

I grabbed each by the hand and walked them to the front door. The locusts were out there flash-popping away, creating another blinding explosion, but I didn't give a damn.

"Rodrigo!"

"Hey, amigo, look this way!"

"Who you got there?"

"Thing One and Thing Two?"

I waited for an unoccupied cab and put up with the attention from the paparazzi. After all, I didn't like what they did, nothing about it—unless they *didn't* do it, and that, it could safely be stated, was the era's catechism.

We piled into a seventies hack and headed back to the Soho House. The ride over was forgettable.

I made a round of drinks, we got to know one another for about seven more minutes, I told them what was going to happen, that we were all on the same team. And we needed teamwork. I unzipped them out of their dresses, stripped comfortably myself, and then we powdered and sniffed off of one another's bodies. Each line placement became riskier until we had nothing left to hide. I shredded bedsheets and made ties. I fucked them both together, then apart while the third party gave erotic boosts from above or below. But it wasn't a one-way street or some form of male domination. They even had their way with me, to satisfy any personal needs they may have had for revenge on the male species—needs that, as I found out, were considerable.

5

THE SHOW; OR NOT

opened sore eyes with aching eye sockets. They were fixated on something wide and white and soothing. The ceiling. For some reason, I feared casting an eye around the expansive space. Rafaela appeared in my periphery, which was a relief. I peered lower and saw that the spacious open room was empty.

I looked to Rafaela.

"They're gone," she said reassuringly. "I untied you."

"Are you sure they're gone?"

"Poz."

"Thank God, I can have breakfast now." I rubbed my wrists, which showed red constriction marks. *"Gracias"* coughed out of my throat.

"I gave them forty dollars for a taxi. You owe me."

"No problem."

She slapped the day's *New York Post* on the bed. "Nice job." Some of my night's antics were featured on Page Six.

I eyeballed her and had nothing to say.

"Anyway, you have an interview in half an hour. Luckily, it's downstairs."

I groaned. When I was younger, and just starting out with the first exhibits of my work, I thought—as everyone does—that publicity and fame and critical acclaim would be exciting and I would love all of it. But demands on my time and energy from both the public and the press became overwhelming and repetitive, and now it was mostly the same old drill, telling the same old stories.

After a decent shower, under a showerhead large enough to provide rejuvenating steaming-hot hydrotherapy, I went downstairs and met with a bunch of journalists to talk the talk for a couple of hours. Then I had a private sit-down with a foreign art publication that wanted to feature my works in France and Italy, and despite my ennui, I had to admit that it was nice for my work to be appreciated. Afterward Rafaela and I grabbed a cab and buzzed off to the Convention Center for the preview show. I greeted everyone warmly, feeling somewhat revived and vital and of this world again.

As I was making my rounds, I heard a commotion, and Rafaela pressed my arm to get my attention. "Look at the door." The Raven was jumping up and down, frantically gesturing, looking gamy and sweaty and still wearing his previous day's clothes. We walked toward him.

The guard looked at us in surprise. "He says he's a friend of yours, Mr. Concepción."

"Yes. Let him in," I said neutrally. As soon as he was allowed inside, he made a beeline right toward me. "Yo, what happened to you last night?" I said, playing dumb. It was the only way. "You got lost—"

"My phone wasn't working! I told you!" he semi-shouted, and that pissed me off.

"All right. Get lost, for real—"

Since some serious collectors were standing nearby, Rafaela guided me away from the pathetic and grizzled Raven to avoid a potentially embarrassing scene.

"What about my five hundred bucks? I need it, Rodrigo!" he called after us, referring to his request from when we were on Tex's plane and I was in the bathroom with the models.

Rafaela spun back and handed The Raven a twenty-dollar bill. "Now go use a pay phone."

This encounter with The Raven, small as it was, was enough to change my mood from upbeat to dark, then angry. It happened so quickly it took me by surprise, especially since I had been savoring the attention and the positive reaction my work was receiving.

I was upset, but I spoke with each of the collectors anyway. Each worth five hundred million to a billion dollars. Schmoozing with the people who would buy my paintings was an activity I normally enjoyed, but suddenly, I didn't care. I didn't like them. I didn't like the way they dressed. Or the things they said. Sure, they were smooth and urbane, but that was all a cover. They were unctuous, too. They were no better than that Israeli host at his whipping post. They might have been worse, because they caught people unaware. Fooling them. Conning them. Cheating them. At least The Whipper played it straight, as in, what you see is what you get. You come, you get whipped. You don't come, you wonder what you missed. And basta.

Here I was, Rodrigo Concepción, a famous artist at the artist's Super Bowl. Art Basel. And I didn't give a shit. I truly didn't. For quite some time now, especially whenever the downtick took over my emotions, the feeling of being disconnected, of disgust and anger at the phoniness I saw everywhere, of dissatisfaction with my own life and even my own paintings, had been building up, and I had had enough. I had always aspired to do better, to improve with each painting—any serious artist does—but during the disconnect, this feeling of discontent seemed to encompass my whole world and was something bigger than I knew how to cope with.

In this state of mind, I was relieved when Art Basel was all over and I could meet Tex and go home. In fact, now it seemed that the best part of the trip to Miami was the Gulfstream flight home. I didn't want to be with or near anybody. Just to be alone with my sleep and my elusive dreams, the ones that would disappear into gray mist and be forgotten upon waking.

When I returned to my loft in SoHo, I lay down and fell deeply into a comatose passage, the most superior sleep of all, don't let anyone fool you. It was needed and well deserved. And during that heaven-blessed sleep, I dreamed once again, and it was the beginning of the most amazing and life-changing series of dreams of my entire existence.

Now I will tell you that first dream, exactly as it happened.

6

LA DOLCE VITA ANCORA

n my dream, I am waking up in a cold sweat. I feel depleted and brain-dead, as one does after a big orange dose of Adderall the night before. Not chips; the full pill. Therefore, the body has little will. I'm temporarily disoriented, too—I don't know where the hell I am, and I don't know how long I've been here; it could be days, weeks, even months. I look around my bedroom quickly and see that the high ceilings are no longer high and there are no columns or murals. I'm not in SoHo. And now I spot the Italian Renaissance brass-handle doorknobs. My cellphone service is Vodafone, the TV doesn't work, and a trip to the bathroom proves the hot water is not hot. That means one thing: I'm no longer in New York City.

I open the dresser, toss on some clothing, hop over a few paint cans in the studio, go outside, and take a neighborhood stroll. I turn the corner, and just up ahead I see a well-dressed guy pinch a girl he doesn't know on the ass.

"*Stronzo!*" she yells at him. The music of Italy, I reflect. I am comforted more than you can imagine. Within minutes I'm perched on my reserved *sedia* at the bar. To draw my faculties to attention, I am sipping "The Rodrigo," seated in the most touristy trattoria in the most touristy part of town in my favorite piazza in the most charming city in the fucking world: the art-for-art's-sake jewel that is Florence.

"Bravo," I congratulate myself. After Miami, I needed a change of pace and a change of place, and I finally did it. I got the hell out of New York.

"*Che dici*, Rodrigo?" Vanni the barkeep inquires.

"Just talking to myself."

"You painters—"

Piazza della Repubblica is a wonderful square, a little pigeon-infested, but that, along with the classical facades and architecture, always gives me a lift. I am a classicist, as it were, the *nuovo* version. The problem with Repubblica is that it's just too close to the breathtaking Duomo, so every tourist and transient ends up flooding through the plaza for a bite, for a *birra* or an afternoon *caffè* or *vino rosso*. But that is precisely what I want. On a daily basis. The most commercial restaurant of all, the Caffè Giubbe Rosse. That way no one will know me. It is so touristy that it gives me unchecked anonymity, as no pure *Fiorentinos* set foot in there unless they need to seduce an overseas client, use the bathroom, or haphazardly spot and target *una bella donna*.

The Giubbe Rosse is a glorious institution, actually, that has a scarlet aesthetic—red tablecloths, red vests on the waiters, red geraniums in boxes in a line near the outdoor tables under the tents. It's truly a toreador's delight. The place took its name from the "Red Shirts" of Garibaldi's forces during the Risorgimento, a badge of honor for liberal Italians, reflected in the silent allusion of the café's blood-red décor. Giubbe has been around since the 1900s, with a long-standing reputation as the thinking man's hub of literati, cognoscenti, and visionaries. Poets congregated here: Montale, Papini, and Soffici. It is the writer's café, the artist's café; the influential magazines *Solaria* and *Lacerba* were launched here, and the memorabilia covers the walls. Though now it is a mere fossil of its former significance, I always feel the ideas, the intellectual courage, and the Futurist passion creep into my bones from the old wooden bartops. Alberto Viviani defines Giubbe Rosse as a *"fucina di sogni* and *di passioni"*—a "forge of dreams and passion." That resonates with me fiercely, and as a modern painter, I feel like I am playing a home game when I am within the walls of Giubbe.

Though next to Milan or Rome, Firenze is a town dead to modern art, it is not dead to me. These are the streets where Brunelleschi looked up, Michelangelo sweated, Leonardo envisioned, and Botticelli breathed—and that's good enough for me. The inspiration surges through me from the city's cobblestone streets, plazas, and quaint bridges. In my still-confused state—how long have I been here?— I have been a Spanish-American expatriate living in Florence, and Giubbe Rosse is my midmorning ritual.

As soon as I stride in, either Vanni or Luca froths up my special macchiato, a blissful blend of espresso, steamed milk, and a healthy spike of Sambuca. They have bestowed upon me the honor of naming it the Rodrigo—even though half of Italy imbibes the same. That and a few filterless Camel cigs toot the morning reveille for my mind and let the blood make its way back to my overworked hands.

It is a Saturday, and I was up late working on a new canvas from memory, from the days when I lived in New York City. On Saturdays I always give myself a little celebratory gift after the caffeine push: I order a glass of Chianti and move from the bar to the rear corner table reserved for me beneath the tents outside.

I have a sketchpad with me and make some pencil drawings to get the circulation going. I always start the day with a flower chosen from the small Holland plates that adorn the walls of my penthouse *pensione* apartment. Flowers require concentration. The leaves, the blossom form—it is a suitable test. I choose the Frederique, named recently after the nineties fashion model. At first my fingers are like five little blind men, not knowing where to go or how to finesse a coherent image, much less refine it, but then they warm up. And the Chianti acts like a slow, soothing interior hearth to my soul as well.

The stem and petals come to life.

There is laughter at a table nearby, which does not deter me from my exercise. But this seemingly mundane cacophony has a twist. There is a singular woman's voice drowning out all others, and it pierces me in an indescribably potent way. It seems I know the voice and have known it for a thousand years, yet I've never heard it before. I lift my eyes from my sketchpad and gaze over to the table beside me, where some friends are drinking prosecco.

And then I see that face. There are others at the table, but they are not her. And like poetry in action, she speaks and claims the voice of a thousand years. She looks at me and gives me a guarded, wry smile. I find myself abandoning my midday calisthenics and flipping the sketchpad to a fresh page.

She speaks up again and laughs a laugh that complements the penetrating voice. It is not a vulgar laugh; it is sweet, measured, very dignified. The voice continues on musically, telling a brief story to the table and haunting me in the process. I am entranced by it, magnetized to it, obsessed, and hypnotized all at once. And to me, her uncommon voice flows like opera.

My hand, steady and disciplined now, is attacking the paper ferociously, lest it miss a single nuance. The sweep of shoulder-length chestnut hair is slightly waved with slow curls as if from the wand of the sea. The facial bones are raised, drawing in deeply the olive-skinned cheeks. Her elegant nose is cut like a diamond, and then those lips—the upper and lower are formed perfectly and harmoniously; they're not swollen or thick but refined and feminine, understated to perfection. Torturing my imagination is a pair of black butterfly oval eyeshades, a couture shape that only Italian sunglass artisans could devise, covering what could only be another exquisite feature.

My eyes dart to and from her face, and I puppeteer my hand, guiding it to the best of my ability. I attempt to calm it, since it is as excited as I am and I don't want it to get spastic. My Chianti is neglected, as I am consumed with my subject.

Suddenly, the chatter dies at the table, but I am too possessed by my rendering to give it any thought. And yet perhaps I should have. There is a reason for the silence.

"Scusi," I hear said in my direction.

I look up.

"Lei è un artista?"

I hesitate before speaking. The woman is addressing me as the others look on. Her hair is swept across her face by a sudden piazza crosswind.

"Signore?"

"Sì," I manage to utter finally as a response to her curiosity. I sense I've been caught stealing. "But my English is better than my Italian."

The woman smiles again coyly, then lifts her glass of prosecco to me, and I remember that long-forgotten Chianti, and we touch glasses. She toasts in appreciation of artists—of all artists, not just me—and it fills me with sudden joy.

"My name is Rodrigo. Please forgive me. I am sketching you. Do you mind?"

She replies while laughing and looking at her friends. "I am flattered," she says in her Florentine-accented English. "Be my guest. But aren't you missing something?"

". . . Of course . . ." I smile, too.

With that she rests the frames of her sunglasses upon her head, offering up the final gift: her eyes. They are green and aqua, like the waters of Sardinia, and I am stunned by their beauty. To me, the eyes of a woman hold all the mysteries of the world, and the eyes of a beautiful woman hold the greatest treasure of all.

An hour goes by, and a couple of my subject's friends peel away from the table and mention their destinations. But my subject stays, projecting her music, that voice that haunts me. With her remaining friends, she speaks of lives foreign to me in a fluid Italian concerto. I am on my fourth glass of Chianti. I feel very warm, and I am driving at full capacity.

Eventually, I see in my peripheral vision that she is getting up from the table.

"Is it finished, artist Rodrigo?"

I add several lightning touches and lean back in my chair. "'Finished' is always a loaded proposition. But, yes."

"My name is Carlotta."

I rise and shake her hand, a light press of soft, slender, elegant fingers meeting my own thick and callused, dried-paint-speckled ones. The combination of ancient voice and eyes weakens me. She continues to look at me.

"So, are you going to give it to me?"

The question takes me by surprise. Not that I am selfish, but I need to keep something of her, and I can't let it go. A rush of nervousness hits me, and I am reduced to a standing awkward fool.

"Uh, no. It's fifty thousand dollars." Instantly, I knew I shouldn't have said that.

The lovely smile dies a little then; it kills me to see that. I am every bit the fool I feared. In the brief silence, I pray to the gods of frescoes that she hasn't taken my crass comment the wrong way.

"Fifty thousand dollars? It took you just a few minutes . . ."

"No, it took me a lifetime," I say, and immediately recognize that I have been doubly rude.

The truth is my sketch does not do justice to her beauty, and I am ashamed of it. I do not want her to have a mediocre piece. That would be the greatest of all my sins. But she could not know that.

Her face contorts. It remains just as beautiful, but a different color of beauty's rainbow. Her mood has been altered, along with her opinion of me.

"It took me a lifetime, too. Bravo, *artista di merda!*"

I am more than an asshole. I am a jerk. A garden-variety jackass. She leaves me standing there dumb, confused, and numb to the touch.

Her remark is to the point and correct. It has taken her a lifetime to become the exquisite creature that she's become, not just her uncommon physical traits but her smarts and instantaneous wit as well. I have spent only an afternoon with her, and already I am possessed and haunted by her. Now, rebuffed, I am obsessed with her.

I tear out of the restaurant looking in every direction, but there are floods of tourists and backpackers mixing in with the *Fiorentini*. I decide on Via dei Calzaiuoli heading toward the Ponte Vecchio. I ascend the quaint little medieval bridge, and at its crest, I see her gazing into the jewelry case of an artisan's shop. She is eyeing a silver panther with ruby eyes. I approach her, so fully relieved I have found her.

"*Mi dispiace,*" I apologize.

She looks up quickly, then stares back into the display case. But she does not move away. "Rodrigo Concepción. The Spanish painter. *Famous*"—she says, then she looks back over at me—"*playboy* . . . and *arrogant.*"

I hesitate and let myself shift from the posturing me of minutes before to the real me. Sometimes I *am* arrogant, on the surface—a defense mechanism, really—but deep inside, where the real me hides, I am shy, even humble. I decide that being vulnerable and letting her see the real me is the only way to get back in her good graces.

"I feel for the panthers, Carlotta. They are constantly annihilated for their beauty. Sometimes that's the problem."

My comment has taken her by surprise. "How do you mean?"

"I mean that beauty can be punished. Like success. And then, of course, you can become a prisoner. To them both."

"Are you a prisoner?"

"Perhaps, yes. But worse than that, I am crude. And unmannered. Please forgive me."

"Forgive me also. I don't often use such language."

"I deserved it. I was fearful that my drawing was, well, less than what I am capable of. Less than what my subject was. I did not want you to even see it."

She just looks at me, but not blankly. There is weight to her gaze. It is not surrender but enough of a capitulation to incite me to try to start over.

"Let me buy you a *caffè.*"

She eyes me briefly and does not look away. She smiles so very faintly. "*Mi dispiace,* I have to go. Maybe next time."

I tear out a page from the sketchpad and extend it to her. She reaches for it, and our fingers graze as she accepts it. Her softness meets my roughness. Again.

She is expecting it to be her portrait. It is not—not this time. She glances at the drawing. "*Grazie mille,*" she says tepidly, and once again produces that reserved curve of her lips which I have already grown to love.

She continues walking, and I know not to follow her. I know to never follow beautiful creatures in the night. They can become very dangerous, and so I watch the danger disappear from sight.

THAT NIGHT I AM SCHEDULED for a dinner date with my old friends Bernardo and Catarina. But I cannot eat, and I don't want my meditations obstructed with small talk, so I cancel.

I am floating and watching myself from above as I make my way back to the *pensione* near the Accademia. As I get closer to the hotel, I hear that voice again, her voice, and I look around, to the corner, up on the scaffold, to an apartment sundeck, but I cannot see her anywhere. I swear I can hear that voice, but the creature in possession of it is nowhere to be found. She is like a ghost.

As I ascend the stairs to my penthouse and art studio, I pass some transients checking out with Giuliana. I am tipsy and exhausted, and it is time for me to rest. That chance encounter with the woman at Giubbe, it was a dream. Was she a tourist? Or native *Fiorentina*? I will likely never see her again. That's what I tell myself. That's what I have to tell myself. It is the most merciful thing I can do.

I decide I can't stand the new canvas I am making from the New York series, and I get up and slash it into strips with an X-Acto knife, and I do it with relish.

I return to bed to die a soft death. "She *is* a ghost, I think." And I say it over and over, like a mantra, until I can say no more.

I hope the ghost appreciated my flower.

7

NEW YORK TOREADOR

My eyes unsealed and I was again befuddled and confused, unsure of where I was. Alfonso strode in noiselessly with a wellness shot and some scrambled eggs, asking me how I felt. My butler's presence in my bedroom snapped me out of my disoriented daze. I was back at the casa SoHo. I knew I'd been sleeping heavily and dreaming substantially. I was feeling invigorated for some reason, if not upbeat and inspired.

"*Hola,* Alfonso, *gracias—*"

"Maestro, you have been sleeping for a long time."

I groaned something Neanderthal and unintelligible even to me. I cleared my dry, raspy throat. "*Bueno.* Rest for the wicked."

The man smiled dutifully with a glint of gold from his rear molar.

"And I think I had a good time . . ."

Once Alfonso glided out, I took a ravenous bite of the eggs and switched on the flat-screen with no sound, just to settle me and infuse me with the colors of the world.

It wasn't long before Rafaela charged into the room, slamming the door against the wall and sending a chip of paint fluttering help-lessly to the carpet like a dead butterfly. She did look beautiful when she was angry, and her rage was unleashed upon my bureau as she rifled through every drawer, tossing each one shut with menace.

"Tell me where, Rodrigo."

I coughed a little. "Where what?" came out half-baked.

"Where the fuck are they?"

"They? Who the hell is 'they'?"

"The sleeping pills! You have been sleeping for two entire days!"

"Two?" I swigged on the cappuccino with another mouthful of eggs. "That sounds wonderful. Good for me."

"You know how much work you have to do?"

That gave me pause. "Well, why didn't you wake me up, then?"

"I have been trying to! I almost called 911!"

"You aren't allowed to do that . . . I don't like 911."

While rummaging through my closet, Rafaela found the little red box from my childhood. She snatched out my vitamin baggie and threw the contents of each pill canister in the toilet and flushed it.

I was still groggy and didn't have the will to speak of the econom-ics involved: she'd just jettisoned a few hundred dollars' worth of meds. I was content to change the channel with the remote and find some new colors. In times like these, ignoring her was crucial, a natu-ral defense against hypertension.

Rafaela tossed off some more targeted vitriol and spiked condem-nation, and that was just fine with me. Eventually, I slid out of bed and removed my pajama bottoms, while Rafaela was still barking like a Doberman. For some reason I slammed the bathroom door behind me, even though I was not so emotional. It was a statement of sorts, just to indicate who was still the boss.

I bypassed the bathtub, already prepared, and opted for a shower. I loved steam showers, and this was the only conscious decision I made. The fact was, I could not get that Florentine dream out of my head. *Who is this girl, and where did she come from?* Had I ever met her, or was she just a creation of my mind, like a new painting, orchestrated and brushstroked during sleep? I figured the steam shower might provide me with some answers.

But it did not.

. . . And where is she now?

I locked myself in the studio and placed a towel at the base of the door to shut out any light or sound or anything else on the other side. All day I sketched and finessed her portrait, dozens of times, to improve upon my disastrous effort at the Giubbe Rosse—I remembered that much of the dream. I suppose it's like, after a thousand victories, you remember only the game you played badly and lost. I paid particular attention to her eyes, which she had shielded most of the afternoon but then revealed gloriously in the golden-hour piazza sunlight with the simple but deft lift of the oval shades. I attempted to infuse the mystery of her within the hazel-green irises of her beautiful eyes and in her delicate mouth, akin to the elusive gaze and mysterious grin of the *Mona Lisa*. Each time I had an inkling I was capturing her, she somehow escaped, the same way she had fled from me that evening at the Giubbe, and then again at the Ponte Vecchio.

As I labored unsuccessfully through the charcoals and then the oils, I kept trying to decipher where I had met her. Had I met her once, albeit briefly, and did she exist after all? There had been so, so many nights of surrealistic nocturnal social clashes with massive intake and indulgence, and perhaps I was recalling her from some lost and out-of-bounds condition that was barely registering on my synapses. But nothing came to mind, and the mystery raged on.

Of course, I tried to deconstruct the reasons for my folly. This girl, this *woman*, meant something more to me—perhaps too much—and I was cracking under the pressure. She was sapping me of my confidence; I was no longer the bold and dynamic Rodrigo, the toreador painter, a matador of art, becoming both the bull and the bully in the process, and taking down one *toro* after another with relative if not arrogant ease. Something about this young woman unmanned me, unglued me, incited my nervousness, and made my hand awkward and tentative, sweaty, clammy, and increasingly unsure. I was capturing something, yes, but not *her,* not *Carlotta di Firenze.* The mere thought of her was turning me into a fumbling art student.

The only allowance I gave myself for such mediocre efforts was that I did not really know this woman; I had not spent enough time with her, and I needed to get to know her better. It was incumbent upon me to seek her out, and this became my mission.

It was not lost on me, either, that this Carlotta was satisfying a need for me psychologically: she was filling a void, a hole, the hole that my present dissatisfying life was becoming. She was an ideal and a perfect creation of my mind; it was my soul's gift to me, it must have been. How else could she be explained? She wasn't in my living room. Or bathroom. Or hallway. She had taken up residence in my mind, at my soul's invitation. Good, soul. Good on you. Help the desperate man in need.

And then I unleashed a rendering with a fury. My fingers were again at my beck and call, and I summoned a work that I would consider my masterwork, if not masterpiece. The feline eyes, lit by the golden Tuscan sun, came alive like twin emeralds. All the shades of green, from lime to mint to sage, were present in those eyes, and she was breathing before me. Carlotta was alive. Then I replicated the formula on all the previous duds and failures, leaving some as sketches and half-painting them while completing others. The series was scintillating, and I was prideful yet protective: I knew in that moment that I would never show these paintings to anyone.

Rodrigo the toreador had returned and imposed his will upon the canvases, making them succumb to his desires. I had tricked myself, my mind had deceived me temporarily, to allow my verve and confidence to reclaim me. This was the only way. And how did I do it? In the most Machiavellian of ways.

On the canvas itself, in the paintings, I had to deconstruct her, degrade her, devalue her, in order to have her, to capture her ghostly all-everything spirit. My soul had responded to the desperation and given me the wherewithal to birth this creation. I sighed in relief when she was done. And when I left the studio, I double-locked the door behind me. I didn't want anyone to see her. Any part of her. She was mine and I would be selfish, for both of us.

Rafaela had been calling and texting me for hours, as I was late for a club opening. I didn't care. But now I was done. My hands trembled as I locked the studio door, and I knew why. There was more to this Carlotta. Though I'd deconstructed her, there was more to the story. I hadn't really stopped believing in her. She was more than a garden-variety muse. And I needed to get to know her better.

I had tricked myself into seizing her portrait. Something fresh and authentic and real had been aroused in me. I didn't give a shit if it would sell, nor would I put any of it up for sale. It would be a series not driven by the demands of a marketplace. But this series needed to come to life, it needed oxygen, it needed to live and breathe. And I asked for mercy.

"Please forgive me, Carlotta," I said aloud. "I have stolen from you. And I hope to repay you in ways I have never paid anyone."

8

MALICE IN WONDERLAND

had come to an agreement with the owners of the Mina Hotel to adorn their lower-level space with my fantasy murals. I had thought the dark, subterranean lounge would be the perfect setting and ambience for my *Alice in Wonderland* frescoes, but after I started, I didn't like the idea at all. I didn't like the surface of the walls I had to paint on, I didn't like the light, and I didn't like what I painted on those walls and in that light. Sometimes it's like that: you don't know what will happen with an idea until you try it. Like it or not, though, I had a contract, and I had to finish what I had agreed to do. I totally understood why even some of the greatest artists of the Renaissance had been known to abandon commissioned works in progress—and had occasionally gotten away with it. But there was no way I would get away with it. I had to keep on painting.

The whole project had been a pain in the ass to do, and now it was opening night. I didn't want to go at all or to do any press, but Rafaela goaded me. I had exhausted myself earlier that evening, and

I followed her without protest, like a dog on a leash. We arrived two hours late, and as soon as I entered, I knew I did not want to be there. The place was crowded but empty. And I still didn't like what I saw on the walls. Made me feel like a whore, like I had sold out for the money, instead of following my soul.

The staff escorted Rafaela and me to my designated booth. When I looked across the room, I detected the unctuous con artists, connivers, strokers, and rip-offs—who had an agenda in a setting like this—slithering in and around tables and booths, identifying big-money targets to whom they might unleash their profiteering deceptions: the art-world heavies, real estate agents, Wall Streeters, gallerists, publicists, lawyers, and also the more reptilian middle-men like themselves, learned in the art of greed and getting their piece. The filler was there, too, the urban underground nomads who had been avoiding the light of day for years and had climbed out from beneath their rocks and emerged from East Village roommate-stuffed hovels to engage in another evening of 100-proof aimlessness.

Just that simple gaze across the room made me angry.

"So, no interviews?" my PR gal, Rachel, leaned in and barked, like a real Manhattan pusherette. She was boasting of all the C-list attendees she'd invited, B-list hopefuls, and A-list pipe dreams. The fact is, the A-listers I knew were across town attending several movie premieres—and that was just fine. Maybe they were even getting to see a decent flick. I chose to ignore Rachel's blatherings and informed Rafaela that I was going upstairs to have a smoke.

"What's gotten into him?" I heard bellowed behind me.

I passed by Molly Boy, a dealer who frequented the club; I'd met him while I was painting the frescoes. I handed him a fifty and told him to give me what he had. I didn't care if anyone saw us. "The sleepy stuff," I demanded.

"Sleepy stuff?"

"Shut the fuck up. You selling or no?" My appropriately candid but uncharacteristic response stunned him, a little like a Pacquiao jab, and his grubby hands swam Olympic freestyle through a run of cargo pockets reserved for his various illicit stashes. He slipped me a palmful of downers.

"Twenty of that is credit—don't forget," I said.

Molly Boy was Hungarian and spoke in a thick Eastern European accent; he had clothes made of tatters and flip-top tabs for jewelry, clothes that made girls gooey—an authentic downtown all-star. His eyes were blackballing, though, and he was too fucked up already to take issue with my newfound frankness.

I was ready to move on, but he placed a jittery, thick Hungarian-goulash paw on my shoulder. "You seen The Raven?"

"Yeah, he's contemplating his life in a pool of sweat, holding on to the one friend who always sticks by him. Fuck off . . ."

"Rodrigo—"

"Hey, Molly Boy, don't ever let anyone call you a loser," I called back to him over my shoulder.

As I climbed the stairs step by step and looked upon my wall art spread high and low, I was leveled with even more disdain. It made my hair stand on end, all the hours I'd spent painting it. However, people loved it, and the place was jumping—it had gotten its liftoff. But I wanted nothing to do with it on this night. Or any other night. I felt as if the walls were closing in on me. If I never saw the frescoes again, I'd be a happy fellow.

Upstairs, I bypassed the crowd outside clamoring to get in, and I reversed back to the lobby bar just to equilibrate, if possible, and give myself some air. I downed a couple shots of whiskey and took an incoming phone call from an old friend.

"Yeah," I responded. "Hey there . . . Congratulations," I added neutrally. "Yeah, we can catch up . . . No, I am excited . . ."

I couldn't have sounded more sarcastic, and my old friend Julia had caught it. I was a heap of exposed nerves with a time fuse and was desperate to get out of there. "No, I'm okay . . . Midnight sounds peachy . . . Yes, I'm sure; just take me far, far away . . . *Bueno.*"

I walked away from the bar, still on the phone. The swollen doorman built of mortar and musclement, who always gave entrée to me and my tribe, accosted me. "Hey, Rodrigo, great party."

"Okay, see you then," I finished the call. I raised a *get lost* finger, but the guy didn't take the hint and considered my dust-off gesture more of a *wait a second* invitation. To extend my preoccupations, I pressed Uber on my phone and arranged my ride while the door jockey was still jawing at me.

"What did you say?" I redirected to the doorman, whom I didn't know.

"Place is slammed—"

"Is it?" He didn't know what I was saying, and I said something only because they were words to say, which pissed me off even more, to be someone's marionette, someone's trick pony, forced to converse with a standing eight-count steroid bag.

"Well—yeah."

"Whatever, door guy . . ."

"What?" To macho over my comment, his HGH-infused and dim-witted brain tried to compensate. "Say, Rodrigo, can you introduce me to a few chippies? I mean, you know 'em all."

And now I was taken aback. But the guy was serious; it wasn't an insult to him, just fat on the cerebellum. Who the hell did this guy think he was, asking me to find him girls?

He said, "I know the groupies, the sluts, but not the high-end—"

"Hey—I don't even know your name!" I snapped. "Now get the fuck outta my face!" Then I shoved him away and charged out the revolving door with a whish.

I sauntered to the corner of Park Avenue and calmed down. Thankfully, my Uber arrived and I slipped inside.

"Where to?"

"Peking Duck. You know it?"

"In Chinatown?"

"Check." I lit up then and watched the smoke billow out of my mouth.

"Sir—no smoking—"

"Just having a quick puff."

The car slowed. "Mister, I said no smoking . . ."

"You're going to tell me I can't smoke?"

"That's exactly what I'm telling you."

"You're a private car and I'm hiring you—you get it? I'm. Hiring. You."

"Put out the cigarette or get out!" The car stopped.

"Turn on the radio. Fuck off."

The guy got out then, a wiry borough baron with the New Yawker accent, and opened the rear door. "Out!"

"Out?"

"Either the cig goes or you go!"

"It's my car, you're just an employee!"

The man lunged at me and I put up a blocking forearm. A scuffle broke out, and some mild fisticuffs, and we half-wrestled upright there, twisting back and forth until I tossed him to the side and walked away.

"You! Motherfucker! Your account is finished! You hear me?" He added some more choice words in my direction, and I gave him a solid uninterrupted look at a place he was welcome to kiss.

I hailed a yellow cab and continued on to the Duck. The increasing—and considerable—amounts of drugs and alcohol I had been consuming couldn't have had anything to do with my heightened feelings of shame and disappointment in my work or with my suddenly short temper. I was strong, and I could handle it.

But looking out the windows of the cab, I did entertain a

notable meditation: *What the fuck is the matter with everyone?* I thought—with absolute conviction. After all, I knew it wasn't me; it must be them, *all of them.* An entire city's worth. It was as if they had all been highlighted with fluorescent markers and they were just carrying on as the daily jackasses they were—but now they were glowing green.

9

DUCK WALK

My midnight dinner date at the Peking Duck was with Julia, one of my closest friends from a few years ago, when I'd lived at the Beverly Hills Hotel. In the time I'd known her, she'd gone from posing in print ads for shampoo to bona fide supermodel. Tonight she'd phoned me after her Fashion Week runway gig and given me the kind of lifeline I desperately needed to get the hell out of that regressive subterranean den. And God bless her.

I dry-throated one of Molly Boy's pills and tried to calm the fuck down. As my taxi glided downtown, I attempted to gain a further sense of perspective. There's nothing like a Manhattan cab ride for introspection. Epiphanies can happen on any fleeting block the eye can frame and capture.

The fact is, I was self-aware enough to know I was off. Or *on,* as it were, depending on your angle of appraisal.

Specifically, I was feeling . . . tangential, like a bold tangent or offshoot of my persona, not like my normal character, which knew how to be polite and play the game and was one people liked to be around.

But this tangent-persona was in no mood for any games. It felt unforgiving and merciless. It was me, all right, but the uncensored me, the fed-up me. I was rude, I was nasty, and the way I was feeling made me want to call everyone on their bullshit. And I was enjoying it. I even felt proud of myself.

It had happened before, this change to the more deliberate, truthful me, but somehow this time it felt different. This was not just a mood swing; it was as if the chemicals in my gut had changed and they were tingling away at the molecular level in an altered arrangement and form.

I supposed it was best for me to disappear, while I was in this state of mind, and let Rafaela handle the business details. But the thought of business didn't excite me in the least. I really didn't give a shit.

The feeling had gotten hold of me around the time of Art Basel, but now it was even stronger. This industrial-strength version gave me a certain power. And that *was* exciting. I gave thought to the new work in the studio that I had under lock and key. It brought a smile to my face.

And her.

Carlotta.

I wanted to know her better. I needed to. I was missing her. My hands were anticipating her. My soul was craving her. Was she real? Or a figment? *Of course she's a figment,* I thought in jest, and laughed evilly—I knew now how to capture her; to denunciate her, neutralize her, even denigrate her, to thwart the power she had over me.

From what I had gathered of her sensibilities, she would have lasted about thirty seconds at that club gig. When I thought of her, just from what little I did know of her, I could see the bullshit of my life so clearly. None of that shit would pass the Carlotta test. The buzzer went off at every shallow interlude, at every phony handshake. The buzzer had gone off on my art, too. Storybook frescoes. *Malice in Wonderland* was more like it.

When I arrived at Peking Duck, Julia was already seated and inspiring a good deal of attention. She signed an autograph and waved off a selfie in the time it took me to check my coat. She stood up, and did she ever look stunning. Her auburn locks were pinned up in a bun with Ivana wisps dangling down around diamond drop earrings. She wore an elegant black shimmering Hervé Léger gown tight to the bosom and pelvis, and her accentuated backside was available for all to see. She was in full glam mode and sucking the air out of the room. And dressed like that, she was also cool enough to go to a place with violent lighting, like Peking Duck.

With the eyes of the restaurant upon us, I meant to peck her on the cheek, but instead she met my lips with hers. She had great lips, and violet eyes like a young Liz Taylor. Since we'd met, she'd become a full-fledged sex symbol, the most coveted configuration of DNA in town. She modeled swimsuits and lingerie as well as high fashion, and lately she'd started acting lessons in an effort to branch out even more. The body was sick. The breasts were genuine, even though she spent most of her time in L.A. surrounded by all that *what I have isn't enough* pressure.

Julia was one of my closest friends, though I hadn't seen her much recently. We had met casually five years before on the garden terrace of the Beverly Hills Hotel, a glamorous hotel that has had most of the world's entertainment royalty as guests.

I was nursing conjugal wounds at the time of my full-time residency, inhabiting a bungalow for months on end after my marriage had ended. I'd turned the space into my own private studio and had painted frescoes on all the walls. The social parade was nonstop and the parties absolutely wild.

Julia was reading at a nearby table on the veranda when we struck up our first conversation. She had just appeared in her first Victoria's

Secret fashion show, and her career was taking off to the point that she was wearing horn-rims and baseball caps to downplay her recognizability. She had been unknown and struggling, and suddenly, she was on top of the world. I was already enjoying my own mild celebrity but was not as well known as I would eventually become.

I had just decided to move back to the U.S. after living in Madrid for a few years. I was wearing a cast on my leg after my ex-wife, Maria, had stabbed me for repeatedly cheating on her. She'd come into my Madrid studio one day and caught me having sex with one of her good friends. I guess that was the final blow. She started screaming, and as her friend scurried away crying and half-naked, Maria went into my room, where I kept an old hunting knife, a gift from my dad. She rushed in with it, serrated edge first. Maria was shaking all over, and I was trying to calm her down; I was convinced she wouldn't do anything crazy. But I was wrong. Not only did she stab me, she tried to up the ante and cut off my member. She missed, but the blade dug into my thigh, nearly severing the femoral artery, which would have meant a long Spanish sunset siesta—the type from which you never awake.

In the movies, when people get shot or stabbed, they can talk and even run—but it burns like a motherfucker, and all I could say before passing out was "Babe, really? You fucking stabbed me! Fuck you!"

When I woke up in the hospital, the police were there, and they started asking me questions. They had already arrested Maria; but I knew she never meant to hurt me, and somewhere in my heart, I knew I deserved it. I told the police it was an accident and that I was not going to press charges.

I saw Maria about a week later, and we agreed that it would be best for us to get a divorce. So with respect to our marriage, we said, "CUT!"—pun intended. And I took the next flight I could book to Los Angeles and left Spain for good.

So there I was, perched on the veranda at the hotel, my crutches leaning against the table, a few feet away from this sweet, gorgeous angel. At some point she came up for oxygen from the book she was reading and noticed this raw exposed nerve of a soul. She asked me, "Hey, what happened to you?"

And I stuttered, of course. "I am—" I began awkwardly. "Well . . . my ex-wife stabbed me. She had a bit of a Spanish temper. Can I buy you a drink?"

She looked at me in my pathetic state and had to laugh. Before we knew it, we were drinking martinis and talking. That same night we went to my bungalow, and Julia did not leave for three days. When we came up for occasional air and fuel, Julia helped me organize and paste up *The Stabbing Diaries,* my new studio collaged mural dedicated to my severed marriage (and a nod to Andy Warhol's assassination creations after the failed attempt on his life). *The Stabbing Diaries* were replete with full-spectrum Polaroid photo coverage of my open wound, X-rays, bloody shirt, shredded jeans, teal hospital gown, original oxygen mask and IV hookups, intake bracelets, and a toe tag stolen from a corridor stiffy, as well as the hospital nurse centerfolds (which became a separate ongoing project, unbeknownst to the hospital heads).

This unique melding of creative minds and bodies blossomed into a romance that lasted almost six months, but Julia and I were both so busy (she more than I, at this point) that it cooled eventually and we decided to remain just friends. But being the single man and the champion of the human spirit, free will, and biological desire that I was, I let it be known I would remain open for any future rendezvous if appropriate or if it suited her.

Little did I know that the offer would be accepted and acted upon. Of course I recognized that perhaps my soon-to-be paramour was attracted by my reluctance to beg for something more substantial between us, which was the kind of attention she was accustomed to. But every now and then Julia and I would hook up and go toe to toe, as it appeared we would again this evening.

Having said that, I knew to never give a woman what she wanted. That worked for the male breed, too. If not the entire human race.

But I wasn't ever sure exactly what Julia was looking for or what she wanted or even how she behaved in a relationship. She would often say, "Rodrigo, you're like a drug—when I need you, I take you, and it always makes me feel better." As it was, I had no issues with being used sexually by one of the most desirable women in the world. So I was faithful to our arrangement and don't believe I ever turned her away.

"Thank you for meeting me," Julia said as I sat down at her table. She was equipped with particularly acute emotion receptors, and her antennae were always up. I sensed she had already absorbed the fact that I was operating at a new frequency, a frequency with which she was not familiar, and she was unsure whether she could assimilate it, much less dominate it.

"Of course . . ." I said. We ordered food and a pair of martinis, and she studied me with a coy smile before speaking.

"We'll always have L.A.," she quipped, and we both had to laugh, she more enthusiastically than I, at the absurdity of it: a mockery of the classic Bogie-Bergman line in *Casablanca,* as in, it couldn't get any more superficial.

"You okay?" she asked.

"Yeah—why?"

"On the phone you seemed perturbed."

"No—*you seem perturbed,*" I said with a smile.

"*No, you're perturbed.*" It was an exercise she'd taught me from the acting lessons she was taking—a Stanislavski word-repetition drill—that was a way to sharpen one's ability to pick up on another's change in behavior and to enhance one's capacity to stay in the moment. We often kidded each other about it.

"*You're guessing.*"

"*Yeah, I'm guessing,*" she allowed.

"You're wondering."

"Yes, I'm wondering."

"Yeah, you're wondering . . ."

"You're curious— I'm *very* curious," she rerouted with new inflection, and with that, she dropped out and broke the exercise. "So what's going on? Tell me."

"Yeah, well, I don't know . . . Feelings aren't my strong point."

"Don't hide. Try—"

"It's in my mind, you know? I've been very abrupt . . . and short-tempered . . . and dismissive with people . . . and you know what? I *like it.*" I laughed, a guttural, boisterous sound.

But she did not laugh. "Okay . . ." she said.

"I mean the honesty of it. Of saying what's on your mind. Of being truthful. I was really being myself. It's a relief."

"It's liberating, isn't it? It's also dangerous."

"But that's just it—I didn't give a shit, and I don't, you know?"

"So how do you feel now?"

"Now? I feel, let me see, the best word is a Spanish word: *tangencial . . .*"

"Tangential?"

"Which translates perfectly, but not necessarily *my* meaning."

"You mean splintered? Or like part of yourself is splitting away? Like a split personality?" Julia possessed a sharp cerebral instrument; she could decipher an emotional grid and get to the nitty-gritty of psychological states in seconds. She was in training, of course, but intuitive, too. She could delineate and define an emotion and produce it behaviorally, living it and owning it.

"No, no. It's more than that. It's more than a split. I'm not divided. It's like I'm undergoing some—"

"Change? Congratulations, Rodrigo," she said, and smiled wryly. "It's a cliché and second only to 'Love is all you need,' but—change is good."

I was still entranced by my meditation. "Like I'm heading off on a tangent of myself, taking a ride, but I can't pull back. It's going one way. Off. The tangent is becoming what was myself, what is me. It's more like a metamorphosis."

"Wow, nice—I hope."

I laughed. So did she, and that gleaming white smile of hers just blazed across her face. "It's literary. It's Kafka-esque."

"*Gracias, amor.* You always keep me in the highest—"

"Esteem?"

"And company."

"Of course I do. I love you," she said.

"You do?"

"Don't you think I do?"

And right then the air went out of my face, and a chip was taken out of my fascination for her. *Here we go again,* I thought. *More actor babble.* "I think you love the idea of me."

"And what's that?"

"The absolute free spirit run by free will. And if you were a man, I bet you would be just like me."

She smiled the guiltiest of smiles.

"Let me rephrase that. You may love what you thought was me. Because I'm a new me now. So, no. How can you be so sure that you love me?"

"If indeed there is a new you—we'll just have to wait and see. Is this transformation for the better?"

"I don't know. I think so. It has to be."

"You're not telling me everything, are you?"

She was smiling again, and my smile broke free as well. "You're so intuitive."

"That one wasn't so difficult."

"I guess not. I'll tell you over dinner."

"I'm staying at the Ritz-Carlton. Is the new you joining me there?"

"When?"

"After Duck," she said, and laughed.

"You mean after dark?"

"Of course I mean after dark—silly rabbit."

We enjoyed another round of martinis and our appetizers and main courses. I spent the entire dinner sharing my dream, the vitality of it, the realism, and the vividness. And *her.* Carlotta. I talked about Florence, recounting the afternoon at Giubbe, and meeting her, and sketching her, and my rudeness—and how it nearly ended in a disastrous way, then it did end without an end, on such a vague note. And I confessed to Julia that I was still haunted by this mysterious woman who had appeared out of nowhere in my mindscape. In a dream that felt so real.

"Have you ever lived in Florence?" she asked.

"Yes, for a few years. When I did the neoclassical series."

"But you don't recall ever meeting her?"

"No, absolutely not. And I mean, after all," I observed, "we normally dream of people we know in our waking lives, or faces that are familiar to us somehow, through the media, television, the movies, even people we've just met. Or don't we?"

"Usually, yes. I mean, it's never happened to me that I remember."

"Exactly," I said.

She sipped from her glass and mulled it. "First of all, Rodrigo, you're an artist, a painter. You're a visualist, and you create images. Perhaps while you sleep, you are creating a portrait in your mind, your unconscious mind, but in this dream life, the portrait depicted is a real-life one—living, breathing, and three-dimensional. She talks. She walks. She makes love.

"But when you actually paint consciously in your waking hours, you craft the non-breathing, non-animated, two-dimensional version. When you see it this way, your painted portraits are images actually captured, yes. But *really* captured, as in trapped. They are not free.

They are in prison, bound by a frame. And maybe you are giving the subjects of your portraits, these prisoners of your imagination, their freedom when you sleep, when you dream. You liberate them. And—"

"And what?" I asked.

"Perhaps you *want* to liberate them. Perhaps painting is frustrating you. Or the way you are painting. Or *what* you are painting."

With that, Julia reeled me back in. "I knew you would have an interesting take on this," I said.

"Have you made love to her?"

"Carlotta? No! I only met her once—I mean dreamed of her once . . ."

"Do you want to make love to her?"

"I—"

"You want to *fuck* her—"

"It's not that . . ."

"Then what is it?"

"I . . . I . . . I want to do everything with her."

10

LA CALA RITZ-CARLTON

I sat at the bar and ordered a Macallan. Some delicate piano with fluid notes was playing. When my drink arrived, I downed the pills Molly Boy had given me, plus a Cialis for good measure, and listened to the floating notes, a welcome reprieve from those thumping club sounds earlier in the night.

Julia returned from the powder room and glided over to me, her hair falling free and emancipated from the formal updo. She looked absolutely ravishing in her shimmering French gown, and she moved as elegantly as a dancer.

She paused before me and extended her hand, gently clasped mine, and tugged me in the direction of the elevator. I followed. There may have been a new me, but not that new. And not that improved. I was still weak when it came to a beautiful woman interested in private biology. A woman in the flesh, that is.

"What do you do when you need a fix, just grab me like a bottle of Advil?" I said, reminding her that she had once said I was like a drug.

"No, Rodrigo. You're not over-the-counter. You're strictly pre-scription fare."

"I'd rather be over-the-counter."

"I bet you would," she said with sly purpose. "No, you're not for everyone. You're riskier than that."

"How so?"

"As in, proceed with caution."

"And with the proper dosage?" I asked pointedly. She smiled and erased the subtext stalemate by kissing me long and soft until the elevator doors opened, inviting us to be swept away on a glorious vertical chariot—and after we went to bed, I was swept away in a glorious dream.

I AM IN FLIGHT, soaring and spearing through wisps of clouds in a clear blue Mediterranean summer sky, held aloft by the thermal wind currents.

I am an eagle, gliding above the Serra de Tramuntana range on the island of Mallorca. I see movement below and spot a donkey train transporting tourists on a sloping mountain path. I coast lower with a flap of my wings and fasten on the gentle curve of the Cala de Deià below, with its shimmering turquoise waters. Farther beyond, the bright blue hue of the cove meets with the sun, and their natural brilliance blends together and produces a delicate purple light, the better part of blue, to form a stunning periwinkle horizon.

I eagle-eye a Swedish-built sailboat floating peacefully in the cove, a fifteen-meter Hallberg-Rassy ketch with twin masts. As I approach, I hear her voice. And there she is again! I land on the forward mast closest to the bow and dig my talons unsuccessfully into the metal crossbeam. Carlotta is enjoying a glass of rosé with another young woman; the two of them are Riviera topless and gazing out toward the sunset. Café del Mar–style ambient music is emanating soothingly from the cabin's interior.

I eyeball her hungrily to absorb what I can, to learn anything new about her. I realize I am witnessing the vacation Carlotta, the Cala de Deià Carlotta, an Italian girl embraced by rugged mountains and a Spanish sea. Her hair is sun-bleached and windblown, her face and fiery-red-bikinied body deeply oiled, bronzed, and ablaze in gold and aqua hues. I can see the glowing green fire glint from her eyes, and the lighter sunburn-free oval-shaped tracings around them where her sunglasses have been. She has a carved, curving figure. Her breasts are not burdensome but full and delicately shaped, the nipples the size of quarters upturned and hard-candied to the wind.

Both girls angle up and gaze warmly and curiously upon me. They seem enlivened by a fleeting brush with a winged brother, another of God's elusive creatures. I wait there with a predator bird's patience and watchfulness. But I am not hunting or seeking prey. I am waiting for the right moment. Timing is everything, even with eagles.

As the sun fades and night falls, the other woman retreats to the cabin's interior, but Carlotta stays on deck, draped in a blouse and wrapped with an African kikoy. Her hand covers her eyes as she peers out to the horizon beyond. The turquoise sea has transformed to a deep Aegean blue. Her brow is creased and her face is a portrait of anxiety, worry, even fear. I don't know her well and have never seen her express any of these sentiments; anger, perhaps, but none from this emotional palette. The two-way radio blasts static-corrupted voices from inside the cabin. Carlotta seems to be combing the waters, searching, looking for something. Or someone. Her countenance remains unyielding and grim.

I want to comfort her, but I cannot. I can't raise my wings. I try again and again, but I am powerless. It pains me deeply, but I am unable to move. It's as if I am frozen like a statue, a vulgar, scaly gargoyle fastened atop the mast, poised as if unwilling to help someone in distress. My face is carved into a devilish expression, I have pointed wings and razor, reptilian claws, and I flash sharp fangs like a dragon bird. I am a Notre Dame gremlin, laughing at her, ridiculing her, in mockery of her loss, whatever it may be. But I don't want to offend or deride her; it's just a mask! It's not me! It's not the real me! You have to believe me, *bella* Carlotta! I'm trapped! Like a bronze sculpture, like one of my portraits held stationary by a frame!

I feel the heat bearing down on me, oppressive and uncompromising. I can move now, and when I do, it's painful. My hand falls suddenly in the water, and my eyes unseal. I hear her voice again and lift from my supine state. I see I am floating on a paddleboard in the middle of the deep blue sea. I hear her call out again, and I twist back around—it is Carlotta, stationed on the bow of the sailboat, advancing on me. The sails have been struck, and I hear the faint murmur of the boat's engine.

"*Rodrigo!*"

"*Sí!* I'm over here!"

"I see you! *Grazie a Dio!* We're coming!"

As the ketch approaches, I try to get to my knees and my skin aches. I have been sunburned, cooked like an Alaskan king crab.

"*Hola, bella* . . . I must have fallen asleep!"

"You did! You are a long way from where we set anchor!" Carlotta tosses me a life preserver and vest, and I catch them, though I don't need either, and it hurts to stretch my scorched limbs to reach for them.

The boat is back-shifted to reverse and idles smoothly beside me. I see a silent Francesca holding the wheel and waving at me, and I salute back. I have to laugh at my good fortune. I could have drifted to eternity with no way back.

"Bravo, Rodrigo! I knew we'd find you!"

"*Gracias,* Francesca! *Dio mio!*" I say, shifting in and out of Spanish and Italian. "You guys saved my life!"

My eyes meet Carlotta's as she says, "We know . . ."

I smile back. Then I jump in the water and raise the paddleboard, and both girls load it on deck. They toss over the rope ladder, and I scale it on shaky burned limbs. Once I am on board, they start razzing me.

"*Guarda,* 'Cesca! We are going to have him for dinner! Lobster!"

"And lobster salad for *pranzo!* Surely we can get two meals out of this guy . . ."

"Very funny . . ."

Carlotta comes up to me, very close, and wraps a blanket around my shoulders. She stands before me and gazes into my eyes, my blues to her greens. Her mouth turns up slightly and her head extends forward, and what does she do to confound me once more? She grazes her lips across mine ever so slightly, not a kiss but a fragile gift that says more than I could imagine. Hungry for anything I can derive from her, I devour the moment fully. We are sailing the Mallorcan coast together, and this is merely day one. There is so much more I want to know about this enigmatic young woman who has appeared in my life in a *poof!*—like magic.

This Cala de Deià sailing sojourn is Carlotta's idea. I suspect she wants to see me in my element—and great, I almost get lost and drown! She has chosen the place and invited her lovely childhood girlfriend Francesca, who has grown up boating on the Tuscan coast and the charming Cinque Terre. Carlotta has chosen our boat, too, the *Monkey Business,* and I am covering all expenses. That is the deal, though I am a little hazy as to how I know all this. I have negotiated my own perk: to be able to sketch and paint the girls. But we never specify when. Or how.

While the girls shower, I straddle the bow up top and count my blessings: how fortunate I am to have come across such a special person as Carlotta. She's refined, enlightened, educated, drop-dead gorgeous, and she'll save your life if you need it! I wash my thoughts with some rosé from a nearby bottle and watch the sun tap-dance on the orange and continuously periwinkle horizon.

The girls join me on deck just in time to see the sun's final pirouette as she dips gracefully over the edge. Francesca speaks of their days as schoolmates in Florence and the trouble they stirred with the boys, of course. They're both the products of overbearing Italian fathers, and they find a kinship in their common stern upbringings, and inspire each other's resultant rebellions. They cover for each other, too, with phantom outings and sleepovers. They are fiercely loyal best friends, the type who anticipate each other's every thought. But there is no jealousy; jealousy is a cancer that destroys any friendship, any union, for that matter.

Francesca excuses herself and leaves Carlotta and me beneath a silvery Mediterranean moon. We're seated on deck cross-legged, the bare hard teak beneath us. My skin is burning, my face, too—it feels highlighted and glowing. Carlotta has me wrapped in a robe, and she serves me hot tea with whiskey. I'm so hot I get chills, and we share a fleece blanket.

I am not hungry, but the plates of food keep coming. Francesca is a fabulous cook. She whips up salads, sliced meats, and pasta. But I am content with my tea and whiskey. Francesca is welcome to join us again, but she instinctively declines. It tells me her act of consideration is what Carlotta would want.

"So, old man of the sea, how did you lose your way?"

"I was paddling with the current toward the sun, and just lay back to contemplate my being," I say with a laugh. "And I fell asleep. When I woke up, I'd lost my paddle and my sense of direction. And then you were there . . ."

"To rescue you—"

"*Amen,*" I say with a bellowed sigh.

"You say that so strongly. Do you need rescuing?"

"Doesn't everyone?"

"I suppose, in some way or another. Or just a hand to hold. At times." Carlotta has never looked more beautiful. She seems not of this world. There is no bitterness.

I am already thinking of where we should do it. As in, share a life. And all the ancillary and adjacent thoughts, of everything that life has to offer when it is shared with someone special. In a very short time, I have come to realize that she is that someone.

"You mentioned contemplating your being? What is your being?" Carlotta asks.

I light up a cigarette then, and she joins me. "My being is . . . in my hands . . . in my art."

She pauses, if for no other reason than to be respectful. "Is that all?"

"It's enough, no?"

"There is so much more to life than what we do, don't you think?"

I take my time with it. Every splintered or corrupted thought I have, she seems to know how to heal it and smooth it over. My instinct lets me know she is right—about so many things. Truths are within us all, but some discover them quicker than others. Some lose their way, following false truths to serve temporary psychological needs. Some take years to find their way back; others never do. When you stumble upon or find new truths and they reveal themselves to you, however it happens, you incorporate them into your life. But all truths are within you. Carlotta unleashes this thought in me as we are speaking. She makes me want to be a better person. A better being. A better soul.

"I do, yes. *Now.*"

"Just now?"

"I think I have known that always. But it has taken me a while to embrace it. I have been following false leads."

"Why?"

"Money. Ego. The dysfunctional one-two."

We sit in silence and take in the stillness of the water, with the shimmering lights of the coast reflected on its glassy surface.

"I have pursued false leads, too," she reveals.

"Yes? That surprises me."

"Really? Why?"

"You seem so grounded."

"You can become grounded once you've hit the ground. The lowest ground. Being grounded often comes with hard work."

"The knocks of life?"

She hesitates and looks squarely at me but says nothing. Which is saying a lot.

"Have you experienced tragedy? Or mistreatment?" I ask.

"Tragedy, in some ways, yes."

"What kind of tragedy?"

"I did not know how to love. And that is tragic."

"That's sad. That's not tragic."

"To a romantic, it's a total tragedy," she says, and we both laugh.

"Do you know how to love now?"

"Yes. I think so. Let's put it this way. I'm a work in progress. But there has been progress. And you?"

"That is a very good question."

She laughs, but lightly, thoughtfully, and not judgmentally.

"I'm not sure how much progress I've made." I wonder then if I should say this or pursue this line. But that is the thing about Carlotta. She inspires me to speak truthfully. And not hide. Or play games. Or even hold back. "But I know the first step."

"Which is?"

"Loving yourself."

"Being honest with yourself, like that, is also a start. And no matter what has happened in my life, there is one German quote I always return to: 'There are no facts. Only interpretations.'"

"Nietzsche . . ."

"So you know it—"

"I heard you say it once before. When we first met. At the Giubbe Rosse. You said it then to your friends."

"Ah, *sì*."

"You want to hear one of my favorites?"

"Tell me."

" 'In dreams, everything is possible.' "

"Ah, yes. So deep down in that Spanish soul, you may be a romantic, too?"

"Of course I am a romantic!" And I belch it like a ham, overcooking it for effect. *"I am Catalan! And I am an artist!"*

"Bravo, yes. Like Miró. Picasso. Gaudí. And Dalí."

"I like the company. *Gracias.*"

"De nada."

"Actually, that is what I was doing when you rescued me this afternoon."

"What were you doing?"

"Dreaming that I was an eagle."

"En serio?" she asks.

"Sí."

"That says a lot about you."

"What?"

"Allora—I once took a class about indigenous cultures," she says. "In some native philosophies, each animal has 'medicine'—special attributes, a lesson for us. An Eagle can be free and follow its heart; it can fly above the mundane into the light that is always available for those who seek illumination. *Troppo pesante*—too heavy?"

"Too beautiful—if there is such a thing. I want to live life by those words—starting now. *Grazie,* Carlotta. Is there an animal for you? Close to your spirit?"

She pauses. "Perhaps," she says with a guarded smile.

"Tell me. *Per favore.* Which?"

"Maybe. Someday . . . when I get to know you better—"

"This might be a way to do that—"

"A girl has to retain some mystery, doesn't she?"

"Amore," I say finally, and it feels good to express it, "you have been the most mysterious person I have ever come in contact with."

"Good," she says, prideful.

"A hint?"

"Someday. *Amore . . .*"

It is time—of course. To kiss her the very first time. If she will have me. But something is holding me back. Not fear. But introspection. Perhaps the eagle discussion has brought it on. I don't know. But I stand up and return to the bow and gaze out over the edge. After several moments, I slowly spin back around and face her. She is still sitting there by the forward mast.

"Why me?" I ask.

"What do you mean?"

"Why have you chosen me?"

"Who said I have chosen you?" She laughs then. I do, too, but less so. She rises to her feet and steps softly toward me. "What I mean to say is, your life brought us together. My life brought us together. There was no choosing."

"But you accepted my soul's invitation," I remind her. "When I was trying to paint you from memory in my studio and couldn't get your eyes."

"Yes. I did."

"You did not have to."

"I know."

"And here we are."

"Yes, here we are . . . Do you want to fuck me?"

I'm surprised by her blunt vulgarity, but she has a caustic sense of humor, with her own brand of irreverence that blends, if not aligns harmoniously, with mine.

"Where I come from, to *fuck* also means to *deceive.* And no—I don't want to deceive you."

"Where do you come from?"

"New York. You know that."

"But I thought you came from here—"

"I was raised here, in Mallorca, but until I met you I was living in New York. And New York stays with you. No matter where you are. Like most places do, but more so. New York is a *more so* city, in every way."

"I understand. Tell me about your friends—"

"In New York? They're all jackasses."

"Maybe time to get some new friends."

"I know."

"In the kingdom of the jackasses, the ass is king."

We share the laugh. "Very clever. Well, you got me. I'm an ass."

"I set you up."

"I know."

"You know about the kingdom of the blind?"

"Yes, of course. One-eyed men are kings. And what of the kingdom of the whores?"

She laughs. "Tell me—"

"The broke one is queen."

"Well, perhaps you don't know this about me, but—I'm broke."

We collapse into each other with a ferocity reserved for decades-old unrequited lovers, in the García Márquez mold.

We are greedy for each other. The hunger is palpable. The avarice undeniable. But we take it easy. We have all the tick-tocks in the world. I taste her flesh. Her lobes. Her lips. Fistfuls of sun-splashed chestnut hair. The softest mounds of voluptuous tissue swallowed nearly whole. Tongue trails feather up the inner thighs. There's gentleness. Mania. Delicate, deliberate preambles to full-body, harsher erotic pursuits. We can't get enough, but restraint rules. Anticipation mixed with playful and tormenting arousal. Driving each other jungle-wild. She seems to know me. What pleases me. And I know her, somehow, some way. This sensorial tease is an instinctual pact, signed without a whisper. At long last. The candle burns beside us, and our movements are glowing shapes.

There is no artifice, no pretending. Smooth, heated petals unfold, flow, and gush a fragrant signature saliva. The festival for a maestro. Perhaps his finest hour. A legato tongue-tip massage spiked with staccato bursts. A precise tempo combined with dashes of purposeful pause. A formula deciphered, discovered, then administered to overkill. Merciless. With timely supplemental explorations to accentuate the writhing, the arching back, pitches and twists, resounding shrieks, bounces, and stutters as if to a bumpy road. Until it can take no more. Curves capitulate, reversing back with a jolt to a hip-swivel over and to the side. A death to the cycle. One of a hopeful many. For us both. Labored breaths die into the pillow and become nothing . . .

We are greedy to please each other.

"I think I'm in love with you, Carlotta."

She says nothing, but her actions scream a response. Reciprocity is on her mind, though it's no requirement. Grateful swollen lips descend in a machine gun of kisses, each one lighter than the next. And farther down to the sensitive skin, arriving at a longing waist. And onward. The engorged member stabs away beneath her chin. It's something she must address. And soon. Or I'll go out of my fucking mind. It's jungle-wild, all right. My thoughts of what could come. She kisses it atop, then lower. She trails down the shaft carefully, cautiously, holding it at the base while treating it like a fragile piece of parchment from centuries ago. Her hands cup the soft stones and massage them until they vanish in her mouth. One. Then the other. All the while her hands grip and massage. Kisses rise up, and she buries the head in her wet mouth while her hand now cups the stones. It disappears altogether from sight, and my eyeballs roll in reverse. She takes a while, she lives it, she owns it. She gets more proactive, up and down, a rise and fall, her hair strewn across my pelvis tickling me, too. She takes even more time and gets to know its every nuance. What was unknown is now known, and knowing she has that knowledge is equally enthralling. She rises up and away and looks at me and offers the slightest shake of the head.

She falls back in slow motion and gently tugs my hand. I see her splayed there, her gorgeous legs parted, her head lying peacefully on the pillow, her eyes glazed and at half-mast. "Make love to me."

I let my chest land softly upon hers and feel her breasts pressed against me. I kiss her warmly, then with everything I have. And she returns it. She nudges me on the shoulder again, and I pull back and smile at her lovingly. To which she nods. The tip goes first and I leave it there; it's time for her to experience jungle-wild. She half-smiles, aware of my plays, my pauses, now. But I will not. Her hands descend my back, and she covers my cheeks with her palms and applies pressure forward. I acquiesce partially, meeting her halfway, and she lets out something guttural, the sound heard from caves to bedrooms for tens of thousands of years. I'm done with my hesitations, and I let it go and let it swim freely all the way to the end. And the pace remains slow for a long while, until I am directed otherwise. But I am not. Not for a while. And we kiss deeply through it all.

The easy all-senses-saturated pace is preferred. Until it is not. Now a double tap to the shoulder informs me.

Legs pretzel around me, and I let it ride hard and fast until our stomachs are slapping each other, until I need to pause so as not to let fly so soon. I wait, and we kiss and pant and laugh, and it's all far beyond the farthest side of beautiful. Until I get another soft shoulder tap and I march on like a dutiful soldier and I feel my lower back and ass being carved and shredded. And the combination of pain and pleasure defines itself. But it's not all about her or all about me, it's about us, and like a conductor to a symphony, I slow down instinctually once again, and the change is welcomed and sealed with more deep kisses, heads writhing and twisting back and forth at maximum lip pressure. She bites my lip and we taste the blood and I feel her swallow it and then I treat myself to the greatest gift of all. I raise my head back and look deeply into her eyes. The room is shadowed so I can't see the twin emeralds firing, but I can make out her expression as I plunge inside her again and again and again. Just to see her eyes registering what is happening below, the privacy of it, the intimacy, the unique profundity, is a source of unfathomable joy—my absolute favorite thing.

Her hands nudge my shoulders to back away, to put me on pause. As I back away, glorious curves spin beneath me until the gorgeous backside is facing me, and she rises up, perching herself on all fours. I comply but soon after receive a slap to my ass like a crop to a horse. A request for more thrust. I grasp her shoulders for balance, then brace her hips and proceed like a battering ram. Methods are condoned and appreciated. She indicates a preference for an even deeper intimacy to bolster our mounting secrets, and the moans and cries indicate we have arrived at what may satisfy her most. Severe domination is welcome, the harsher the better. I clutch her breasts and knead them like two loaves of bread as I hammer away. I change grip and pull her to me, to the rhythm of my forward thrusts. I cannot hold back. It's all too much, and I suddenly begin to shudder. And I succumb and cry out. I withdraw and reverse. The searing milk flies forth and covers her beautiful ass.

We lie back awhile, sufficiently exhausted, and say nothing. I feel irritation if not pain in places. She has left marks. I have left welts. We spin in and kiss lightly. I think she is smiling in the dark but can't be sure. The candle's flame went out a short while ago. We have scratched and clawed and ground ourselves down to the bare mattress, the twists of sheets nowhere to be found. A loving sexual greed at its finest. Rarest. Chemicals deep in the gut have been altered. Forever. For me certainly. For her, too, I believe.

Before passing out, I have an idea. "Let's make love to the sunrise."

"Hmmm?" I hear her groan. "Sunrise?"

"When the orange, fuchsia, pink, and violet fuse together we can greet it. Wouldn't that be fine?"

"It would be quite an accomplishment," she says with a yawn.

But I am thrashed and depleted. And in the groggiest of fogs. I desperately need to pass out and recharge. After all, this is merely day one.

WHEN I AWOKE, I saw the chandelier first. Then the moldings. Pricey, unoriginal paintings adorned the walls of an immaculate, luxurious room. Confused, I scanned the bedside table and found a notepad with the Ritz-Carlton Hotel letterhead. I popped out of bed and stubbed my toe on the carpet while sauntering unevenly to the nearest window. I looked at the view of Central Park, and below at the passing cars. I had indeed been an overnight guest at the venerable hotel.

I heard the shower blasting then, at the other end of the suite. I passed several suitcases splayed open, each blossoming with jeans and dresses and sprouting more brassieres and panties. I spotted the shimmering black Léger gown draped over a club chair.

The noise of the shower came to a halt. Julia emerged soon after in a cloud of mist, her head wrapped in a towel turban. She was startled when she saw me standing there. "Whoops, you scared me. Morning, baby—"

"*Buenos días . . .*"

"You okay?"

"Uh, uh, yeah. A little disoriented."

"I ordered your favorite—*huevos rancheros.* They should be here shortly." She was rushing to get dressed, and it took all of a minute. "My car is waiting for me. I'm late! We start shooting in an hour in Brooklyn."

"Shooting what?" I asked.

And she was at the door already. "A Chanel ad . . . See you!"

Just like that, she left.

I collapsed in the club chair. I wasn't feeling well. It was a combination of anxiety and perhaps paranoia. I heard a knock on the door, and I rose and ambled over to answer it. I wasn't hungry, but I would, at the very least, take Julia's breakfast order. I opened the door, and to add to the morning of surprises, it was Julia once more. She had a panicky buzz in her eyes.

"I need to ask you. Did you dream of that girl again last night? Carlotta?"

There was a beat of silence between us, as I did not know how to answer. I looked into Julia's eyes, which reflected her hurried morning. Yet there was something else distilled in there, too, almost a nervousness or even a hint of jealousy. This was important to her, and so was my response.

"Yes. I did."

She looked me squarely in the face, and I saw something die in her piercing violet eyes. And with that, she emitted a sigh that sounded like the last breath leaving her body. She wasn't in any hurry now. Her emotional receptors, so refined and highly developed, had been overloaded. She looked as if the arrow of hurt had bypassed her heart and pierced her soul. Nodding sparely, she pivoted and walked down the hall without uttering another word.

As I saw her slip into the elevator, I knew we would never be together again, at least in that way. There would be no more liaisons of mutual convenience or late-night invitations. She now saw my nocturnal interlude as a transgression of sorts, despite the fact that we had just engaged in the most profound and intimate levels of sexual activity, resulting in our best sex yet. But she also perceived—as I had—that I had been making exploratory love with someone else, not her. That was the peak of insult. And perhaps humiliation.

I called reception for a razor, and when it arrived, I luxuriated in steamy hydrotherapy under the expansive showerhead. As I imagined a jungle rain cascading upon me, I tried to piece the evening back together.

I remembered too many details, and that indicated one thing and one alone. I had been with Carlotta after all. I could not explain it in real-life terms, other than there must be a parallel universe at play.

Because Carlotta and I *had been together.* Of that I was certain. I knew everything about her, right down to her personal biological scents. Hot flashes of memory hit me as I dried off and shaved, and the more I remembered, the more vivid the specifics of the evening became. On that boat. In the Cala de Deià. When Carlotta saved me at sea. When we made love for the first time.

I got dressed, and as I lifted my jacket, the baggie full of Molly Boy "vitamins" fell to the carpet. There were some left, thankfully. It made me wonder if the sleeping pills had induced my surreal dream state. And my current grogginess. But I concluded that was not possible—my memories were too lifelike.

The breakfast Julia had ordered arrived, but I had no interest in *huevos rancheros,* or any food of any kind, for that matter. I lit up a cigarette instead and sat at the table nearest the windows. There was another Ritz-Carlton pad lying there. With a pencil I found in the desk, I immediately got to work on a sketch. I tried to recapture Carlotta's face from my fresh memories of our Spanish voyage. I had made it my mission to get to know her better, and now that I did know her, truly and deeply, in the most intimate of ways, I had high hopes that my expanded knowledge and fresh perspective would be reflected in any new creation.

It wasn't that I was being an opportunist, simply taking from her for my art. It was just that everything about her moved and inspired me to reach for new heights. She was my magical muse, as it were; but most of all, without a doubt, I was in love with this remarkable woman. I counted the hours until I could see her again.

I turned my phone back on and spied the numerous texts Rafaela had sent me to remind me of an appointment I had at the SoHo studio with Jean Paul, my art dealer. He had flown in from Paris strictly for the visit, and was bringing with him a few well-heeled French collectors who wanted to see some work for a potential show at the Centre Georges Pompidou. I was already several hours late. I was still clutching my phone when she called again, as she had apparently been doing all morning. Jean Paul was very upset that I hadn't shown up, as were his buyer colleagues, and they were already on their way to the airport to return to France.

Rafaela of course read me the riot act, and I of course told her I didn't give a shit and hung up on her. I didn't give a damn about meeting Jean Paul or his merry band of French collectors. He was the type of art-world opportunist I needed to stay away from. Even Carlotta agreed that I should not surround myself with my dysfunctional group of friends and associates any longer. Enough was enough.

Eventually, I tried to reach Uber to arrange for a cab downtown, but found that the company had actually terminated my account after the Peking Duck incident. *Motherfu—!*

I hailed a cab the old-fashioned way and headed downtown, back to my apartment, cut a sharp path past Rafaela, who tried to launch in on me, and locked myself in the studio. On the way in, I'd grabbed a bottle of Blue Label to serve as a one-two punch, along with an eight ball of yeyo I pulled from the nightclub utility baggie. Sufficiently jacked, I began to re-create my recent otherworldly sojourn in seaside Spain in order to put it to canvas for a new series.

I labored through the night, from detailed charcoal sketches to a vast array of oils. It was an explosion of color, passion, and love in many forms. Channeling a new energy, I was inspired like I hadn't been in ages. If ever. This was the new me, the real me, and the best reflection of me. And I was proud of my fresh creation, the beginning of the most personal series I had ever undertaken. I was being truthful to myself and operating from a place of raw instinct. I had given birth to a new universe, *my* universe. I called it *The Parallel Universe,* and by morning it had come alive, in all its otherworldly intent, and I with it.

I had been reborn—and now I was ready to sleep.

11

MEETING OF LESSER MINDS

I am walking down Via Cavour toward Carlotta's apartment with unparalleled excitement. I can't wait for her to see my new works. To keep Carlotta from seeing the paintings before they are ready, I have been visiting her rather than having her come to my studio. She says she has not seen anything of mine in a while, only in some magazine before we ever met. So I have asked her to wait and not Google anything. I don't want her to see my old canvases. I'd like her to see only the new ones now, especially since they depict our vacation in Cala de Deià. They will be like giant postcards, a gift to ourselves that we can privately share. Later I will show her the old pieces, perhaps, so that she may see the progression—but only if she asks to. I want her to appreciate my work. I want her to be proud of me. More than anything, that is what is important to me.

In the front entrance of her building, I ring the buzzer to her family's apartment; she lives there alone when she is in the city, and is staying another night before heading back to the vineyard in Gaiole.

Her parents rarely visit the city anymore, as they are semi-retired and for the most part have left the business in the very capable hands of Carlotta. My Carlotta. She runs the family winery now—a business well known for making some of the finest Chianti in Tuscany—as the chief manager and sommelier.

I text her, but she does not respond. A neighbor who has seen me there before and recognizes me as Carlotta's friend opens his own door.

"Have you seen Carlotta?" I ask, likely too animated.

"I haven't seen her today," he says, but he opens the door to the lobby for me anyway. I climb the stairs instead of taking the elevator, too antsy to wait for it to return to the ground floor. I am huffing and puffing as I knock on her apartment door, and I place my other hand on my heart to calm the pounding in my rib cage.

"Rodrigo!" someone calls out, and there is more knocking. But I realize I am not doing the knocking. Is someone else knocking on a door down the hallway? Who is calling me?

Knock! Knock! Knock!

"Rodrigo! Open the door!"

"What? Who are you?" I am disoriented.

"It's Rafaela!"

"Rafaela? What are you talking about? I'm traveling!"

"Please open up!"

"I am in Florence! Go away!"

What the hell is going on? I blinked and looked around, struggling to wake up, and saw *The Parallel Universe* paintings. Apparently, I passed out on the couch after working all night. *The Universe* informed me that I was in my studio in the loft in SoHo. I recognized the furniture and saw my New York mobile phone on the table. But I still wouldn't let anyone in. The studio was off limits now.

"Rodrigo! Open up!"

"Rafaela! Go away! I want to be left alone!"

"It's important!"

There was no way I was coming out. "What I'm doing in here is important! *More* important!"

"Please, this is *very* important!"

"You can't come in here!"

"I don't want to come in there! I just need to talk to you!"

"Yeah—what about?"

"Rodrigo!" she yelled, and Rafaela rarely did that.

"What do you want from me? *I'm retired!*"

She hesitated a moment. Then she said it earnestly, her voice now controlled and calm. "You haven't paid me in weeks. I'm sorry. But I need the money."

It was just about the only thing she could say to get me to come to the door. Appealing to my sense of honor. Dammitall!

"What time is it?"

"It's nine."

"It's too early."

"Nine in the evening."

I'd slept through the day. But so what? I didn't give a flying fuck. I'd given birth, and that takes a while. And I needed to recharge for the next installment.

"And it's Thursday. You've been in the studio for three days . . ."

Thursday, I thought. *That's impossible.* But then I gazed around the studio and saw about twenty canvases. It must have been three days. I couldn't have done all this in one night. *Holy shit!*

"Rodrigo . . ."

Whatever. I needed to do what I had to do. I didn't feel guilty in the least.

I rolled off the couch and stumbled across the floor in my jeans and socks, no shirt. At the door, I turned and rested against it and gave another look to the freshly blossomed series. It filled me with happiness. Even the Eagle was eyeballing me from atop the *Monkey*

Business mast to remind me of my connection to the divine. I put my finger to my lips and said to my new family, to all my little brothers, "*Sssssshhhh.* Our secret."

I unlatched the chain and twisted the double locks. I opened the door about four inches. Rafaela's face appeared in the crack.

"Go write yourself a check, bring it to me, and I'll sign it."

"I can't."

"You can't? Why not? I give you authorization—"

"Your checks are in the safe."

"*Porca miseria!*" I cursed in Italian. "Here, let me give you the combination."

"You made me vow to never let you do that. Please—"

"Do it!"

"I won't!"

It was a stalemate, but Rafaela had been good to me. Even now she was showing me her uncompromising fidelity. I remembered, too, that I had my stash of tranquilizers, sedatives, baby Adderalls, and other assorted "vitamins" no one knew about hidden in there. Rafaela would surely throw them out if she saw them. I had to comply.

I released the latch and stepped out and quickly double-locked the studio door behind me. I hurried past her. I was going to be quick—I needed to get back to the studio.

I burst through the door to the study and there they were, seated in a semicircle, looking up at me. I was in absolute shock. Rafaela followed me in and closed the door, locking it behind her.

I knew instantly what this little congregation was about. They had come to confront me. All of them. My attorney, Alan Steinberg, was there. Jean Paul was there. Alfonso, of course. My general practitioner, Dr. Sands. Tex—Tex, of all people!—was seated next to him. Even Rachel, my PR gal, was there. Rafaela settled herself in one of the two remaining chairs. The last one was poised opposite the semicircle, reserved for me.

My eyes fixated on the table before them and a pile of apples in a bowl. "How about them apples," I said.

Dr. Sands disregarded my attempt at hollow charm and spoke first. "Rodrigo, we've come here together for one reason, and one reason only. Because we care—"

"I know why you're here," I said. I was about to call them out and tell them that I knew they were fearful I'd lose myself to my true art, the one that turned off the money tap. *Their* money tap. But I held my tongue, for one reason and one reason only. To bide my time. I knew where I had to go and what I had to do. I had places to be and a *Universe* to create, and I would not let them interfere with my travel or work schedule. But what they had going for them was numbers. So I had to play it cool and smooth and gay and breezy and yes the fuck out of them all.

And that's exactly what I did.

"So, okay, cherished friends and confidants. I realize I've been acting somewhat erratically, if not recklessly, but you're not here to play Pictionary, so bring it on."

They hurled it at me. Each one took a turn to explain how I had disappointed them, hurt them, or showed behavior that worried, even scared, them. One right after the other. Even Tex. If anyone needed an intervention, it was *him.* But when you have that kind of money, no one ever tells you the truth. On some level, I should know.

The sum of it all was that I showed a great deal of restraint and concurred with everything they said. I admitted that I was wrong— dead wrong—and they were right. I agreed that they were completely justified in their concern for me. I confessed that I'd become worried for myself, worried that my faculties were in disarray, my world had lost its axis, and I needed help—and would seek it. I thanked the good Lord for them, these wonderful, spiritually connected, high-minded peeps, and, man, did I feel fortunate to have them in my life. I even agreed to see a professional colleague of Dr. Sands at Cornell Medical the following morning so that he could conduct tests and perform a psychiatric evaluation.

I was A-OK with everything. If they'd asked me to bend over so they could shove a red-hot poker up my ass, I would have flashed cheeks with a gracious grin.

There would be no need to strap me to a gurney, no rags stuffed down my throat so I wouldn't swallow my tongue, no burly orderlies to manhandle me, no needles to the arm to make me a docile chimp, no IV units, and no physical restraints while I violently fought them off in a kicking, screaming fit. There would be none of that. I took it nice and slow and easy and tame, with the resistance of a teacup Maltese.

Those *pricks.*

I simply asked Rafaela to get me a shirt to cover myself while I opened the safe and took out my checkbook. I scratched off checks to my staff and gave them raises on the spot. I asked everyone else if our accounts were up to date. Jean Paul, of course, asked for five grand. Though the oily son of a bitch still owed me a fistful of euros, I gave it to him without protest, to boost my profile, to display a hint of magnanimity and psychological balance. If I'd had some chocolates from the holiday sampler series, I would have passed them around on a plate of my finest china.

I made only one request, which was more of a proclamation. "I was up late last night, and I'd like to be of clear mind for tomorrow's evaluation, so if you will forgive me, I'm going to retire and get some rest."

I thanked them all for coming, for having had the courage to come forward; I admitted that their actions did in fact show the deepest form of love, and I expressed how much the little gathering meant to me. I told them I loved them all, and I hugged each and every one of them, surviving even a cheek brush with Tex's spray-tanned face and atrocious cologne. When I waved good-bye with a hearty big-toothed

Mallorcan dazzler, I think my gold molar cap glinted in their direction with a *ding!*, little darlings that they were.

With that I sauntered peacefully to my bedroom, like a model patient embracing the notion that knowing you have a problem is three quarters of the battle—and I had articulated it just like that to serve as my final gesture of sportsmanship as well as my parting words.

When I reached my bedroom, I wanted to puke. But my state of perturbation did not last. I was already starting to pack, and thinking about my future and what I must do to get from here to there. Without this infestation, without these blockers, without the people I'd just left downstairs. And *with* my new family, my new universe, my *Parallel Universe*. And with *Carlotta*.

I'd never looked so forward to the future, regardless of where it might take me.

TWELVE O'CLOCK HIGH

The clock hadn't even struck midnight when I rocketed out of the SoHo loft. I didn't have much of a plan other than to escape its confines after making a quick revisit to my combination safe for some essential traveling gear—most important, my baggie of vitamins. I had already packed my passport. I was paranoid, I admit, but I was trying to think two steps ahead of them. If they confiscated it, I would be locked in their world, and I might never be able to get back to my parallel universe and Carlotta's world again. I could never finish painting my *Parallel Universe* series. Because this psychological evaluation stuff could undo me. Because it would give them an accredited professional opinion. And therefore grounds. The beginning of the end. Of my end, too.

I hit the money machine and withdrew a lot. I needed cash—nothing that could be traced to my movements or whereabouts.

And then I just moved. Onward. By foot. Without a care in the world. I'd made a good stand against my overpaid staff and their intervention team. I had won my freedom, and now I would blow with the wind.

I decided against a cab. Again, I didn't want anyone to have a track on me. I turned off my phone, too, hoping to thwart any geo-locational attempts, in case Rafaela got chummy with some surveillance folk.

I avoided all the known hangouts and boîtes. I would go where no one knew me and no one could find me. I was taking a me holiday and didn't plan on it ending too soon. I just needed a proper hole in the wall, I thought, a crack of daylight. In this universe, it was all about me, in the now, and no one else.

I marched uptown as far as Washington Square Park. I lit up a cigarette and moseyed around the big arch. There were clusters of night crawlers, as usual. I took a seat on one of the benches and contemplated the galaxy.

I was looking to achieve liftoff, to travel and see the world and the woman I loved. It was as easy as one, two, three. The first guy came and went, and I let him. He tossed me some lures but seemed too sketchy. A second street urchin came around; he seemed like a guy I could work with, but he didn't have what I was looking for. The fact is I didn't know what I was looking for, just where I wanted to be. It was the third one who was giving off the proper pulsations. Now all he needed to be was holding—whatever it was I needed.

"Hey, want Molly?" he sent my way.

"No, no Molly." I checked him out and liked his vibe; I thought our sensibilities could be in alignment. It was the only test, and I'd gotten pretty good at it. "What else do you have?"

"Got evathin', brother. K, pot, coke, meth, too, got some rockin' meth—"

"Anything else?" I said with intent. "I want liftoff."

"Ah, I got you. You're a high roller. Don't got none here, but I can take you—"

"Take me—"

"For commission and cab fare back."

"Done."

We hopped in a cab and arched over the Brooklyn Bridge soon afterward. His name was Jesus, and he told me he had about sixteen nationalities in his DNA. "I'm an ambassador to the world, brother. A United Nations all-star."

"Good on you."

We pulled up in an industrial section of Greenpoint, all warehouses, some already converted to private residences. We got out of the cab after I paid the fare, and the Ambassador rapped on a warehouse door. I saw a panel in the door slide back, a window peeper. Not long after, locks unsnapped, and a big guy with an automatic rifle opened it up.

"Jesus, what we got here?"

"Yo, Disco," the Ambassador said, "we got a high roller."

"You know him?"

"Yeah, yeah. We grew up together. Shared the same crib."

Disco smiled with a twist. "It's your funeral."

"No, man, he's cool. Like the summer breeze."

The Ambassador tapped me then, and I gave him two hundred-dollar bills. "Pleasure doing business with you, brother."

"And you."

The Ambassador disappeared into the night, and I was on my own. I stepped inside, and as the big guy held the gun, another wiry sort stepped from the shadows and frisked me. When he finished, he offered a short nod of approval to his armed colleague.

The three of us walked through an enormous space that was so dark I could barely see. We arrived at an old elevator. The door opened, and the wiry guy and I stepped in. Then we went down, way down. At least a few floors. I could hear noise; music, actually.

A couple more doors were unlocked, and I entered the subterranean paradise. The decor was somewhat Oriental, somewhat Parisian, like some kind of fantasy place. Red velvet was everywhere, even on the walls. A few lamps with red shades and red lightbulbs gave the entire space an otherworldly hue. There were lounge beds and club chairs and tables scattered in groupings around the large room, softly lit by a sea of candles. Asian girls were everywhere. Beautiful ones, too. The high end. People on beds were kissing, snorting, fingering, shooting. I opted for a more private affair.

An exotic cocktail was passed to me from a tray, and I was escorted by a beauty in heels to a room. My room. For me—only me—and any company I wanted. The room was furnished with the same kind of table, chairs, and bed that I had seen in the public room, plus a mini-bar with spirits. My personal valet was an elegant Indonesian beauty who introduced herself as Akira. She was dressed in maroon satin, her lips and nails painted to match her dress. She poured me a double Scotch and gave me a kiss that tasted sweet. She let the kiss linger, but when I didn't reciprocate, she stepped back and bowed deferentially. "Call me if you need something," she said in a soft, silky voice that was as sexy as the rest of her.

"What do you have that's good for me?"

"Everything, sir."

"Like—?"

"Cocaine. Crack. Heroin. Propofol."

"What's that?"

"It makes you sleep. You don't sleep?"

"I sleep. My trouble is when I wake up." Unsurprisingly, I decided on the propofol. Akira left the room and came back soon after with another woman, named Melanie, who was perhaps Filipino, Malaysian, or Eurasian—I couldn't tell. Melanie rolled the IV unit into the room, and I stretched out on the bed before exposing my right arm. Melanie tied the tourniquet and gave me the stick, and I watched my veins swell as the milky substance began dripping like honey.

13

DREAM PLAYERS

Carlotta is waiting upon my answer. *Back, back, back . . .* I'm going way back . . . all the way to when I was a schoolboy in Mallorca . . . We are sitting in the hot tub on the terrace of her apartment, with a glorious sweeping view of the Duomo and Brunelleschi's dome. It's a starry Florentine night, not a cloud in the sky to veil the crescent moon. I can almost make out a face on it, with its crater eye and long protruding chin.

She is sitting in my lap, beautifully nude, and we are sipping a particularly excellent prosecco from her own vineyard.

"Well—?" she says.

The steam is rising from the churning water. Carlotta gets up from my lap and moves opposite me to let me recount my story. She has asked me about my life, about my past and growing up. I have a feeling there is more to it than a simple question, that something specific is driving her curiosity, though I can't be sure. Since I have no fear of discussing anything with her, I ask her about it: "Why do you want to know about my past life? Talks of the past can be so boring."

"Don't make it boring, then," she says. "I'm sure you can make it colorful."

"I'll try."

"Rodrigo, I love being with you, and I just want to understand what makes you who you are, how you became *you*. There are so many things I don't know. But if you prefer not to, we can talk about it some other time, when you feel like it. Maybe you'll even want to share your past with me someday."

"*Amore,* I want you to know everything about me. I don't wish to hide anything. Some things I just can't remember."

"I don't hold you responsible for telling me those things, then," she says with a smile that reflects silver off her white-white teeth.

I'm glad she is asking about me. She really does want to know. And I want her to. Trust is the foundation of everything, and it starts right here.

I tell her of my days as a schoolboy in Palma. That I wasn't cut out for school, that it didn't seem to fit me too well. I was always getting in trouble, being sent to the principal's office. I smoked and chewed gum, and when it came to girls, I tried to round as many bases as I could get away with. Carlotta produces the mild beginnings of a smile at that.

"One day everything changes. I'm playing hooky like usual, hiding behind hedges so the teachers don't see me. I stay around the schoolyard because I still want to have fun. And I can't go home. This big guy with huge hands sees me crouching there having a cigarette, and he taps me on the shoulder and catches me by surprise.

" 'Hey, what are you doing out here?'

" 'Nothing.'

"He looks down and sees my sketchpad flapped open. It's the one class I like—art. And I sketch a lot. I like to sketch faces. Especially of the pretty girls, and then I give the drawing to them. It often pays off with a kiss. Sometimes more. Sometimes less. I don't do it exactly for that, but I see how it affects people. I like the way they smile when I give them a gift that is so personal; it makes me feel good. And the more I draw, the better I get. And then I start to paint. And that evokes an even bigger response from people.

"'Are you an artist?' he asks.

"'Yes.'

"'What kind of art?'

"'I'm a painter.'

"'How long have you been painting?'

"'I can't remember a day in my life without painting.'

"'Really? *Bueno.*'

"Just then I twist out my cigarette, and I begin to sketch. This man. And he watches me. He says, 'I'm an artist, too,' but I'm too busy with my sketch to answer him.

"'What's your name?' he asks.

"'Rodrigo Concepción,' I tell him.

"'My name is Heriberto Carrion.'

"I look up from my sketch then. 'I have heard the name,' I say. Because he is a legend where I'm from. People talk about him, but I have never seen him before. I have seen his work, though—he's a sculptor.

"And he says to me, 'I want to see everything you have done.'

"'Okay.'

"'Say—I need an assistant, too. To help me with my studio. And my work. Come around after school—'

"'How about now?' I say.

"The big man with the big hands does not turn around to answer my impatience. And my frustration with school. But he does spin around to say, 'Nuance. That is your gift.'

"That is how it all began. I went to his studio every day. I helped him in the preparing of the clay, and I swept up the floors. He made the most amazing creations. He's not well known outside the region. He kind of does it for himself. He never seems to make it in the marketplace, because he won't sell out. He will only do what he wants to do. But he gets by. Yet he has this huge amount of knowledge. And a library filled with works by all the masters.

"He made me study art history from all his textbooks. It was like going to school—but this time it was a subject I loved. He taught me everything about painting, about usage of color, perspective, space, chiaroscuro, about choices of subject matter. And he encouraged style. You cannot teach style. But you can tease it, nurture it, and bring it out—once the basics are digested. And he fed me the food of art and made me digest everything. Big canvases, small canvases. And I started to paint at his studio. I had my first show at fourteen. And I continued to work with him for several more years."

"You owe a lot to him, no?"

I have to pause. I feel a rush of tears to my eyes, not enough to run down my face, but the emotion sweeps over my body. Carlotta perceives my misty expression and extends her hand and places it atop mine.

"Of course. I owe him my entire career."

"So he never makes it himself as a sculptor?"

"He does," I say, collecting myself and my thoughts. "Everyone knows him. But his work is considered intellectual. He's so smart that he conceives of pieces with these layers of thought, rather than things that are pretty or aesthetically pleasing to the eye, things that people want to look at all the time and have in their homes. But he is successful enough to have occasional shows and make a living. And he is well respected in the Spanish art world because he's so knowledgeable. Artists come to him for advice, that kind of thing. He's an artist's artist."

"Is he still alive?"

"I think so."

"What do you mean? You don't know?"

"We haven't been in contact. The last I heard, he was in some kind of hospital." I pause and clear my throat. I cannot bring myself to tell her that I know exactly where he is.

Carlotta seems to eye me in a funny way. "So what did you do after your early shows?"

"At sixteen, I quit school and moved to Madrid. Had my own apartment. And I turned it into a little studio, hanging everything on the walls. Then Heriberto hooked me up with a curator who gave me a room in a gallery to show my work. And it sold. And then I got my own gallery for my own works. I was really young, but my paintings were selling. That is when I met my ex-wife, Maria. She was an aspiring opera singer, and was studying at a conservatory. We fell in love and planned a life together. We got a nice apartment in the city, not too far from where she grew up, and we had lots of friends. And dinner parties. And I continued to work, and she helped me with the finances. And things were going really well. And then . . ."

I laugh now, a nervous laugh, almost out of embarrassment. I know I am getting to the tricky part of my story.

"And then what?"

"May I kiss you?" I maneuver across the tub and kiss her softly.

"Continue, please . . . Tell me . . ."

"And then I explode. My stuff begins to sell for a lot of money. And I'm all over the press. And I have shows all over Spain. Then France. And Italy and London. And I become the new-new thing in the European art world. Not as well known as I am now, but this is when it starts. And this is when I change."

"How so?"

"Well, I start to lose my respect for everything. All the temptations are there, and I stay out all night drinking, doing drugs. I'm an outgoing person, too, and I have enjoyed this kind of mind expansion. It feeds the art. But it's a problem if you're married. Women are throwing themselves at me. And it's not that I don't love my wife, but it's just to have this little experience here, this one there, and each one is kind of wonderful, and you get in a cycle. Did I get married too young? Of course. But we were in love, and that was the most romantic thing we could do. And I went with all of that, too, because I am a romantic, but . . ."

"You cheated on her, yes?"

"Yes. And I am ashamed of it, and of this part of my life. But, well, here it is. I want you to know."

"Go on," she says more reservedly, and finishes her glass of prosecco.

"Maybe this isn't such a good idea."

"No, please. Don't mind me. I'm not judgmental. I understand. More than you know."

It's nice to hear her say that. It's perhaps the nicest thing I can hear at this juncture of my story.

"So the affairs keep on, and I'm traveling, and she's not coming on all the trips, and that leads to other things. Plus, I'm getting really well known, and that takes it to another level. Even the people who don't normally want to be with you, want to be with you. And the snowball builds and builds, and before you know it, you're in this wild, fantastical trip of total chaos. You don't know which end is up, and you do things, silly things, irrational things, deceitful things, and you have to tell stories and fibs, and they get bigger and bigger as the snowball gets bigger and bigger, and, well—"

"When did this all stop?"

"One afternoon when my wife walks in on me and I am having sex with one of her best friends."

"Her friend?"

"Yes. I know, bad. And my wife has had enough. She tries to cut off my balls. She misses and stabs me in the thigh and just misses the artery that would have killed me, and we decide to get a divorce."

I look at Carlotta, and I can see she is a little crestfallen. And I am crushed. And yet I can also see she is trying not to show this. We exchange some kisses, but we do not make love.

We get out of the hot tub and put on robes and sit on the warm shaggy carpet in the living room. We each have another glass of prosecco and kill the bottle. I ask her if she has any Scotch. She points to the bar, and I pour myself a double shot before continuing my story.

"And that is when I decide to leave Spain and move to Los Angeles and live in the Beverly Hills Hotel. I'm wearing a cast from my leg injury, and I hang out on the terrace and meet all the folks staying there, including many celebrities. I turn my bungalow into a studio, and I have parties and go to parties all over the Hollywood Hills, Beverly Hills, and Malibu, and I meet all the actors and actresses, agents and producers. I sell my art, too, to famous people, and get their endorsements, and the word spreads, and I make more of a name for myself. I try to take America right from that hotel. And I do.

"And there's more partying and serial relationships and mind expansion, but now I am not married, and I am free to explore my new life in a fresh new setting with new experiences, and my art reflects this change. My art matures and so do I, in a certain sense. There are still the same temptations I experienced in Spain, but now it is on another level, with really famous people and on a global scale.

"Things just continue to get bigger and more indulgent, but at the same time, I am able to handle it. And not. Because some things get wilder. People come to my bungalow and graffiti the walls, and there are girls, girls, girls—with L.A. agendas—girls who will do anything to gain status or money or access to rich and famous people—they are looking to get a leg up, and they end up getting, well, two legs up . . ."

Carlotta is tipsy and laughing now, and she's warmed back up to me. I hope she thinks I have come out of this dark tunnel I am describing, and I can't wait to get to the end of the story to tell her that, to drive that point home.

I continue, "And people are attracted to you because you're famous, and they attach themselves to you to go along for the ride and see what they can get out of it, too, but you don't care—it's fun, it's a blast, it's L.A., it's America, and this is where you can make it really big, so the show goes on for a while. Until that changes, too."

"How?"

"Well, I am becoming a monster. I am more famous now, and the experiences are right at my fingertips. And I am an artist. I want to consume and produce, consume and produce, not people but experiences. All the experiences—good, bad, sexual, crazy—all to feed the art. Because in the end I am an artist—not a playboy, not a drug addict, not a hedonist; those are the vehicles you use to get your art where you want it to be. But it takes a lot out of me, and by the time I leave L.A., I am just drained. So I am looking for a new challenge, and what is the biggest challenge in the world for a modern painter?"

"New York."

"So I move to New York and buy a loft apartment in SoHo with an amazing roof terrace, and hire a manservant named Alfonso. And my works are well received and I am a celebrity and I have a lot of money in the bank. And then I fall into the same patterns that others have, but now in a New York big-city way: you meet everyone influential, from old money to new money, and everyone you haven't met wants to meet you, and there's Page Six, blasting your fame. Then there are the great restaurants, and I have shows, and there are trips to Art Basel and shows there and trips to European cities, the Biennale in Venice, and back to Europe but now with a bigger name and better galleries to show my stuff, and it's selling and I'm making more money than ever. And this goes on for years, too, until that changes . . ."

"And what change is that?"

"You come to a point where you see the artifice in it all and the empty nature of it, and it's not fulfilling anymore. It can be fun, but, well, so many artists now are marketers, and it's no longer pure art, like it was in the Middle Ages, the Renaissance, or even when Picasso painted in the twenties and thirties . . . It's the twenty-first century, it's a tech explosion, and everyone is an artist or a writer, and especially since I met you, I have come to the realization that I don't really like what I am doing or how I am living—but worst of all, I don't like myself because of it.

"I want something more fulfilling. I am an artist who still wants to produce work, but my mind-set and perspective have changed. That's the big difference—the change within me. I've done the other stuff, and I am depleted, emotionally spent, and perhaps spiritually starved. Not perhaps. *Definitely*." I take another swig and finish my Scotch. I am getting drunk, and the looser I feel, the more uninhibited I am in my discussion with Carlotta. "You mind if I have another?"

"Help yourself."

I make my way over and pour myself a triple shot. I take some ice from the icemaker and toss it in the filled glass.

"Tell me more about Heriberto. Did it end well between you two?"

"Well, no. Not from my standpoint. Not because anything bad happened. But once I hit it big, I never turned back. I never contacted him. I deserted him. Like I deserted a lot of people. But he was special to me in my life. And I rationalized my dismissive behavior by making myself believe he was jealous of me and all my success, when that had never been the case. The fact is, I didn't need him anymore, and I threw him away.

"He was a victim to my ambition. And ego. Because that comes into play, too. You want to believe all the great things everyone is saying about you, that you're amazing, you're a genius. And that twists your mind. It makes you forget. You forget where you come from when all the money and fame arrive. You don't want to give credit. And people who helped you, you put them in that diminished box of 'Well, *he* was lucky to have worked with *me*, because I didn't need him. It could have been anyone, because *I'm that great*—I made *him* a star.'

"And Heriberto, the wise, circumspect, savvy man he was, I'm sure he must have felt all that, that this was what I was doing and what I had become, and it must have hurt him. I am not proud of it. In fact, I am very ashamed. Because I owe everything to this man. My whole career. My whole life, for that matter."

She looks at me squarely for a beat, until I look away. It is a lot to take in. But I'm hopeful that she is encouraged by my honesty, by the fact that I do not try to hide the deeds of my past.

"Do you still take drugs, Rodrigo?"

In Carlotta's world, drugs are not a part of my life. "No, not at all. I quit all that. I'm the healthiest I've been in years. I'm ready."

"Ready for what? A new change?"

"No. A new life."

"The *next* change . . ."

"The next *life*. Ooh, that doesn't sound so good." I stand up then, a little wobbly, I might add. "Want me to spell it out?"

"Spell what out?"

"My whole life."

"If you want."

"Okay, I'll spell it out for you. I've lived the high life. I'm acclaimed. Wealthy. Forty-nine years old. Lived all over the world. I'm colorful. Passionate. Tortured by a decadent life. And the trappings of money. And fame. I'm desperate. For something more. Out of my existence. I want the real love. To be able to trust and be happy. But I've been unable to break free. I have a gorgeous SoHo loft that doubles as my art studio—"

"Hold on, *caro,* you live in Florence. Your studio is here—"

"Wait a second, don't interrupt me," I say drunkenly, beginning to toss and slur my words. "Where am I? *Was* I? Oh yeah. I have an Italian butler, Alfonso. And Rafaela, a beautiful Colombian assistant. She's more like a confidante. And life coach. I paint by day, wait for the night. My two employees clean up the mess I make in the process. I'm a classic lady enthusiast. Incorrigible playboy who parties till dawn. Consuming everything along the way. Waking up with assorted women, sometimes more than one. My 'friends' are a billionaire and a pimp. But I'm—as in me, Rodrigo—I'm Machiavellian. I'll hang with the people who buy and support my art. And bring me ladies. And this hollow, hypocritical setup is, well, it's my life . . ."

"But that was before, when you lived in New York, right?"

"I'm just telling you how it is. I behave objectionably, but I'm likable, and people want to spend time with me. I'm my own protagonist in my own story. I'm sensitive. Thoughtful. I'm a divo sometimes, because of my fame and the fact that I can get away with almost anything, but deep inside—and I think you understand this already—I am still humble and my heart is pure. I want to be better, to do the right thing, but sometimes I make bad choices.

"I have a passion for life, generosity of spirit—but I also see the lies and can expose . . . the deceit around me. But I'm attracted like a moth to a flame . . . to the fame and glamour. And trapped in the excess. The success, money, ladies, the world at my fingertips, have left me depleted. And empty. I go to Art Basel . . ."

"Rodrigo, you're a little drunk."

"I'm being honest here. Full disclosure."

"And you're repeating yourself."

"That's okay. I'm with the lady I love . . . I can tell you everything, right?"

"*Sì.*"

"You appreciate my honesty, don't you?"

She pauses then. "Yes, I do."

"And I go to Art Basel every year—"

"You said this already."

"*Please don't interrupt me . . . gracias,*" I say. "And I play the town with all the decadence it's known for. But I'm crashing. On a downward spiral. I've hit rock bottom. Carlotta, I am truly, truly, truly—"

"I'm listening—"

"—at a crossroads. Of my life. I'm at peace only when I sleep. When I wake up it's the same hollow, hedonistic routine . . . into more debauchery and decadence. I have inconsistent rest patterns . . . and fractured sleep . . . due to my crazy, crazy hours . . . and drug and alcohol use.

"I have not been able to remember my dreams—in dreams, everything is possible. But I have been without them. That constitutes a hole. In my life. And work."

"Rodrigo. It's time to go to bed. I don't like seeing you this way."

"No—hear me out! Full disclosure, remember? I'm giving you what you want. You asked for it. And I'm telling you . . . But suddenly, that changes—"

"What changes?"

"Forgetting my dreams . . . After three nights of partying, my body forces me to rest. I sleep for two days. And during sleep, I meet a woman in my dreams. Until now I have not been able to love a woman in what I would consider to be real love, a pure love, with neither of us having an ulterior motive, because of the contamination of the world I live in. So I am stunned by this meeting. To the point that I want to see her again. But only sleep can bring her back. I'm haunted by her—in a beautiful way—and I fall in love with her, with her beautiful soul and her physical beauty. And she's there waiting for me, in my dreams. All I have to do is show up. It changes my behavior. My patterns. I arrange my days for her. It becomes all about the night, but in a different way than before. It's all about the sleep now. And seeing her again. I start sleeping during the day, too. To be with her. I become obsessed with my dream life. I take sedatives to induce more sleep. As my love affair with my dream woman gets more intense, all I want to do is sleep—so I can be with her. And you know who this woman is?"

"Rodrigo—" Carlotta stands then; she doesn't want to listen anymore.

"You!"

"I think I've heard enough."

"Wait a second—"

"This is crazy talk, Rodrigo. You're scaring me, okay?"

"This obsession turns my life upside down . . . I lose track of what is my real life and what life constitutes my dreams. Until there's a total takeover . . . by my nocturnal fantasies . . . which are no longer . . . fantastical. My dreams become my real life . . . and my real life I treat as a dream. How do you like that?"

Carlotta moves out of the living room and disappears into her bedroom.

"Hey, where are you going?" I call out.

"Time to go to bed."

"With you? Anytime . . . *amore* . . ."

"No. Not with me."

"No?"

"Not tonight. You take the guest bedroom."

"Really? Was it something I said?" I down the rest of my Scotch and pour another. "Do you have any Blue Label?" I blast out. "Guess not."

With my fresh glass, I move unevenly to her bedroom. The door is closed. "Knock, *knock*. Who's there?" I burst through the door. "It's me! The *Eagle*! Remember?"

"Yes, Rodrigo." The voice comes out of the darkness from the other side of her room. "I remember."

"And what are you? What animal? Still haven't told me—"

"Another time."

" 'Cause remember, I'm the Eagle . . . I fly close to the heavens, close to God. Looking for enlightenment. And salvation! Are you going to save me?"

"No, Rodrigo. No one can save anyone—but themself."

"Kinna harsh. Well, I've got it rough, then. 'Cause I have another problem." And I walk deeper into her bedroom and stumble and fall down.

"Yes, you do."

"I know—I have a lot of problems. But I have one major, major problem. Know what it is?"

"No."

"I have to decide . . . what is my dream life? And what is my real life? I mean, who's real? Who are the players of my conscious dreams? And who are the players of my unconscious dreams? Or is everyone a dream player, and life is one complete dream from beginning to end? It is said all over the world, in every language: 'You are the man of my dreams. You are the woman of my dreams.' There has to be more to that. Are we just players in one another's lives? You, me, everyone? It's possible, no? Because in dreams, everything is possible. I leave you with that thought."

"Buona notte."

"Buona notte, Carlotta . . . *Ti amo* . . . Oh, and another thing—"

"Please, Rodrigo, I'm getting angry now . . ."

"Just one more little thing?"

"What is it?"

"I made some new paintings."

"You told me already."

"Not entirely. It's a series . . . of installments. Like chapters. To a journal. My dream journal on canvas. Been meaning to tell you, but my past got in the way. Funny, the past always gets in the way. It's called *The Parallel Universe.* They're about you. Us. I'm not selling them. Won't let anyone see them . . . except you. I think you're going to like them. Hope you do, anyway. But they're in New York—"

Carlotta remains silent.

I think she should have more of a reaction. "Well—?"

"In New York?" she finally asks.

"Yes. I will have them shipped over."

"Shipped from where?"

"From my apartment. They're locked up. In my studio."

"In your dreams, Rodrigo. In your dreams."

"You're teasing me now. Is that all you have to say?"

"That, and congratulations."

"Grazie . . ."

I get up off the floor and stagger back out of the bedroom.

The conversation reminds me that I have to call Rafaela and tell her to ship the new series to me. But the fact is, I do not want her to see the work. She'll show it to Jean Paul and sell it. I'm going to have to figure that one out. Maybe I can get Tex or The Raven or Alfonso to do it. Or my attorney. Yes, that's it. I'll have Alan Steinberg send it. He should be happy with me now. After all, I agreed to the psychiatric evaluation.

I hope I can get some X-rays. Of my brain. I love the black, and the texture of the plastic the X-rays are on. I can collage them into another series.

Like I did at the Beverly Hills Hotel. After the stabbing. With my bloody jeans. And make light boxes for them. The X-rays lit from behind. So you can see the brain. And skull. And teeth. Very electric.

I'll call it *The Intervention*. No, better yet. *The Electric Palette Diaries.*

With X-rays of my mind.

Fuck that. It's the same old narcissistic shit. It's a New York idea all over again. I will never paint about New York again. It represents everything I hate. Everything I am leaving behind. Shame on me for even thinking it. I have left that exoskeleton. Like a snake, I have shed that skin. I have metamorphosed. I was a larva in Spain. A caterpillar in L.A. I was wrapped in a cocoon in New York. And now I am free. A butterfly.

But butterflies don't live long. Only two weeks. They dance in the air with all that brilliant color. For just two weeks. I've always felt for butterflies. They bring such joy to the lives of children. To everyone. Then they die.

Fuck that. I'm no butterfly. I am an Eagle! I'm immortal!

I must be really drunk.

I slip into the guest bedroom and lie down. But I can't sleep. I glare at the ceiling for half an hour and ride the tangents of many splintered thoughts. I go back and forth between the universes. I would like to get all the dream players in one room. And give them a piece of my mind. And tell them I've figured them all out. That I know what they're up to. They can't fool me!

I am still a little cocktailed, and maybe it's better not to wake up all grouchy and hungover at Carlotta's. I wonder if I have been saying too much. I have been known to do that. But she knows me. She loves me. For a love like this, it's full disclosure. Even though she hasn't spoken much of herself. Because I am better now. I have jettisoned the liars, the cheaters, the manipulators, and found my new universe. My *Parallel Universe.* With Carlotta. And it's all breaking as peachy as a Monet sunrise. Or sunset.

Before I know it, I'm back on the streets of Florence. Not much going on at this hour. But you feel like you are stepping back in time. I walk past the Duomo and down a network of little left-right alleys to the side street that leads me to my *pensione.*

I trudge up the stairs and snap open the door to my flat. I step inside and head right to the studio. And *porco dio,* to my utter shock and surprise, the new series is right up there on the wall to greet me, accosting me, saying, "Where the hell have you been?"

I don't know what I have been thinking. It must be the excellent prosecco. Of course it is. Carlotta's a professional who produces superior vintages. Best of all, I don't need to contact Rafaela or anyone else to ship *The Parallel Universe* abroad. *The Universe* is surrounding me. Even the eagle looks happy I'm back home. He has been giving me the eyeball a lot lately. Probably because I have been saying I am an Eagle, and he wants to remain top bird.

"There's room for both of us in this town!" I yell to him.

I better behave. The eagle has got serious juice with God. The One who lives in Duomos worldwide.

Perhaps I said too much to Carlotta. You can do that, you know. Say too much. Then you lose the mystery behind a love. And yourself. Some things you must not give away. You lose power when you do that. When you offer everything or give too much. You can become lost. You must preserve your power. I will preserve my power.

I *am* an Eagle.

Who needs a nap.

14

THE NEW INSTALLMENT

In my studio in Florence, the morning after my long talk with Carlotta, I have a hangover but still remember that I may have confessed too much. There is nothing I can do about it now, though, so I decide to get to work. I'm nearly finished with the newest installment to *The Universe,* a prequel to the first. I have gone back in time to when Carlotta and I met. The first installment is comprised of works from Cala de Deià, so the new chapter of *The Universe* consists of paintings from Florence. I start to attack the canvas, me and my cigarettes. They're the last vice I possess. Cigarettes and alcohol. But I'm not drinking while I paint. I don't even suffer loneliness anymore. Nor do I long for the company of serial partners to compensate for it, like in past realities. That had been a vice. Another type of drug. Now I have one partner. I have the best partner, and that is more than enough.

I toil away for many hours, and it dawns on me that I haven't heard from Carlotta. I decide to phone her, but there is no response.

I send her a text thanking her for the great evening and apologizing for getting a little tipsy.

I do remember her telling me I was scaring her. It is our first quarrel. But she understands I am undergoing a transformation. That is why it's important to let her know about me and my past life. So she can understand fully where I am coming from in my journey, and see the arc of progression.

But I cannot concentrate on that now. I have to get this canvas perfect. This is the most challenging and important one. I've already covered poses at the Giubbe Rosso, the Ponte Vecchio, walking the Florentine streets. I did the head-shot portraits and close-ups, even one with sunglasses. And I hope she finds them worthy. Carlotta is the consummate muse, a gift from the portraiture gods. But this portrait on the easel before me is the one I have been waiting to do for weeks.

I will do more than one of this. Perhaps I will make it its own sub-series. I run off ten sketches, some just the head and eyes, others full-bodied.

My charcoal renderings depict the creature compact. Well muscled. Thick chest. Stocky build. Legs short but thick and mighty. A robust, stout head. Its jaws immensely powerful. Large paws, round pads, razor claws. Short tail. Impressive bone-crushing canine teeth, fangs of several inches. The brownish, tawny yellow coat covered in dark rosettes for camouflage. Then smaller dots and irregular shapes within the darker markings. Some resembling butterflies. Which must work well in the dappled light of a forest habitat. The spots on the head and neck are solid and dark but form a band on the tail.

I need to express the solitary, opportunistic, stalk-and-ambush nature that comes to fruition in that exceptionally powerful bite, more powerful than a lion's. A bite that can pierce the shells of sea turtles. And then there's that unusual killing method. Its canines spike directly through the skull of its prey to deliver a fatal strike to the brain. And all of that needs to be reflected in one place and one place only: the huge eyes—gold and reddish and glittering like Spanish doubloons, with round pupils and irises—and the fearless, merciless, lethal glare contained within them.

Majestic. Solitary. Elusive. Mysterious.

That's what I need to capture in my poses. This is *The Universe*'s fiercest challenge. I feel like I am up to the task like never before, and I get to it with a fury. I administer the oils and incorporate color like never before. I work through the day and into the night. Then into the next day. And the next night. And this goes on for a week.

And I go back and forth. From a dangling tree pose to a portrait, to stalking, to a jungle nap. Mouth open with fangs protruding to an indiscernible jungle smile. Layer upon layer, addition upon addition. I undo and repair. And constantly add more shading and color and check consistently for nuance. Nuance is the crucial element. That is what my mentor, Heriberto Carrion, has told me is my gift. That is what I deliver.

I take my time with this fresh chapter of *The Universe,* not trying to rush. And what I have created is a bomb. It is an explosion.

I am very proud.

15

A SHOW OF ONE

am happy, painting in Florence. I call Carlotta each day when I take a break for light food; I do not want to eat too much and neutralize my real hunger. But she does not answer, and she has not contacted me. I figure she must have gone to the country to take care of her responsibilities to the business and to see her family.

Now the new chapter of *The Universe* is complete. I decide to take a walk and air myself out. I am floating, really, and so thrilled with gratification that I utter a silent prayer of thanks to God as I walk. I have never done that before. I walk along the River Arno and cross one of the baby bridges and look down the river and see all five bridges spanning it in the distance.

My next stop is the Giubbe. I sit at the bar and have a Rodrigo, and the barkeeps tease me because I have paint all over my hands and clothes. As I'm explaining the futurist movement to a German tourist couple and letting them know that the Giubbe was the birthplace of it, I receive a text at long last from Carlotta: *Ciao, Rodrigo. Mi dispiace to have not been in contact. Can you meet me at the café at the Accademia in one hour, per favore?*

I text her I will. I love the Accademia. I'm glad Carlotta has chosen such a Rodrigo-friendly and art-centric place. It is why I came to Florence in the first place, to be surrounded by the works of the masters: Botticelli, Brunelleschi, Leonardo, Raphael, Michelangelo, the list goes on and on. The town may be dead to the modern art movement, but to me it's alive, and I'm thriving in it.

When I arrive at the little café, Carlotta is seated at a table in the back. She is sipping tea. When she sees me, she rises, but the sober expression doesn't leave her face. I approach, and she steps away from the table and extends her cheek to allow me to give her a disappointingly amicable and reserved peck on each one. Nothing more.

She says nothing and we settle into our chairs.

"You're such a mess," she says with a weak smile. "You must have been working."

"I have been. Nonstop."

"The colors on your hands are mesmerizing. Such a wide variety."

"Jungle colors."

"What were you painting? What types of stuff?"

"It's a surprise."

When I say that, her expression reverts to the more complicated grim one, and she takes a deep breath. "Do you want a *caffé* or something?"

"No."

"Rodrigo. I have been doing a lot of thinking."

"Thinking's good. Mind expansion."

"Yes, you're right. But I have been thinking about us."

"Okay . . ."

"I love you. With all my heart I do. But I cannot be with you."

I am stunned to hear this. It is much worse than anything I might have thought she would say. It is too much to take in. I immediately flash back to the last night we were together and realize I have gone too far; I have told her too much about myself. She did warn me that I was scaring her, but I never, ever could have imagined that it would lead to this.

"Let me explain," she adds.

"Please."

"You have told me a lot about yourself."

"Too much."

"Perhaps. But I asked you to, and it was a fair question, I think. But having said that, I have not been fair with you in return. I have not told you much about myself. The fact is, I come from a traditional Florentine family, meaning a traditional Italian family. My mother and father have been married for forty years. But my father has been equally traditional with his endless infidelities. He is like a lot of Italian men who marry their sweetheart to give them their children, and then they assume the right to be with as many women as they wish. Mistresses. It's almost a part of our culture.

"It has always been very difficult for my mother, but especially in this day and age. I don't want that type of life. I have seen my mother's suffering, and it hurts me. I don't wish it for myself. I don't wish it upon any woman.

"And with respect to you, I know how you have changed, and I understand how your life has progressed. And it seems logical that it would evolve the way you described it. I am not judgmental about it, obviously, or I would not have let you get this close to me. But a leopard really does not change his spots. And maybe not today, or tomorrow, or next year, or five years from now, but as a professional artist who needs experiences from which to derive inspiration, you will eventually feel the need to have one of your changes. And we will be in the very situation that I am telling you I don't want. And I will be in the same situation my mother has been in all her married life. So, I am here to tell you I need to stop seeing you."

My brain goes completely numb and I cannot speak. My whole world centers around Carlotta. Not just my emotions and my thoughts but my work, too—what I want to paint now, what I *need* to paint now, the way I express who I am becoming and who I want to be. There is a catch in my throat and I can feel a mist behind my eyelids. I remind myself, *Carlotta taught me that I am an Eagle. Now I must behave like one.*

"Okay," I finally manage to say.

"I'm sorry, Rodrigo."

I already know her well enough to know it is useless to argue with her right now. Is there anything at all I can say to keep the door open even a little bit, so I can try to reach her in the future? I have to try. "I feel so much gratitude for your honesty. And the way you have told me this, it helps me further understand why I love you so much. It lets me know, well, it's out there—people of your integrity. And perhaps at last I am looking for the right things in someone."

"I think you are. And I know it has not been easy." Carlotta's eyes are welling with tears now. "And I know I do love you."

"And I love you."

She reaches forward and clutches one of my rough, paint-splashed hands. "How is the work going?"

"Come to the show sometime. You're the only one with a ticket."

She attempts a smile, but her chin quivers instead. "I'm not that strong . . . Maybe someday." She tries to regain her composure and clears her throat. "I have something I want to tell you. But now—"

"Now what?" I ask.

"—I can't remember." She has a relapse and brings my hand to her bowed forehead, hiding her face, which is contorted with emotion.

Eventually her head lifts up. The lids to her beautiful emerald eyes can hold back the tears no longer. They pour a series of tiny silver droplets down her cheeks as her chin trembles again.

"Don't lose faith, Rodrigo. And don't slip back. To former ways. That would be a shame, you know?"

"I won't . . . I'm an Eagle."

And she smiles through her tears. She looks down and strokes the top of my hand with her thumb while studying it. She bends low and kisses it.

"So many beautiful colors," she says as she rises and then quickly runs off. Through my own tears, I can see her twist back, and a final *"Ti amo"* crosses her lips, but her fractured voice can't produce the sounds, and nothing comes out.

16

MAKING TRACKS

I t was all very hazy. A gentle hand stroked my forehead and brow. My eyes unsealed, but my vision was still blurred. I looked around in a foggy daze and gradually recognized my surroundings: my private room in the subterranean drug den in Brooklyn. I was still lying on my back in bed.

Akira was sitting next to me. Her shimmering black hair, smooth immaculate skin, and full, deep red lips looked beautiful in the soft candlelight. She was still wearing the same glamorous skintight red satin dress, with the same elegant string of tiny pearls suspended from her vulnerable thin white neck. She was as feminine a creature as I'd ever seen. When she noticed that I had become more aware of my surroundings, she smiled, showing her snow-white teeth.

"Hello, Mr. Concepción."

"W-where am I?"

"Don't worry. You are back," she said in that gentle, silky voice. "I was worried about you."

"What a . . . nice way . . . to come back. How long have I been out?"

A voice called out from behind Akira. It was Melanie, the dosage technician. "Over a day!"

"Really?"

Akira nodded and smiled sweetly again and swept my bangs gently off my forehead.

"You be careful. Very dangerous what you do," Melanie remarked.

"You took care of me all this time?"

"I was worried for you. You were very sad."

"I'm a sad man."

"You were crying. A lot. For hours. It made me sad. They were going to take you in an ambulance. But I said no. I said I would take care of you."

"God bless you, Akira." I brought her hand to my lips and kissed it. "Akira, can you do something for me?"

She nodded the shortest of nods. "I will do for you whatever you wish." She squeezed my hand.

"One more. I have to go back."

Her expression changed from warm glow to more serious. "That would be very dangerous."

"I'm fine. I'm strong. Like a bull," I said, and added a smile.

"I will see what I can do." She let go of my hand and stood up. I reached inside my underwear and found the hidden stash. I handed her a thousand in cash before she left the room.

I sat up and put my face in my hands and rubbed my eyes. When I tried to get up, I was unsteady and tipped over. On the second try, I made it over to the bar and poured myself a Scotch. I downed it and poured myself another.

Dangerous or not, deadly or not, I had to go under again so I could see Carlotta in Florence. Akira had brought me back to waking life in the Brooklyn drug den before I even had a chance to try to change Carlotta's mind and win her back. I couldn't imagine life without her in any world or universe, dream or otherwise.

Akira came back in and said, "One more. But you are finished after that."

"Thank you, Akira. Last time," I agreed, and settled onto the bed again, holding her soft hand.

Akira said, "But you must promise—you will come back to me."

I eyed her profoundly and produced a spare nod, as if to say, "I promise," though behind my assurance there was little more than hollow conviction.

I felt my arm being tugged and pricked, and I saw the world in sepia before I drifted blissfully off in a luxury ride to heaven.

17

PRIVATE AUDIENCE

I don't know how long I have been back in Florence painting, but it seems like it's been a long time, maybe months. Much as I try, I cannot get in touch with Carlotta. Instead I am concentrating on work, so I can have everything ready to show her when I do find her. I am in perfectionist mode, consumed with fine-tuning *The Universe.* Adding brushstrokes here and there, deepening color panels, providing supplemental shadings; I have even signed each work with a fresh and improved "RC." I want everything to be completely new in this private and personal period—no connection to past oeuvres.

There is a knock on the door and I call out, "It's open!"

Arturo, my neighbor, a fellow tenant from the floor below, steps in and informs me there is someone outside who would like to speak with me.

I take the coffeemaker off the flame and turn off the burner. I ease down the stairs, taking my time, thanking my neighbor for checking with me before allowing any unknown visitor entrée.

I pop out the front door, and to my total shock, Carlotta is there, standing before me. We greet each other warmly with twin pecks, and I'm heartened that she's perhaps come for a visit.

"Can you come up?"

"I have to go, Rodrigo. But I came to tell you—"

"Just for a moment . . ."

She hesitates. "But only a minute."

We climb the stairwell, slip into my foyer, and ascend the steps to the studio. I open the door and let her enter first. Carlotta scans the walls momentarily and emits a sharp gasp.

She drifts to the middle of the room, spinning. She takes it in. She is silent, with her hand to her mouth. For over a minute she doesn't utter a sound.

I stir a little cream into my homemade macchiato and ask her if she would care to have one. She doesn't hear me. I fade back to the kitchen to light the burner once again.

I reenter the space where she's now seated on the couch, and I see her wipe her eye. She seems to be mesmerized by the Cala de Deià horizon and sunset sub-series. The boat, the water, the rescue. She pays particular attention to the five eagles, taken from different locations and angles. Flying, soaring, floating upon upcurrents, on the bow, and on the mast. Then the *Eagle Eye Triptych*—three angles taken from the eagle's own vantage point. I suspect she may be entertaining memories of that vacation.

I'm filled with much joy. It would have been enough that she has materialized before me in the flesh, that she has come to visit. But in addition, she seems to be appreciating what is before her. She is the only audience ever intended, and she is moved. It is one of the happiest moments of my entire life.

"Are you pressed for time?"

She doesn't answer me. She doesn't hear me. She is transfixed, which is always a positive indicator that your efforts—all the planning, the preparation, and the execution—are validated. There is nothing more satisfying than to earn the appreciation of those you cherish most, and the respect that comes with it.

"Rodrigo," she whispers, as if in church. Respectful. "You have taken my breath away."

"Really? It gives me such joy to hear you say that. I'm overwhelmed, actually. That you approve."

"Approve? *Rodrigo.* I'm completely—I don't know what to say. These are masterpieces. That's the most obvious thing I can say. That anyone could say, in any language. *How marvelous . . .*"

"Do you have time still?"

She nods quickly.

"Come," I say. She follows.

I maneuver across the space and tug away a large drop cloth that is covering more works stacked against the far wall. These are the seascapes and landscapes from the Cala series: the cove, the beach, the Serra de Tramuntana mountains, the full range and singular high peak formations, the donkey trains. There are twenty-five in all. I flip through one by one. I get to the Tramuntana mountain sub-series—the full range captured repeatedly from the same angle and composition, but taken at different times of day, with different light and different weather.

Again her eyes well up and she does not offer words, only intermittent shakes of the head. As she moves from one canvas to the next, tear droplets fall from her eyelids. Her chin trembles.

It surprises me that she is reacting to the high peaks this way. They are just mountains, after all. Then I realize I am an insensitive dolt, an imbecile. She is perhaps envisioning the beautiful time we enjoyed together. These manifestations are no longer paint on canvas but postcards to us, celebrations of the time we shared. These postcards, caught in the slow mail of life, have been delivered to her in giant size, all at once, with an impressionistic haze and a concentrated intensity. That must be the reason for her emotional response.

Her reaction is even more gratifying because now she is experiencing the emotion that fueled me while articulating them. My emotional
grid has been properly transferred through paint and brushstrokes on
canvas.

She stands next to me as she studies one piece after another. I feel
her hand gently clasp mine. With each piece she sees, she grips my
hand tighter.

I cannot help but recall witnessing the tears in her eyes when she
told me she could not be with me, and how starkly different it is to
see them now, in this context.

I step back and go to the kitchen to pour her a coffee.

"May I?" she asks as she begins to flip through the rest of the
stack.

"Of course!"

I return and hand her the coffee in a mug.

"*Caro,* I am so proud of you."

"I didn't have room for everything."

"You mean there's more?"

"These are the initial forty-five. There are twenty-six more." There
is not enough wall space to hang the entire two initial chapters of
The Parallel Universe, composed of seventy-one works in all.

"*Dio mio.* Where are they?"

"You want to see?"

"Don't play games with me!"

I laugh. She has caught me; I *am* playing. And why? Because I am
the happiest man on the planet. I have to pinch myself to know this is
really happening. Her. Me. In my studio. And for a private audience.

She walks behind me down the corridor. I open the door. The
room is dark, as the shades are drawn.

"Stay here, *per favore,* it's dark."

I move through the space to the far wall, to reach the blinds that
have been blocking out the day for weeks on end now. I need the dark

to effectuate an endless time continuum, to help me finesse the blossoming *Universe* in constant conditions, without being distracted by the changing light of different times of day.

I locate the wall switch and flip it. The motorized blind begins to rise with an old-world metallic racket and at an old-world snail's pace.

As yellow light slowly floods first to the bottom of the room like water in a bathtub, indistinguishable gray shapes begin to pronounce themselves. With more light, the gray transforms and the shapes begin to take on color.

"*Scusi,* please forgive the mess . . ."

She says nothing.

Soon the entire room is filled with light, and the chaotic condition of my large bedroom reveals itself—paint-covered clothes strewn everywhere—in addition to a four-wall display. Suspended around the room is the final sub-series of *The Universe*'s second chapter, the prequel to Cala, comprising the day we first met in Florence.

"Carlotta?" I call out. "Come on in. It's ready for you to see!"

The noisy motorized window blind stops, and I hear the faint sound of crying. I dash back to the bedroom door to Carlotta and find her leaning against the door frame, her face in her hands.

I clasp her hand, and she spins toward me and collapses into me. "I'm so . . . so sorry."

"Nothing to be sorry for. I'm here. You're here. All is good. *Tutto a posto.*"

"B-b-but," she stammers, "how did you know?"

"Know what?"

"That is my totem animal."

"Which? I do not know." I scan the *Animal* sub-series, arranged across and down in the order that I have painted them.

"That!" She points to the head-shot portrait of the true beast—captured close and in tight, with the huge golden eyes, the menacing expression, the exposed slashing incisors, the broad head. A fierce portrayal.

"*Panthera onca,* yes. The Latin genus name for 'panther.' The sub-series is all panthers."

"How did you guess, then?"

"I don't know what you mean . . ."

"You asked me so many times. I never told you. The panther is . . . *me* . . ."

"That's—"

"*Sì, caro!*"

"I did these from memory."

"What memory?"

"Of our first day together. I found you on the Ponte Vecchio. At the silver artisan's shop. You were admiring the panther ring in the showcase when I caught up with you and gave you the drawing of the flower. That's what this installment is about: when we first met. It's a prequel. Because this happened before the first installment. Though I painted it after."

As she takes several deep breaths to regulate her breathing, I go to the kitchen to get her some water. When I return, she says, "Our last night together, you were speaking about parallel universes. And contacting New York. Like you still lived there. I thought you were losing it. Or had lost it. You seemed crazy."

"I was drunk."

"But it scared me. I was so scared, Rodrigo."

"I'm a scary drunk."

"But—all along you had processed me, you *knew* me, so incredibly well—more intuitively, intimately, deeply than anyone ever before. Including my parents."

"Coincidence."

"*Mah!*" she exclaims. "No such thing. Not in this life. Instinctively, you knew. You discerned the very essence of my being. You felt it. And you expressed it. In paint. You may not have done it consciously. But part of you knew." She gives it more thought. "Maybe we are all dream players, like you said. Passing in and out of one another's dreams. And that is life—just one big dream."

My reaction is to twist away, albeit imperceptibly, as my arm hair stands on end. I will stay away from this line of conversation. For now, at least. I am afraid to talk about it anymore; talking about it might make it all go away again.

"I'm sorry I doubted you, Rodrigo."

I don't say anything. What is there to say? And what purpose would it serve? What do I have to prove? All of this is good enough for me. For the second time in recent days—the first being my actions during the intervention by my "friends" in SoHo—I find myself exercising restraint. From ego. And from senseless psychological needs for vindication. Or revenge. Or to be right all the time. Or to get credit.

And even during this time away from Carlotta, I haven't gotten freaked out, jealous, bitter, or vengeful.

And then it occurs to me: perhaps I really am reformed. Or getting there. I have endured many hardships and survived a dark past. And now I am seeking a higher consciousness. I am invoking spirituality. I am operating on a higher plane. I am soaring close or closer to heaven in order to connect to the divine. I am following my proper path. I've really become Eagle. I've taken flight. And I'm on my way.

"What are you thinking, Rodrigo?" she asks softly.

This prompts me to formulate a question for her. "You taught me about Eagle. And I think of it every day. It's even in my work, as you have seen. So I am asking you—what does the Panther mean to you?"

Carlotta considers my question. Her face and eyes are still wet, and the mascara has run down her cheeks in distinct tar paths. She looks as beautiful as I've ever seen her.

"That's a very good question. Basically, it's that you can be too afraid of the darkness to see the light, and you should confront your fears and have confidence that the answers will come to you." She hesitates again. "But as you can see—when I doubted you, I gave in to fear. I lost sight of Panther. And then I arrive today, and there he is. The Panther portrait, right on your wall, staring down at me."

"Yes, but there are other factors involved," I tell her. "Like one's family. One's upbringing. What one has gone through in life. The challenges. And you have had challenges. Things have to be weighed. And considered. I don't think you gave in to fear at all—"

"How can you be so sure?"

"Because you're here. Are you here?"

". . . Y-y-yes . . ."

"You have come back. That took confidence. And faith. You just needed time for more answers. Perhaps you have some answers now."

At that moment a tear makes its way down her cheek, refracting the window sunlight like a tiny diamond.

"Yes, *amore mio,* I do," she says with a weak smile.

I'm hopeful and encouraged to hear her utter the word *amore.* "Love" has returned to our intimate language.

"And maybe now you can have trust in the future."

Carlotta leans in and kisses me so very lightly on the mouth, as if still asking for forgiveness. I can feel that her lips and breath are heated, as if she is running a fever.

"*Amore?*" she says.

"Yes?"

"Make love to me. Now. *Per favore.*"

It reminds me of the first time we made love. I lead her to the bed and undress her piece by piece until she is beautifully nude before me. I undress myself, and our bodies meld together. I look into her eyes, which a few minutes ago were red from crying, but are glossy and sparkling now as they register the slow rhythmic penetrations within her. The tears stream down our cheeks, but they are tears of joy, for both of us. She has missed me as much as I have missed her. Our lovemaking is the reward for having found our separate ways back to each other, with our Life Forces being exchanged and now passing through each other to form an unbreakable bond.

Afterward, we lie side by side on the bed, holding hands, and talk.

"What made you come here today?" I ask.

"I had something to tell you. And I'd forgotten it. Remember? I mentioned it at the Accademia café."

"Oh, yes."

"I came here to remind you. Of your mentor."

"Heriberto?"

"Yes. I had a dream about him. You must track Heriberto down and pay him a visit and find out how he is—if in fact he is still alive."

"He's alive."

"Then you must find him and tell him what you told me—how you feel. That will be good for you to do. Good for both of you."

"So you do believe in dreams?"

"More than ever now. I think you are right. In dreams, everything is possible."

"And Heriberto came to you?"

"Yes. He would love to see you. He told me so. In my dream."

"And I would love to see him. Now that I am ready. That feels right, yes."

A pause, a comfortable silence, before Carlotta speaks again. "Do you believe in God, Rodrigo?"

"No, not one god. I believe in them all. The gods of all religions. The faith is the same. And so is the love. God is love no matter what name or shape He takes, no matter who tries to possess Him and call Him his own . . ."

"I agree. God is in every one of us."

"I believe that. Everyone has a piece. That's why there are many gods."

"You make me a stronger woman."

"You make me a better man."

"I love you, Rodrigo, so very much."

"I love you pretty much more."

We are lying there in my bedroom with the *Animal* sub-series of *The Parallel Universe* surrounding us, enveloping us. I spin back and into the arms of the woman I love, and we exchange knowing, hungry looks once again.

"You sure you didn't come here for anything else?"

"Well, the make-up sex, of course, *caro.*"

"Thought so."

We make love then, again and again and again. And later that night, with Carlotta's sleeping head resting upon my chest, I have a dream that I remember, that I will always remember:

The Great Spirit looks down upon Mother Earth and sees the Panther and the Eagle. The Panther, trusting with open heart in a future with the soaring Eagle, derives courage and confidence from his strength and leaps forward in the face of considerable darkness. She borrows a brush from him and paints her own portrait of grace and nobility for all to see.

The Eagle, inspired by the Panther, sheds all that had soiled and weighed him down and takes flight, soaring higher and higher through the clouds and mists, getting closer to the heavens than ever before.

And the Great Spirit praises Panther and Eagle. They have met their challenges head-on, with courage, strength, and integrity, and are the better for it. They make love in each other's arms and rejoice in the gifts they have given each other. Then they fly forth with humility and gratitude. They have garnered the golden blessings of the gods of all religions. The Great Spirit deems it so.

I wake up from the dream in the middle of the night. I watch Carlotta sleep sweetly beside me. I caress her twitching cheek and kiss her softly. I stretch the bedspread up and over her exposed shoulder.

I rise from bed and make my way into the studio. There I climb the ladder and remove a canvas from the wall. In the bedroom, I reclaim another from the *Animal* sub-series and replace it with the one taken from the studio. Now, hanging from the wall, side by side, are Panther and Eagle, floating together like kindred, harmonious spirits.

The Parallel Universe is now united.

"Rodrigo?"

"Yes, my love?"

"I've missed you in my sleep."

"No need to worry. I'm always there."

18

ASIAN ANGEL

Rodrigo? Wake up. Rodrigo, wake up!"

"What is it, Carlotta, my love? Did you see Eagle and Panther?"

"Wake up! Rodrigo! Come back!"

"Where?"

"To me, Akira. I'm right here. Come back to me now . . . That's it, open your eyes. You can stop sleeping."

The world was identifying itself to me, making its presence felt: colors and shapes, words spoken, and soothing music.

"Rodrigo. Welcome back."

I could see her now. She was wearing a sapphire satin dress. Her hair was swept to the side, and diamond-fire drop earrings dangled beneath her chin.

"I'm happy you came back."

"What day is it today?"

"Today is Friday."

"And I've been here how long?"

"Three days."

"Holy shit." I tried to sit up and didn't make it the first time. *"Wow . . ."*

"Did you have a good time?"

I angled over at her and smiled. "I had a *great* time."

"That's good. For you."

"I have to go. I have to get on a flight. Can you get me my stuff?"

"It's ready. I have it right here."

On a table was my jacket. My shoes were on the floor, and I put them on. My money and passport were in my pants. I had to clear my mind and figure it out. I couldn't go back to SoHo, since my friends and staff had confronted me and revealed their plans to make me take psychological tests. Now that I was producing paintings I had no intention of selling, I was worried that such testing could give them a foothold. To do something more. To take control. Of my work, of my money, of my life. After all, I knew what they were after. And it had nothing to do with my mental health.

No. I was definitely not going back to Manhattan.

"Akira, perhaps you can help me."

"How?"

"Tell me, can you drive me to the airport? JFK?" I didn't want to leave any taxi records that could be traced back to me.

"Uh, well. Maybe. When?"

"Now."

"No, no. I can't right now. I'm working."

"Let me speak to your boss."

"He will not let me."

"I can be very persuasive when I want to be."

Within fifteen minutes, we were entering the ramp to the Van Wyck Expressway heading south. It was nighttime, though I hadn't been sure until we left the warehouse and hit the pavement. I'd bought Akira for the night, making the Asian underworld drug-den proprietor an offer he could not refuse.

"You might be the most important person in my life right now. You know that?"

"Really?" And she laughed a high-pitched, girlish giggle.

"You're the most trustworthy woman in New York. I trust you more than anyone."

"Thank you."

"But I want you to know, I'm in love with a woman. Very much in love. In my former days, that wouldn't matter. But, well, I've changed. I need a new team around me. Maybe you can come work for me."

She said nothing, but the look on her face implied, "Doing what?"

"We'd think of something. Where you work now, it's dangerous, you know? You could get in a lot of trouble."

She was silent and remained so for a while. Then she said, "I'm with a guy, too. I don't think he would let me. He's no good. He treats me bad."

If I'd heard it once, I'd heard it a thousand times.

"He owns the club where I work. That's why you stayed a long time, because I asked him. And because you paid a lot. Even though I wanted you to stop what you are doing. You are killing yourself, Mr. Concepción. You are a good man."

I hadn't thought of myself that way in a long time—a good man. Betrayal, disappointment, and anger had built up in me a self-defense system, and I had become a user, a taker, a narcissist. But hadn't I begun to change all that during the time I had just spent with Carlotta?

"Are you okay?" Akira asked.

The overpowering emotions of the past three days, especially the draining task of keeping my two lives going, hit me all at once. My eyes began to flood, and I cried.

Akira put her hand across mine and squeezed it. "Is everything okay? What's going on in your life that's making you so sad?"

"I have two. So it's . . . a lot."

"Two lives?"

"You think that's possible? To have two lives?"

"I don't know."

"You probably think I'm crazy. Like everyone else."

"Maybe you're searching for a better life. Searching is good. I'm searching, too."

"You deserve the beautiful life you are searching for, Akira."

"Thank you. But it doesn't come easy. There's nothing wrong with working on yourself."

"You have a beautiful soul, Akira. I know it's tough, working where you do. If you are ever in trouble, please call me, okay?" I wrote down my number and placed it in the console. "When we stop, you give me your number, too."

"Thank you, Mr. Concepción."

"Rodrigo. Always Rodrigo."

"You're a nice man. I could tell. I liked you very quickly. That never happens."

"Akira?"

"Yes?"

"You're an angel. You've helped me get where I need to be—twice. I believe you came into my life for a reason."

"Maybe, yes. Angels have helped me, too. That's why I am here."

She drove up to the airline terminal, and I got out. Akira got out, too, and gave me her number. Then we embraced as if we had known each other for a thousand years.

There was a midnight red-eye to Madrid on Iberia. I could get a connecting flight from there to anywhere I wished to go. I bought the ticket in cash, waited for an hour, and boarded the plane.

And just like that, with liftoff, I was on my way to another life.

19

PARALLEL NO MORE

The plane touched down in the afternoon at Madrid-Barajas, where I had a two-hour layover.

During the long flight to Madrid, I'd had plenty of time for a nap. Even though it had been only a few hours since I'd left the drug warehouse, I was a little twitchy and glad of the opportunity to rest and to sleep. I let Carlotta know I was heading to Spain. I invited her, too, but she had a wine festival to attend in Fiesole, where she was going to introduce some of their new selections to the vendors. She was happy that I was making this excursion, and she liked the idea of Ronda—my proposed destination for a cozy shared getaway. I thought we might rent a house there, and suggested that Carlotta join me when she had wrapped up business in Fiesole. In the meantime, I could turn the house into a studio, as was my habit, and embark upon the next installment of *The Universe*. I planned to get some fresh Spanish supplies in Barcelona to enhance my color palette.

After the plane landed in Madrid, my first move was to buy a Spanish phone in the airport and make a few important calls. First I contacted my bank in New York and had them wire money into my Spanish account in Mallorca. It was the very same bank in which I had deposited the contents of my little red box all those years before, and requesting a transfer brought back a wave of nostalgia. Having organized what I hoped would be my hard-to-trace monies, I placed several calls to real estate brokers to find a nice *finca* or ranch or villa up on the hillside in Ronda.

Then I boarded my flight to Palma de Mallorca. We landed in Palma around sundown, the beautiful pinks, reds, and peaches flooding the plane windows. From Palma, I would go to see Heriberto in Valldemossa. I had been thinking about this ever since Carlotta had encouraged me to go and visit him. I looked forward to seeing him again after all these years, albeit with some apprehension.

I decided to stay in a modest, low-profile two-star hotel in Palma rather than drive northwest to Valldemossa in the dark of night. I ordered some tapas at a cantina close by, though I wasn't very hungry. I hadn't been eating much since, well, before I went to the warehouse in Brooklyn; but even before that, in Florence, my appetite had waned when I was finishing the *Animal* sub-series. (My normal eating habits in New York had been embarrassingly gluttonous for a person my size.)

As I lay in my hotel bed, I realized I was feeling much better. That subterranean interlude, those three lost days in Brooklyn—during which I had no memory of eating—had taken a lot out of me and left me depleted. Scattered. Run-down. Perhaps even depressed, thanks to a post-binge crash.

But I'd slept well on the plane. My nerves and anxiety had calmed, my faculties had been restored, my sensibilities were realigned, and my mood was rebooted. Everything seemed to be functioning in proper working order. In fact, I hadn't felt this good in a while. It was like the pressure was off. I felt whole. Unified. Relieved.

And why? It felt as if my two worlds had found their overlap and come together, and now I could just relax. And be myself. And live. And produce my art. And most important, be with the woman I loved.

I was exhausted from the trip, but I was still wide awake. Before I eventually drifted off to sleep, I thought to try Carlotta again. But her phone just rang and rang, so I left a message that I'd speak to her the following day.

The next morning, I got off to an early start and opted for an anonymous taxi instead of a hired car. I hailed it right outside the hotel.

The beautiful coastal hillside village of Valldemossa, eighteen kilometers northwest of Palma, was only a thirty-minute drive. The quaint fishing village, now a repository of Spanish culture, had a long and sometimes violent history dating to shortly after the Trojan War. The inhabitants had fought many invasions (and even pirates) in the old days; in more recent centuries, they had been host to many famous guests, among them the Polish composer Frédéric Chopin and the French writer George Sand, who had lived in the monastery after it was sold to private owners.

Valldemossa was also a gateway to the Serra de Tramuntana mountains, a spectacular range that had already provided the rough and ragged topline I had painted as the stunning backdrop for Carlotta and me during our sailing voyage to Cala de Deià.

Once again I began to have professional aspirations and designs in mind. As we wound through the beautiful roads that led to Valldemossa, I pictured the area's delicious portraiture potential: luscious landscapes, local rituals, indigenous quirky color, and of course the sweeping Mediterranean overlooks. All of which could be targeted for Part II of the *Universe* series, which I would call *The Unified Universe*—*The Parallel Universe* being Part I.

This was a day that had been a long time coming, and frankly, my visit with Heriberto was long overdue. I was finally going to spend time with my old mentor, friend, and colleague—and the more I thought about it, the more I realized that this visit was perhaps the subconscious reason for my unexpected return to Mallorca, when I needed to hide out from my staff and friends in New York. Heriberto had been on my mind for years. I mean, how could he not be? I painted every day, and his influence was always with me, but not only in spirit. I did think of him, the man himself, more often than I cared to admit once upon a time.

Before I met Carlotta, I had become contaminated. Poisoned. By the galloping rot of fame and money. But it was not only the trappings of success that had corrupted me.

The problem resided in one place and one place alone—within me. I was the problem. I had always been the problem. Otherwise, the more-money, more-press, more-girls, more-success complex would not have gotten me. The more, more, more machine would not have been *able* to get me. My problem was within me. It ran right to my core. It was my soul that was corrupted. Tarnished. Contaminated. Buried beneath all the other layers of false, misleading, deceiving drives, such as ambition and ego. These drives had taken my soul hostage and buried it in a shallow grave with a few air ducts. It was barely alive, barely able to get enough oxygen. It was suffocating. But thankfully—my soul was still there. Waiting for me to reclaim it. To let it breathe again.

And I had help—my dear Carlotta. She had come to my rescue in the nick of time. Before my pilot light went out. Before my soul could be suffocated. Carlotta. The woman of my dreams. The woman in my dreams. The woman who was the center of *The Unified Universe.* The woman who had inspired me to make this pilgrimage to see Heriberto in the first place.

We were ten minutes into the drive to Valldemossa, and the thoughts of my behavior toward Heriberto were putting my stomach in knots. Though I hadn't told Carlotta, I had known where he was all along for a reason I had not wished to make public; nor, for different reasons, had Heriberto. I started to sweat. And get woozy. It was making me sick how I'd treated this man. I'd given myself a long overdue shame-on-you sermon, and here's the kicker, *I actually felt ashamed!* My body was responding accordingly, and it did not feel good.

I asked the driver to pull off the road. When the car came to a halt, I opened the back door and dry-heaved; I had eaten very little in several days, so my vomit was nothing but a vile mix of bad air and bile vapor. In that moment I knew my body was trying to rid itself of any residues and bacteria from my former life.

I had seven heaves and was hoping for more. I wanted it all out. There were years' worth of contaminants lodged in my system. How can you get them all out at once? I assumed it would take time. I closed the door then. The driver was heartened that I hadn't soiled his cab, and we drove on.

One thing was clear: I was not yet healed, either mentally or physically.

But forget about me. *I'm sick of me!* What about *him*? What about Heriberto? How did my behavior make *him* feel? He was not a contaminated soul. He was a giver. He gave to me. His time. His knowledge. His love. His food. A job. A paycheck. A place to go. And stay, if I ever needed it. He gave me everything! And to be forgotten like that must have wounded him deeply.

He must have thought, *How could this boy I helped educate, helped raise, turn his back on me, completely forget me?* And he was right. Because he was never out for riches, or fame, or success in those terms. He was in touch with his soul. His soul was not buried. He knew early on that it was better to give than live a life of personal greed in all facets. What he cared about, very simply—what really mattered to this man I had neglected and ignored, who had been so good to me in every way—was *helping a little boy realize his dream.* That was all this man cared about.

The tears flooded down my face in a torrent that didn't stop until we arrived in Valldemossa. The driver let me off in front of the fourteenth-century Carthusian monastery, which was now a nursing home.

I needed a little time to collect myself, so I walked the grounds. I sat on a bench. I contemplated the remarkable structures of the converted monastery. Each brick had been laid with love and faith. It represented the best of human nature, monuments erected for the purpose of helping others, and now, all these years later, they still were. A healing place, a place for the well-being of mind and body, a place for people who had lost their way, mentally, physically. This was now the home of Heriberto. I considered it a suitable place of peace, tranquillity, and natural beauty, staffed by his own kind of folk—people trained in the art of caring for the needy.

I stepped into the nave of the ancient church—the Palau del Rei Sanxo, which was near the monastery—and said a prayer to all the gods of all the religions. It was too deflective, too assuaging, too self-absolving, too self-serving, too greedy, too arrogant—it was all *too much*—to ask for forgiveness, so I didn't dare waste the church's time. Instead, I prayed for my old friend Heriberto.

I tried to call Carlotta to let her know I had arrived but already felt uncomfortable being here. Once again, she didn't answer, so I tried to leave a message on her machine. Why wouldn't she answer me? We had been through enough together now that I ought to be able to reach her at any time, even if I was perfectly awake and clear in thought, as I was now.

In the church, I had thought about what I wanted to tell Carlotta: at first my intention in coming here was to get Heriberto's forgiveness, or some form of redemption, at the very least. Now that I'd had time to consider it carefully, I realized I wanted nothing from my old friend but to share some time together without the thought of receiving anything in return. I wanted to take nothing from that. Though my improper conduct toward this man who had given me so much had haunted me for years, as it should have, this trip wasn't about me—not this time. This visit would be all about him and whatever I could give him.

I was confident Carlotta would concur.

20

HEAVY SEAS IN VALLDEMOSSA

The grandiose monastery, with its spectacular Roman facade, was partially set into the hillside. When I went indoors, I walked through medieval barrel-vaulted corridors on my way out to the gardens; I went through the gardens and on to the sanitarium. It was a separate modern building, a hospital, really, with state-of-the-art medical equipment.

I checked in at the front desk. That morning I had notified the staff that I would be coming, and I was on time.

Marisol, the middle-aged head nurse, guided me down a long hallway that led to an offshoot wing reserved for the Alzheimer's patients. I passed a number of them, mostly elderly, who, bless their hearts, had seen better days. Some had chins that rested flat on their chests, others walked slowly on walkers with slow death creeping in their eyes, still others were being pushed in wheelchairs, and some were able to drive their own motorized models.

"Though his condition has deteriorated, he's actually quite lively. And very fantastical." Marisol winked at me. "And that's good. Being upbeat is the key ingredient to mental health, especially as patients age."

"You mean he's positive?"

"Very. Others in the ward are more depressed. And depression brings on, well, an earlier passing."

"Gracias, Marisol.*"*

"De nada, Señor Concepción.*"*

"You know me?"

She laughed. "Who doesn't? Are you forgetting your fame and fortune? Your career? Not to mention all the press? And the Internet?"

I was embarrassed. In my former days, I would have happily taken these winds of praise until my head was blown up like a beach ball.

"You're a celebrity. If you're big in America, what do you think you are here? You're Spanish, after all!"

I remained silent but smiled sparely.

"If you have a moment, some of the staff would like to take photos with you. And maybe have you sign one or two of your books?"

I had to pause, but I nodded; what else could I do? "Of course," I said. "But, Marisol, I would like them to say nothing. I don't want anyone to find out I was here. Or that I'm even in Spain."

She looked at me with a perturbed expression, which was not my intention, since I didn't want to set off any alarms. "Is everything okay?" she asked.

"No, no, I mean, yes . . ."

"I only say that because I'm good at what I do. And you look a little, shall we say, preoccupied. And anxious."

"Perhaps we could talk after. I have some things on my mind, I mean, that I'd like to get off my chest. Perhaps I could speak with one of your professionals . . ."

"Let me see what I can do."

"Gracias."

"And not to worry, Señor Concepción. Privacy has been our business for seventy-five years," Marisol said.

"I know that—it's one reason I wanted Heriberto to come here, where he would have both privacy and excellent care," I told her.

"To this day no one has ever known that you have been the anonymous benefactor for Heriberto all these years. And I commend you for that. Beyond your fame and success, that says everything about you and the type of man you are. But we have always kept your secret, and that will not stop now."

I nodded, knowing I still had not done enough. *"Gracias."*

"De nada."

Marisol stopped at the last doorway and gestured for me to go ahead and enter. The room was pleasant enough, and gave my old friend a stellar sweeping view of the ocean.

"So he's optimistic?"

"He's beyond optimistic. He's animated. And very creative." She added a wink.

My former master was dressed in a hospital gown and sitting up in bed. A wisp of white bed hair rose from his scalp. When I approached the bed, I noticed he was holding something in his hand and looking off at the turquoise vista through the window.

"Steady there," he said, then tugged at his lower eyelid, warning me in the European way to watch or pay attention.

"Hola, Heriberto.*"*

"Tell me your credentials, sailor."

"It's Rodrigo."

"Fine name, fine name. But have you ever been on a ship?"

I turned back and eyed Marisol. She smiled and shrugged. Then nodded as if to say, "Just go with it."

"Uh, yes. I have been on a ship."

"What seas?"

"Well, the Mediterranean."

"The Mediterranean is for pussies and playboys."

I started to slide into the visitor's chair.

"This is no time to sit, man! Heavy weather. Get up!"

I rose to my feet, and he lifted the pair of binoculars he'd been clutching, angling them out to sea.

"Winds're coming from the west at forty knots. It's going to be a humdinger. Check the two-way—"

"Sir? I wanted to come here—"

"No time for idle chatter, I have a ship to sail, so don't tell me about your petty problems. Strap on a pair of stones and get on that radio."

I angled over and saw the ancient Zenith radio from the fifties, the plastic yellowed and browned with time. I spun the dial until it clicked. I could see the appliance was not plugged in.

"We're listing. You feel that?"

I saw it in his eyes. What had been brilliant slate blue was gray. He'd lost almost all his hair, and he weighed about a third less. But his hands, always the genius behind his sculpture, were massive still. What this man used to be able to do with his hands! I always thought Rodin had nothing on him. But the market had spoken. He no doubt would have achieved more if he had played the game just a little. But that wasn't his thing. I'd respected him for it then. I loved him for it now. I saw in his eyes that he had no idea who the hell I was. At that moment, I was just another deck swab on his ship. Battling the sea and the oncoming storm.

"*Mare mosso . . . cinque . . .*" he said, mimicking an Italian coast guard radio transmission: "Rough seas . . . level five . . ."

I would press on.

"Heriberto—I came here today to see you after all these years. I apologize for not coming sooner. I apologize for a lot of things. You were the most important figure in my life, even more so than my parents. And you were like a father to me. All that I have achieved, if

I've achieved anything, is because of you. You helped me pursue my dream—to be a professional painter—and with your knowledge and teachings, which you passed down to me, you put me in a position to attain that dream—"

"*Mare mosso . . . sei . . .*"

"And—"

But he cut me off. "The swell has picked up, man!" he said excitedly. "It's three meters . . . If it gets any bigger, we could go over! Man the life jackets!"

"And I have succeeded. In certain ways. But not in others. I'm working on that. It hasn't been easy. But I'm trying. And I think I'll get there—"

"*Mare mosso . . . sette . . .*" he interjected.

"But for years I traveled around, thinking only of myself, and what I needed, what I wanted, and grasped for it all greedily, only to want more of it—to the exclusion of everything else. And everyone else. Including you. I'm ashamed. If I knew then what I know now, well, I like to think things would be different. I would have seen much more of you. And we could have worked in the studio together . . . like we used to . . ."

"*Mare mosso . . . otto . . .*"

Tears were filling my eyes. My voice was beginning to crack. ". . . You doing your brilliant bronze . . . creations . . . and me doing my portraiture . . . and I'm sure my work would have been executed better . . . with more thought, more depth . . . done with more precision . . . and passion. With you nearby. You lit a fire in me . . . it's been going ever since, and bless you for that, Heriberto. It is no one's loss but my own that I haven't seen you more . . . *big loss . . .*"

He was combing the seas with the binoculars again and said it very faintly: "We might have to follow those trawlers . . . it may well be our only hope . . ."

"Maestro—" I said suddenly.

"Don't just stand there, sailor, turn up the volume on that radio! We're talking a force-nine gale!"

And he was glaring right at me. I spun the dial once more.

"Go down into the galley and fetch me a Scotch! Gonna need a little liquid courage . . ."

I broke down then. It was what I used to do for him. Make him a Scotch on the rocks every evening at six. I can't be sure this was a sign he remembered me, but I like to think it was. It had become my drink of choice years later. In my petty, pitiful homage to him.

"Mare mosso . . . nove . . ."

"Maestro—" I appealed to him again. "You are a master sculptor. There is magic in your hands. You hold a wheel now. The wheel of a ship. But you are not a ship captain. You are a maestro of great works of art. I know. I have seen your genius. Everything you taught me has urged me to come back to you now. And that's why I am here. To tell you. You must come back. Come back to life, come back to us, and fill the hole that has been left. In our lives. And in the world of creation. The world of men and women, as simple and pathetic and error-prone as we all are, we need your gift. We need your magic. The magic of your hands. And it is within your grasp, the grasp of your magical hands, to set yourself free. Release those hands from the wheel, get off the ship, and come back to land. And make more beauty. The world needs beauty, and she is ready for the return of the Maestro."

I approached his bed and reached forward to clasp his hand.

"Don't you dare touch an officer!" he yelled. "I'll have you put before the Naval Tribunal!" And then he threw a tantrum, a blast of accusations and threats in a maritime theme, including having me thrown in the "brig." His diatribe went on and on until Marisol returned with an orderly. Heriberto demanded to have me thrown off the ship if I didn't leave. I faded back a step.

"I love you, Maestro. May heaven's choicest blessings be showered upon you . . . and please come back."

And that just caused more of a reaction, as he tried to wrestle and fight off the orderly, until Marisol could give him an injection.

But I didn't wait for that. I was already in the garden.

21

THE MEETING IN THE GARDEN

Are you Señor Concepción?"

I was hovering in a daze but snapped to and spun around. "Oh," a woman said with a short gasp, as if frightened. "I do recognize you. Good morning. I'm Ana Paola."

"Rodrigo, *por favor.*"

She was blond, very pretty, medium height, wearing a white lab coat and white pants that were snug enough to reveal a slender, shapely figure. Her top was low-cut, and she had a trace of cleavage showing. I was still unsettled by the afternoon's events, and I felt ashamed for noticing.

"Marisol suggested I come meet you. She said you wanted to speak with one of the doctors?" she said.

"Uh, yes."

"We have light staff today, and our normal patient-intake girl is out. I'm filling in for her. I'm going to ask you a few questions, if that's okay."

"Yes, but—"

"I know privacy is a concern. And, well, just to let you know, it's not an issue. No one will ever know you visited us. You have my word." She uncapped her pen and raised her clipboard.

"*Gracias,* Ana Paola."

The questions she had for me were rather basic: personal information, medical history, prescribed medications or drug use, reason for appointment. The usual things.

When the interview concluded, a comely young colleague of Ana Paola's joined us. And as she approached, my breath slowed until I stopped breathing altogether. This young woman was a Mediterranean bombshell.

Her eyes were big, blue, and clear like a swimming pool, with eyelashes so long and feathery they almost appeared fake—but weren't. She was deeply tanned, with high, sculpted cheekbones, a very feminine button nose, and a perfect, rosy mouth that smiled easily. Her brown hair was slightly reddened from the sun and pinned up in a tight bun. Her lab coat was draped over her arm, and she walked with a slow, confident stride. She wore a white mock turtleneck spandex top, and her ample rounded breasts bounced fluidly along as she walked. For a doctor, she oozed sexuality, and I gave her the benefit of the doubt: she wasn't even trying. Her nameplate said "Dr. Volita," and as I read it, I could barely hear being introduced to her. I scolded myself for my thoughts as my face flushed with telltale embarrassment.

"Señor Concepción. This is Dr. Volita." Ana Paola repeated the introduction, and I snapped out of my reverie. Mercifully, I had my sunglasses on.

"Please call me Rodrigo," I stuttered.

"Desideria, *por favor,*" she returned. "Enchanted to meet you. I have seen your art, and I like it very much."

"*Gracias,*" I said, and left it at that. There's nothing worse than acting like the brat artist who, after receiving praise from people who have been moved by the art, then dashes their complimentary appraisals. It's such an overwhelming show of disrespect. Because what you're really rejecting are other people's imaginations, dreams, and at times, their feelings about themselves. Besides, once you've finished a work, it's no longer yours to lay claim to. Art belongs to anyone who looks at it. Each person's reaction is unique, based on all the things that have happened in his or her life. To denounce someone's interpretation of art is to denounce the person—and this is never okay to do, even if you are the original artist.

Marisol returned to the garden. She was carrying two of my coffee-table books and three calendars. "It's all they had at the bookstore."

"I'm sorry, if I'd known, I would have brought something. Next time."

"Will there be a next time?"

I turned and saw that it was Desideria who'd inquired.

"I believe so. I want to check in on my old friend from time to time."

"Ah, the *Capitano, sí.*"

"If you could keep me informed of his progress, I would be most grateful."

"For the great artist of Spain, of course!"

"Here, Desideria," I said as I handed her the book I had just signed.

I took several photos with the hospital staff. Though I usually despised this sort of thing, this time I didn't mind at all. These young professionals had dedicated their lives to helping people, elderly people, no less. If their intentions were coming from a good place, I knew I must give goodness in return.

I gave the girls my private email address and promised to invite them if I ever had another show.

"You mean you're not going to have a show?"

"No. I'm doing personal work now. Just for me." I smiled, too, because it made me happy to say so.

Ana Paola said, "Did you know George Sand wrote *A Winter on Mallorca* right here?"

"In Valldemossa?"

"No, right here at the monastery, before it was converted. When she lived here with her lover Frédéric Chopin."

"Oh yes, that's right."

"We are in a great artistic surrounding. The ghosts of artists are here, too."

"Why don't you paint here?" Desideria said. "If books can be written here, surely paintings can be rendered, no?"

"I'm sure you are quite right about that."

"What a place it would be to paint."

"Yes, I'm thinking of doing the monastery before I go. And perhaps other landscapes and local color. I did the Tramuntanas already, from the sea, anyway. But I was thinking of capturing them from inland, looking out to the sea. The jagged peaks and slashing valleys."

"There are places you don't know about," Ana Paola said.

"Really nice secluded beaches. And coves. Very private. We found them by boat."

"Why don't you paint *us*?" Ana Paola said. "We're local color, aren't we?"

For some reason, my temperature was rising. The interplay was stimulating, and I found these two to be incredibly simpatico. I had tremendous respect for the selfless, caring creatures they were. It was just prurient coincidence that they were both physically alluring as well.

"He doesn't think we're worth painting."

"No, that's not it. It's just that, well, I'm doing other things right now."

"Like what?"

"Well, it's kind of a secret. But not woman portraits. I know I did a lot of that before, but now I'm more disciplined to the requirements of a new style."

They both glared at me, not satisfied.

"Because I know I can do better," I tried to explain. Even though I did not want to go there, I wanted to make sure they would not feel personally insulted.

I looked over at Desideria in that pregnant, silent moment, and she was eyeing me with a sparkle in her eye and her iPhone held aloft and accessible, as if to take my impending number. When I smiled at her and didn't take the bait, she turned her head with a slight flick and raised her chin, almost taking on the pose of an elitist snob with her nose in the air. She was not used to having someone reject such an offer. It might never have happened before.

The girls had to go back to work then, and I had an appointment to meet with one of the doctors. So we said our good-byes, and the two walked off with the items I had signed for them.

22

THE APPOINTMENT

At Marisol's suggestion, I went to the hospital coffee shop and had an instant macchiato. I had about fifteen minutes to wait before my appointment with the distinguished Dr. Bartolo Abreu. He greeted me in the coffee shop and then escorted me to his office. He was immaculately dressed, and I took particular notice of his periwinkle Chanel tie.

We sat down in his tastefully appointed office, which, like Heriberto's room, had a spectacular view of the sea beyond. Dr. Abreu had me sit opposite his desk on the smooth, soft suede seafoam couch. There was a Miró print on his wall, and that made me feel instantly at home. We exchanged light chitchat, as he seemed interested in me; we spoke of Heriberto briefly, and I informed Dr. Abreu of our long association. With respect to me and my reason for being there, I was more candid than I had been with Ana Paola. At the same time, I didn't really know how to express what I was feeling.

"It's as if another dimension has revealed itself to me. Growing up, if there was one subject I didn't mind besides art, it was science. And I learned of the scientific method. 'Show me the proof' kind of thing. And I believed in that. But more recently, I have been open to more ways of looking at things."

"What ways?"

"Well, there seems to be no explanation for astrology, and yet there seem to be patterns that are valid. There is no explanation for spiritual events. Or extraordinary feats, like the Pyramids, the Mayan installations, Stonehenge. And yet they exist. And you hear it stated how little we use of the human brain, only five percent or something. The majority is unused, and something must be there, but it is not activated. I mean our brain is smarter than we are, it must be, all the knowledge of the universe lies within it. I believe that—and what has been happening to me seems inexplicable. As in no scientific explanation. For that functioning five percent, anyway."

"What exactly are you referring to? What has been happening to you?"

"Well . . ." I began, and chuckled nervously. "I have two lives. A dream life. And a real life. But I'm not sure which is which. Recently, I have come to realize they are becoming unified. It's one big unified life. Or one big dream."

"Are you in a dream now?"

"Maybe. Am I?"

"Do you take drugs?"

"Never, in my dream life. But I have, in what would seem to be my real life."

"What do you take?"

"I'm glad you asked." I withdrew from my jacket the baggie and handed it to Dr. Abreu. "There's Adderall. Perhaps you could tell me what the others are."

"You take these by prescription?"

"No. Recreationally. In my New York life."

"Well, this is Xanax. And this is Vyvanse. This here is"—and he unscrewed the cap—"this is cocaine."

"Sorry."

"And this, this here, *hmmm*. This looks like"—he scratched on it to taste it—"this is MDMA or Ecstasy; Molly, they call it, too."

"Check."

"This looks like a horse pill. A horse tranquilizer."

"That's Special K. Ketamine."

"And this is— How did you get this? This is risperidone."

"Molly Boy."

"Who?"

"I have a supplier. In my so-called real life. But don't tell any real-life cops. They will put me behind real-life bars." I thought I'd better not mention the three days of propofol.

The doctor laughed. "Risperidone is a very serious drug. It is for schizophrenics, really. And this supplier, he gives them to you for recreational use?"

"I guess." I had a flash of concern then. "Uh, Dr. Abreu—I have to know. Is this a judgment-free zone? I'm going through a lot."

"Don't worry, I'm not here to judge you or your habits, but let me give you an example. Heriberto takes risperidone—"

"Really?"

"*Sí.* And it calms him, actually, because he can become very animated on that boat of his."

"You mean he's like that all the time?"

"For as long as he's been here, twelve years now. He sets sail every day. He thinks his bed is a ship and he's sailing right on the water there. On the Adriatic. On the Mediterranean. The Aegean, because he likes to go to Greece. And through the windows, he sees the weather, and as the weather goes, so does his daily voyage. And every day is a new day on the sea. Like rebooting. Sailing is something to look forward to each day. It's what gets him up in the morning."

"We had stormy seas today. But the sun was shining outside."

"That was because you were there. He wanted to scare you away with the rough seas. What size storm did he say it was?"

"Force nine."

"Yeah, that's heavy weather. He wanted you to go."

"You mean he *really* wanted me to go—"

"You can't take it personally. And it's not you. It's anyone new. If Marisol or I were there, he'd be sailing in the beautiful sunshine of today. Really, it's what the window tells him. Or what he sees in the binoculars. Unless there's a stranger in the room."

"He was also reading off Italian tide and swell reports."

"Yes, well, he sails the Adriatic, usually. The Italian coast. He did that as a boy, apparently."

"I do remember him telling me about that."

"If you think about it, it's not a bad way to go. I mean, he gets to be on the water the rest of his life, if you want to look at it that way. It's very peaceful. With respect to his condition, sailing is his brain's way of coping with the frustration, with his disease, and it miraculously conjures a fantasy for him. It's a survival mechanism, really, propagated by the brain's need to compensate for the losses caused by Alzheimer's.

"In his case, the risperidone calms him. In someone without any schizophrenic tendencies or Alzheimer's, it can induce fantastical thoughts and reveries."

"Dreams?"

"Yes. How long have you been taking risperidone?"

"I don't know. Just recently, I believe. But my dream life has been with me longer, I think. But that's the thing. My dream life seems to be my real life, like it's more real than my real life. Is it possible that my brain could be jumbling things?"

"How do you mean?"

"That my brain is doing things in reverse. That my so-called dream life in Florence, where I seemingly live in my dreams, is actually my *real life,* and when I sleep there, I am really then dreaming, and that becomes what is considered my real life, my life in New York. In which case it's not a dream at all, it's a fucking nightmare, because I don't like what is considered my real life. Sometimes I act like a monster in New York.

"But in Florence, I am in love and spiritually connected—I'm an Eagle—and I'm doing the best art of my life. So when I go to sleep in my flat in Florence, I have nightmares.

"And the nightmares are New York and all the things I get into there. Doing cocaine off titties. Banging girls up the ass till their eyes pop, you know? And it's my brain that is reversing things, twisting it around, and making me believe the New York–life nightmare is the real one when it's not. That's what I think is happening."

"But you realize you have cocaine on you now. And since you don't do drugs in Florence, that connotes New York, doesn't it?"

"I know. That's why I'm confused. 'Cause I also just spoke to Carlotta. So I'm wondering if the two worlds have come together now, unified—and I can't wait to paint that series!"

"Who's Carlotta?"

"She's the girl I'm going to marry."

"And she lives in New York?"

"*No!* She lives in Florence! She's—well—she's an amazing person. In so many ways. You would love her, Doc. We're going to take a house in Ronda. That's where I am going to propose to her."

"Paint what series?"

"*The Unified Universe.*"

"She's Italian, this Carlotta?"

"No, she's a Panther . . ."

I sat back in my couch then, relieved. I'd gotten it off my chest. This doctor really got me. He was someone I could work with, and

I could feel that, too. I saw him taking a lot of notes then, which I hadn't registered before.

"I mean, yes, she's Tuscan," I added as an afterthought.

"Claro."

"I don't want any of this to get out. I don't want anyone to know any of my plans. In New York *or* Florence. That's like twice the heat on me."

"You have my word."

"Do I seem a little, uh, under the weather to you?"

"No, you seem fine."

I pulled the T-shirt away from my chest to stretch it out. It was oppressing me. "You probably think I'm totally crazy."

"Well," he said with a smile, "some people would think you're crazy to give up the life in New York, I'll tell you that. I mean, eyes popping and all."

I broke up then. This guy was fucking cool, and I felt I could trust him. I couldn't wait to tell Carlotta about him.

On second thought, I recognized that was not the best idea, because I didn't want to scare her, to let her think there was something wrong with me, that I was crazy-artist damaged goods, or that I'd lost the top floor. I had to exude confidence. Because if I worried, she'd worry. No need to upset her now, when it seemed to me that things were starting to piece themselves together nicely.

"Tell you what, Rodrigo, why don't we do some tests? I'll set you up with an fMRI brain-imaging scan and see what we come up with—"

"You mean to see if I have some sort of condition?"

"Well, there are indicators that can be detected if there is a potential condition, yes. Sound good?"

"Yes."

"The process takes about an hour. Why don't you head back to the cafeteria or sit in the garden? Our chief radiologist, Dr. Volita, will come get you shortly."

23

FULL EXAMINATION

took a stroll past the gardens and along the ancient fortification that walled in the church and monastery. It was a clear day, not a cloud in the sky. I gave thought to the new series I would paint and choices of subject matter. Was it going to be all nature? Or some figures, too? Any animals? The fact was, I needed to stick to the theme. Whatever was part of *The Unified Universe* was fair game.

"Are you ready?" Desideria was waving my way with a warm smile. I picked up my pace to meet her, and we strode through the gardens together.

"Hi, there."

"You nervous?"

"No, should I be?"

"Not at all."

We proceeded inside the hospital and continued down a corridor to the new wing, still partly under construction, that housed the radiology department.

"We just moved into this wing. The place is a little cluttered. I'm going to call one of the maintenance guys. In the meantime, slip into this if you would—"

"Desideria, is there any way I could keep the scan you do today? I like to use things like this for collaging."

"I'll check with the doctor. Maybe we can get you a copy."

I stepped into the changing room and took off my clothes. "Everything?"

"Yes, please! So that you have no personal items on you . . . Nothing but the smock."

I emerged then and sat in the chair beside the MRI machine and waited. "Can I ask you something? What exactly is schizophrenia? Dr. Abreu mentioned it in connection with one of the drugs Heriberto is taking, though in his case, that's not what it's for, as you know."

"Schizophrenia is a chronic, disabling brain disorder that affects about one percent of people. It may cause them to hear voices, see imaginary sights, or believe other people are controlling their thoughts. These symptoms can be frightening and often lead to erratic behavior. There is no cure, but treatment can usually control the most serious symptoms. Why? You think you may be a candidate?"

"In dreams, everything is possible," I said.

"Ah, yes, I love that saying. As you may know, we're going to give you what we call an fMRI: that stands for functional magnetic resonance imaging. It's a little different than the full-body MRI; the fMRI just scans from the neck up and maps brain activity." Then she asked, "How do you feel?"

"A little tired. Jet-lagged."

"It's easy to drift off in there. But try to remain still, okay?"

Then she slid me inside the machine as if she were closing the drawer of a bureau. The sound of the machine whirred all around me, and it was noisier than I thought it would be.

24

MRI DREAMS

Carlotta said, "*Amore*, I've been waiting to hear from you. How did it go?"

"Not so well. Heriberto doesn't remember me."

"No—!"

"It's that bad, sadly. He looks well enough. But he's bedridden. And he thinks he's a ship's captain. As soon as you enter the room, it's all about the voyage he's taking, and his bed is his boat."

"I'm so sorry, *amore*. But I'm so proud of you for going to see him."

"I left all my information with them and told them I would be back periodically. I told him I love him."

"Of course you do. You always have. It has just been buried in there. You've made a tremendous transformation already, and I'm so proud of you."

"I love you."

"How is the work going? Have you chosen your subject matter yet?"

"I'm getting ideas every day. The mountain formations, the flowers, the donkeys, the church, the monastery."

"How exciting! What about portraits? What about Heriberto?"

"I thought of that, but it makes me too sad."

"No! You must do it! You love him, and he must be part of your new series, to reflect where you are spiritually, your refreshed and revitalized soul. Anyone else?"

"At the hospital, there are two people: this woman doctor, a radiologist, who is very interesting and very beautiful, and a nurse. They are incredible people who live at the monastery and have given up their lives to help others—terminal patients and downtrodden people and some who don't even know their own names."

"*Amore,* what are you waiting for? Put them to canvas," Carlotta said.

"*Sì,* I have thought about it, but then I felt bad—that if I did it, I would be spending all this private time with them, and, well, I didn't think that would be fair to you. So I have not offered to paint them."

"Rodrigo, it will be all right. I trust you. Don't hold back!"

"*Ti amo, amore mio.* Would you like to come and help me with the series? Be my assistant. Come tomorrow!"

"*Amore,* I cannot. I have the festivals now, we are introducing all our new wines, it's very important."

"Always the consummate professional . . . Then we will meet in Ronda?"

"Yes, Ronda!"

"And we will go see a bullfight!"

"If you wish, *amore,*" Carlotta said.

I sensed an interruption. "*Amore?* What is it?"

"It's over," a voice said.

"What's over?"

"The fMRI. You're finished. Wake up, Rodrigo. It's Desideria."

I opened my eyes as she was sliding the drawer out of the bureau—me out of the machine.

"You were in a deep sleep," Desideria said. "But fortunately, you didn't move your head. So we got what we wanted."

I raised myself to sit upright. "Wow. I was really out." I looked around and was reminded that it was the radiology room. Then my hazy gaze panned right back to Desideria. I shook my head to clear my faculties.

"You have an appointment with Dr. Abreu at twelve o'clock on Friday to go over your tests."

"Two days from now?"

"Yes." Desideria then smiled the sweetest of soft smiles. "It's been a pleasure working with you," she said.

"Listen, I'm going to stay around for a few days, to plan more of my new series of canvases. I've been thinking about what you and Ana Paola said, and I would like to feature you in some way. In what way, I'm not sure yet. But—would you be willing to take the time from your work to pose for me?"

Her smile erupted, and she nodded quickly and exaggeratedly.

"And Ana Paola, too?" I asked. "Can you contact her?"

"*Sí.*"

"When can you take the day off? Tomorrow?"

"For this, of course I can. And tomorrow is Ana Paola's day off, anyway."

"Perfect. We will go to those little places you know about. *Bueno?*"

"I can't wait."

"Can you do your own makeup?"

"All my life."

"Especially the eyes—we will need extraordinary eyes."

"Don't worry. There was a time in my life when I had thoughts of becoming an artist. There is still something left of those thoughts. I can do eyes."

"Desideria, I'm sure you can do anything you put your mind to."
She approached me and extended a sealed prescription envelope.
"What is this?" I asked.

"Dr. Abreu wanted me to give it to you. He said it belonged to you."

"Oh, right."

"Did he prescribe anything for you?"

"No. What is contained in this is, well, for a different kind of flight." I left then but paused at the door and turned back. "I am giving you and Ana Paola an assignment. I want you to choose the animal you think is closest to your spirit, and text me tonight with your choices. Tomorrow I want you to be that creature, breathe it, live it, and own it—all day long. Can you do that for me?"

"I feel so honored you have asked me to pose for you, and Ana Paola will, too. In the spirit of making art, we will be happy to do anything you ask of us, Rodrigo."

"*Gracias.* We will all soar and make art together! Okay?"

25

SPANISH BEAUTIES

had rented a two-bedroom suite at the Hotel Valldemossa that gave me a sweeping view of the Mediterranean. I prepared for the following day by choosing various locations. I would take my Nikon D800 to capture the day, so that when it was time to go to canvas, I could be refreshed and reminded of all the places and colors we had seen.

In my earlier days, I did things haphazardly, recklessly—as in anywhere, anytime, with little forethought. And that's a viable creative process, but this was a transformed me. I still embraced spontaneity, but I had learned discipline—and with that came preparation. Taking the camera was part of that diligence, to record everything, something I'd never done before. The big difference was, I was hoping to maximize my talents with all resources available to me. And the integrity I sought now in my work came from one place—Carlotta.

The two Spanish lovelies were to pick me up in front of my hotel at six in the morning so we could start the day with the colors of the sunrise. I was waiting for them when Ana Paola pulled up in her brand-new lime green Volkswagen Beetle convertible. The girls were wearing sunglasses, their hair blown wild. Both were wrapped in African sarongs—Ana Paola in turquoise, Desideria in fuchsia.

I had one request. "Let me see your eyes."

They lifted their sunglasses. Their eyes were painted with a rainbow's worth of colors, tastefully done; as they explained to me, one depicted a Spanish sunrise, the other a Spanish sunset. And dark mascara to underscore it all. Their eyes popped like jewels. Just what I'd been hoping for.

I had asked them to choose an animal spirit to embody for the day. "I am a hummingbird," Ana Paola avowed. "Dancing in the island air."

"And I am a *mariposa*—a beautiful Spanish butterfly fluttering in the Mediterranean winds," Desideria said.

I jumped in the backseat of the car with my canvas bag. It contained my camera, cigarettes, two bottles of champagne, and the baggie from Dr. Abreu that held my vitamins.

I gave them only one direction: to take the exhilarating drive on the MA-10 coastal road that went from Valldemossa to Andratx. From there we could venture off to wherever we wished.

We were in search of the charms of the Tramuntana; this would be Mallorca at its wildest, where valleys sliced through jagged peaks and cliffs plunged abruptly to the sea. Little villages made of golden stone were precariously positioned on hillsides that rose above olive groves and citrus orchards.

I wanted to use that view as the backdrop to the sea: I was now looking out on the Mediterranean from within the Tramuntana—just the opposite of the Cala de Deià series of paintings, which looked from the sea toward the jagged mountains.

I sensed that this spectacular drive would be a sojourn into the heart of creation. And some exotic and unforgettable canvases were sure to come of it. In this way, *The Unified Universe* was painting itself already.

As we motored along high above the sea, the light from the sunrise was a splash of watercolors—peach, mauve, violet, fiery red, orange, pink, and magenta—an appropriate backdrop and gateway to our creative mission.

We toured alluring little villages like Estellencs and the vine-draped Banyalbufar, founded by Moors in the tenth century, where stone-walled terraces tapered down to the sea. We ventured onward. The coastline of the Tramuntana was punctuated with bays sheltered by steep forest-cloaked cliffs.

At the end of the hairpin coastal road was our reward and our chosen picnic locale: Cap de Formentor, a wild peninsula that appeared to flick out like a dragon's tail. We skipped the busy main beach in favor of a tiny, tranquil, unoccupied cove called Cala Murta, huddled below the wind-buckled peaks. It was an easy hike on foot.

After we had a picnic lunch of cheese, fruit, chewy bread from a roadside stand, and white wine, the girls swam while I remained on the beach.

I thought of Carlotta, as I did often, but today, while the girls splashed in the water, I thought in particular about her encouraging me to paint the girls: "It will be all right. I trust you." I said a prayer then and thanked all gods of all religions for bringing her into my life.

"Rodrigo? Do you have another destination in mind?" Desideria asked.

I told them I didn't.

"*We* do," they said in tandem. "But it's a surprise."

26

HUMMINGBIRD AND
BUTTERFLY IN FLIGHT

We hiked back to the Beetle. The girls had a Mallorcan surprise for me, and I couldn't wait to see it. Having grown up on the island, I was well aware there were places I still hadn't explored. We got back on the MA-10 and serpentined our way eastward, eventually through Alcúdia and beyond, to the Cap des Pinar peninsula, known for its pretty coves with a sea of bluest blue—a favorite of boaters, as the jagged coastal cliffs made passage virtually impossible by land, even on foot. It wasn't long until we veered off onto a dirt track, making for a bumpier, woodsy ride.

The girls chatted animatedly. They were laughing nonstop and singing, and it was a festival of good cheer. It appeared that their brief sabbatical from the monastery was quickly becoming the time of their lives.

Desideria spun back toward me suddenly. "Who are you calling, if you don't mind me asking?"

"I'm calling Carlotta—"

The girls exchanged quick looks.

"I told her I would keep her posted on how everything was going."

"Well—tell her the Butterfly and Hummingbird say hi!"

"Can't get through. No signal up here."

Ana Paola stopped the car in the middle of a heavily wooded area. It was about three in the afternoon when we began our hike, and the sun was slashing through the canopies of the thick treetops. We had trekked almost two kilometers on the footpath when Desideria made me pause as she drew a bandana from her beach bag. Then she tied it around my head and blindfolded me. "Like we said, it's a surprise!"

I did not protest. I was sandwiched between the girls, and they steered me along the path.

We stopped abruptly, the bandana was lifted from my eyes, and I was able to look down, from high above, upon the most dazzling beach I'd ever seen. Called Platja des Coll Baix, this immaculate, deserted white crescent was embraced by pine-speckled cliffs that dropped off steeply a good hundred feet below. There was a shabby wire ladder in place; it would require effort, strength, and care to negotiate it safely. It looked borderline dangerous.

There was no question this uncommon setting would find its place in *The Unified Universe.* I could envision about six canvases already.

"We came by boat the first time," Desideria said. "And heard that was the only way."

"Then someone told us about the footpath," Ana Paola said.

"I'm in awe!" I said. "In my own backyard, no less."

The girls smiled proudly at my reaction to their excellent choice.

"Thank you so very, very much," I said. "I just hope we can climb back up!"

The girls scaled down the ladder like ninjas. I slung my bag over my shoulder, and by observing them descend the ladder, I managed without pause to get down to the beach.

From then on, the afternoon unfolded like magic. We had the entire sweep of white sand beach to ourselves. I drew out the camera and set it on manual. The girls perched on their towels to sun themselves and warm up. I took a lengthy stroll and recorded the bay from every angle. When I returned, the girls had opened a bottle of champagne.

They were Butterfly and Hummingbird, and they flew and danced and twirled and spun, and I photographed. They lay in the sand, they stood tall, they oiled their skin, they sat up, they went to all fours, they did whatever they wanted, without any fears, distractions, or judgments. It was pure, it was innocent, it was naughty, it was sensual, and it was very revealing. They did not hold back. They were as professional in following my directions as they were in their daily work.

We shot through the golden hour of the afternoon Mallorcan sun, which shimmered on the water like gold coins.

That day on the beach was transcendent not only for the girls but for me, too. I was filled with an unbelievable high, a raised state of consciousness of some sort that helped me to realize something about myself.

When I was young and naive, I had been hurt and betrayed by women I loved, women who just wanted to use me for their own personal gain. After that, whenever women opened themselves to me, exposing themselves for my art or in my personal life, their vulnerability gave me the feeling that I could get back at them, get revenge, for what I had suffered when I was younger. The taker in me was aroused by the act of seducing and then conquering the fresh subject at hand, like a canvas that could be bought or sold. Sure, it had led to erotic fantasies and the imagination running wild, but it had also led to the production of art.

But as Carlotta had seen so clearly, in the end, it wasn't about art as much as it was about me and what I could use and consume. The first chance I'd gotten, I had strayed from my wife and indulged myself however I pleased. I had looked for love in the places I was least likely to find it, and where I was most likely to meet the kind of women I could never trust.

As I was packing up my things to leave this idyllic setting, perfectly chosen by the Hummingbird and the Butterfly, I realized that all the behavioral rot of my former days was because my sensibilities had not been in proper alignment. I had had no spiritual connections. I had been drawn to the wrong things, running on the fuel of vanity and ego.

But this glorious day in the Tramuntanas was different. I was genuinely enthralled and uplifted, and in my heart, I could find nothing dirty or sordid about the beautiful, sensual art we had made together.

Perhaps my prayers had been answered and I had indeed metamorphosed into someone worthy of Carlotta's trust. I had encouraged these two wonderful young women to soar and to make sublime art with me, without my feeling that I was deceiving them or taking anything away from them, as the old me would have done. And they had made me feel exalted to be a human being. I left the beach that day feeling proud.

27

DAY INTO NIGHT

The dining room at my hotel was not busy, and we had little difficulty getting a choice table by the window with a view of the lights of the quaint town. The girls drank champagne and I ordered Scotch. I brought the camera to show them their work, and they were exhilarated by the viewing. Each thought the other had never looked more beautiful, and I had to concur as much as someone who had known them for only two days could. None of us could wait for the results on canvas. I offered to pay them a day's rate for their work, and they rolled their eyes and waved me off.

The conversation turned to Carlotta. I had tried several times during the day to phone her, but she had not answered, nor would the machine take a message.

"Do you have any photos of Carlotta?" Ana Paola asked. I did not, but I had some phone photos of paintings of her from *The Parallel Universe* series. Which then led to an explanation of both the *Parallel* and *Unified Universe* series.

"Do you think there's a possibility you engage in a little fantasy about things?"

"How do you mean?"

"Well, with all these dreams, isn't it difficult sometimes to differentiate between what's parallel and unified, and what's real and what isn't?"

"Definitely."

"I mean, I wish you no disrespect, but isn't it possible that you imagine or conjure events, even people, in your highly fertile imagination? Remember, we are not only professionals, we are your friends now. We mean well when we ask you these very private questions."

"It's possible," I answered.

"Carlotta is real?" Ana Paola asked gently.

"She is."

"But we see you making calls to her, and she never seems to pick up. And you don't have any actual photos of her."

Desideria spoke up for the first time. "Does Carlotta ever call you on the telephone?"

"Well, no. But she's very busy and she knows I am, too. We talk as much as we can."

"But, as you say, she appears in your dreams."

"Well, I don't want to get into the medical or science jargon, because that's why I had a meeting with Dr. Abreu. And you know a little of it, Dr. Volita. I feel like there are people and events that are a dream and those that are not, but I feel that Carlotta—and our life in Florence—is real."

"Let me add, Rodrigo, at the hospital we share information on patients. We need to, in order to be in the loop, so we know how best to handle a patient."

"I'm not a patient. I just had one meeting."

"I know," Desideria said. "But what Dr. Abreu is looking for is something involving the brain, as you know. And I'm not saying it's true, but there is a possibility that there are things you may be inventing for yourself—for any number of reasons. This does happen to people. An imaginary world may be invented that is more comfortable to the person. Sometimes that fabricated world exists inside the patient's mind to make him happy, or to take away pressure from real life . . ."

"That's what makes dreams beautiful—you can be who you want, meet whomever you want, and do anything you want while you are dreaming," Ana Paola added.

"I'm not delusional. These things really happened. Carlotta is real."

"Well, you know, Heriberto has his delusions, and there are very specific scientific reasons why he has them."

"I'm not sailing a ship, okay? I'm not fighting off heavy weather!"

"No, I'm not saying that."

"What are you saying?" I asked.

"That I think you might want to keep an open mind."

"An open mind to what—?"

"What you consider definitely real and what you don't."

I pushed back in my chair, becoming somewhat annoyed by the conversation. "Are you guys real?"

They looked at each other. "We think we are."

"Well, there you are."

"But we can prove we're real."

"How?"

"Do you have your phone?"

"Yes."

Desideria dialed me from her phone. And my line started ringing. "Hello, Rodrigo? The famous painter? The god of two universes?"

I had to laugh.

Then she hung up.

"Point well taken," I said. "But at the same time, maybe that phone call happened in a dream. And if you were part of another reality, it would not appear there. In my other life, Carlotta could say something similar when I'm with her: 'Those hospital goddesses never call you, no?' And I have other proof—"

"Go on . . ."

"The proof of my change, of my evolution, of my embracing of the spiritual. I was a selfish hedonist playboy when I met her. She has helped make me a better person."

"She has? Or you have made yourself a better person? Subconsciously, or consciously, or within your dreams? Perhaps you were ready for a big change and your mind steered you that way, to what you were seeking, to fill the void in your life—"

I had had enough of the conversation at this point. "This *must* be a dream . . . On that note, I think I'll finish my Scotch out by the pool."

Ana Paola and Desideria exchanged exasperated looks, clearly recognizing the futility of any further discussion.

I walked out to the patio to make my phone call and looked into the pool's glowing turquoise depths. Once again Carlotta's line rang and rang without any response or recorded message.

Our discussion at the table, combined with my consistent inability to contact her, did make me wonder once more if I was in the reverse dream—the theory I'd expressed to Dr. Abreu. That this plane of existence was not real, even the day I'd spent with Desideria and Ana Paola. The proof was that I couldn't reach Carlotta. I knew she was real—she was the realest thing in my life—and yet I couldn't communicate with her. Perhaps I was caught in another dimension, trapped between the two universes. I figured I would just have to play it out until I woke up from the present dream state.

And with that, I ordered another Scotch.

WHEN I WENT BACK TO MY SUITE, the first thing I noticed was the plastic baggie of pills on the table. The pills represented my life in New York. I knew that was where I had obtained them, and I knew I had brought the baggie to Europe. It further convinced me that what I was doing now was a dream. And that my life with Carlotta was the root of reality.

My fresh analysis went against my previous theory of the unified universe and meant that the two worlds were still separate—but in the reverse. How could that be? That didn't make sense even to me.

Was I losing my mind? Who could be speaking in such terms and be sane? I couldn't really answer that question.

I decided to turn away from introspection. I made a conscious decision to set myself free from these confusing thoughts, at least for the time being. And taking a hit of Molly seemed a good way to do that.

"Molly Boy doesn't mess around," I said out loud, appreciating the quality of his product, and then I realized what that meant. It was another indicator that my New York reverse-dream life was real, but now I wasn't so sure about the day and the dinner I'd had with these two hospital goddesses.

Did the girls even exist? The rest of the hospital certainly existed, but Nurse Goddess and Doctor Goddess might have been total products of my imagination in my dreamscape. After all, I had a pretty damned good imagination. I was a real professional when it came to imagination.

Perhaps we had never met and I had never even been to see Heriberto. But that couldn't be right. I knew I had seen my mentor; I'd told Carlotta about it. I even remembered *not* telling her about Dr. Abreu.

So maybe I'd left the girls a long time ago, after I had signed books and calendars for them.

Maybe we did go on our road trip today and make some very sensual art on the beach, but it ended when they dropped me off, and I was asleep now, having conjured this evening by the pool in my dream as a continuation of the day together.

Or maybe we just had dinner at the hotel and argued and they went home.

Who was I to argue with two goddesses who might not even be real and who were having a party in some hotel suite located in some remote corner of my mind?

I think I passed out then.

28

WORLDS TO JUGGLE

When I woke up, I was alone, curled up on the couch. My hotel room was completely clean, the bed still made. I was wearing my T-shirt and sarong, and I had a colossal hangover. After getting dressed, I noticed a dinner napkin spread on the table. There were two bright lipstick prints arranged vertically side by side, forming the shape of a butterfly.

I needed to move quickly. I had an afternoon appointment with Dr. Abreu, and I'd scheduled an evening flight to the south of Spain. I was groggy and had that spike working away in my skull, but I made it to the hospital with a few minutes to spare and headed down the hallway to the doctor's office.

Dr. Abreu, again dressed immaculately in a charcoal suit, Chanel tie, and Guccis, waved at me to come in. As I entered, he stood up and said, "Come with me. I want to show you something."

I followed him down several corridors to a familiar-looking wing. We continued to the last room on the right. As we approached the open door, the doctor raised his hand and indicated that I should not enter. Instead, we stood there in the hallway and observed Heriberto: to my amazement, he was out of bed, bending over and working—unbelievably—on a mound of clay. I watched him knead the clay to warm it, the requisite preparation for shaping it. On the windowsill, I saw an already completed sculpture in clay, a ship at sea. It was intricate and extraordinary for clay, which can be difficult to work with and can crack or even fall apart; but that did not surprise me. What surprised me was that Heriberto was working and that the magic was still in his hands.

"Congratulations," Dr. Abreu said to me.

"For what, Doctor?"

"You broke through to him. I heard what you said to him two days ago. Something must have registered, to release him from his maritime fantasies. Apparently, he shot up in bed in the middle of the night and said, 'I am Maestro! Maestro lives!' He did pause before adding, 'But I'm a ship captain, too!' The mind works in mysterious ways, Rodrigo."

Tears welled in my eyes. I was elated. "I can't tell you how— I can't even express the words."

"I know."

"May I—?" I said, indicating a desire to see Heriberto.

"Not today, and not for a little while. We'll let him be, to get in the routine, and not disturb him—not that you would, but it's just playing it safe."

He wrapped his arm around me, and we left the Alzheimer's wing. "Shall we get a cup of coffee?"

"Sure."

As we walked toward the cafeteria, I looked out the window and saw Ana Paola pushing an elderly lady in a wheelchair. She saw me and waved amicably. But I wondered—maybe that entire road trip had been a dreamland fantasy. Perhaps we had dinner and that was all, and then I got drunk and passed out. Her lack of enthusiasm at my sight certainly would indicate as much.

Dr. Abreu and I sat at a table in back and ordered two macchiatos, which were welcome, in my current state.

"I want you to know I have what may be considered good news. The brain-imaging scans came back negative, so there are no physical issues involved here."

"I'm not schizophrenic?"

"No, not at all. At least nothing detectable."

"But there are times when an abnormality like that remains hidden?"

"Rarely, Rodrigo. I think you're fine. Maybe a little stressed, maybe something else. And this is what I wanted to warn you about. Those drugs you had—the cocaine, the risperidone, the powerful hallucinogens. If you are doing this frequently, or combining them, I mean, who knows what the outcome could be on the brain."

"You think the drug intake may be causing—how do I put it so I don't describe myself as a total lunatic?"

"Alternative perceptions?"

"Yes."

"It's possible. Perhaps more than possible."

I sipped on my coffee, a big healthy swig.

"Not to sound like a square, which I know I am—I'm a doctor, by definition a square—but you may want to consider staying away from those recreational drugs altogether. They can enhance volatility and cause mood swings."

"But I don't really take them. I mean only in one life. Not the other, so, well . . ."

He eyed me for an extended moment, perhaps beginning to understand me better. See me in the whole rather than the half. Because unlike most people, I had two worlds to handle. He was used to people of one dimension. But I had twice as much ground to cover. I wondered if he would charge me twice as much.

"Have you ever been tested for bipolar disorder?"

"Like I'm a manic depressive?"

"Yes."

"No, never."

"It's something to think about if your alternative perceptions persist. But overall, I would say, Rodrigo, as far as visits to the clinic go, this was a pretty good day."

"Thank you."

"And I thank you for your help with Heriberto. You did in five minutes what my staff has been unable to do in twelve years."

"Well, we do have history."

"Yes. That often helps. Or hurts, as the case may be."

I left the cafeteria and checked my watch. I still had time to catch my flight. I passed through the garden on my way out the front of the hospital. I made a quick stop by Heriberto and checked in on him from a distance. He was still at it, attempting a new creation. It was a man's bust. On closer inspection, I thought it looked an awful lot like me. I told the nurse attendant I'd be back to visit.

As I emerged from the hospital, a voice came from behind me. "Rodrigo?"

I spun around and it was a vision—Desideria wearing a pair of bell-bottom jeans, hippie beads, and a glowing yellow T-shirt. "I was hoping I'd find you," she said. "How did it go?"

"Fine, I received a clean bill of health."

"That's fantastic."

I nodded and remained silent. I felt uncomfortable for some reason.

"I want to thank you for yesterday," she said. She stood there and smiled. "Are you okay?"

"Yes, I'm fine. A little hungover, but—I guess I drank a lot of Scotch last night."

"You did. Are you in a rush or something?"

"I have to catch my flight to Málaga."

"You're leaving today?"

I nodded. "Now."

"Well—I'd like to see your artwork sometime."

"Yeah, sure. Let's stay in touch."

I didn't think anything intimate had happened after dinner, and I was almost too terrified to ask, but there was that napkin with the red lipstick butterfly kiss on it, and I had to know. "Desideria? Did something happen last night?"

She studied my face and peered into the depths of my eyes almost clinically. "No, Rodrigo. Nothing. Nothing happened." She paused, then nodded with a smile. "Good-bye," she said.

"Good-bye, Butterfly."

We pecked cheeks, and she turned and walked away.

Back at the hotel, as I put my clothes and camera in my bag, a thought hit me like a shovel dug into my chest. I remembered then that when I had dreamed during the fMRI, I had told Carlotta about Desideria and Ana Paola. She had told me to paint them, that she trusted me. That meant they hadn't been part of any New York reverse dreams or any other dimension. They were *real*.

I took a taxi to the airport and tried not to think about anything.

When I boarded the plane, I got out the camera in search of more hard evidence. I went to view the memory card, but to my amazement, there were no pictures. None. And yet we had been looking through them at dinner the night before—if there had been a night before, given this new clue. Maybe there had been no excursion to the beach, either. I was so fucking confused.

But not about one thing in particular. I wrote a text to Desideria: *Precious Butterfly. I'm so sorry. I'm mixed up. I have to work some things out. I'm so grateful we met. Thrilled we made beauty. Please continue to fly, Butterfly. Love always, Rodrigo*

The most convincing hard evidentiary fact I could hold on to was that I still had the baggie of vitamins from my New York life. I debated trashing it altogether, as the doctor had suggested. My thoughts seemed increasingly jumbled. I was mixing universes and dreams, and reversing everything over and over, but my best guess now was that the universes were unified. I couldn't think about this anymore. It was all too much.

I needed sleep, and flights were always good for that.

"*CIAO, CARLOTTA.*"

"Rodrigo, where have you been? I've been trying to get ahold of you for two days."

"Really? I've been trying to contact you, too, and I couldn't reach you, either."

"Listen, I'm coming in three days, okay?" Carlotta says.

"Okay. Great."

"How does the house look?" she asks.

"I haven't seen it yet."

"No? Where are you?"

"I'm flying to Málaga now."

"I can't wait to see you, *amore.* Is anything the matter?"

"No, no. Just had too many Scotches," I respond.

"How did it go with the girls? Did you get some inspiration?"

So I really have told her about the girls. "Well, some, yes. I took some photos, but they didn't come out."

"What do you mean?"

"I mean there are no photos on the camera."

"Not even of me?"

"I've never taken any of you with this camera." I'm thinking that sounds bizarre, actually. I mean, why have I not captured Carlotta on any camera or phone? I need to tell my mind to shut the fuck up. It is only serving to disorient and bewilder me. "I don't know what is happening."

"Maybe the girls took them. Were they risqué?"

Wait a second. She's right! The girls probably took the memory card so nothing would happen with the photos, in order to protect themselves. I think they trust me, but who trusts anyone anymore? What if the photos got in the wrong hands and ended up on the Internet?

"I feel like such a jackass." I clear my throat. "Some are risqué, a little. The girls had never done a shoot like that before."

"Nudity?"

The sensual imagery of the girls twirling on the beach is assaulting me and making me sweat. "Uh, some . . ."

"Do they excite you?"

What I need is an end to the splintered thoughts. There are too many splinters in splintered thoughts. Splinters hurt, too. "T-t-the photos?" I stammer. I am feeling pretty insecure.

"*No, the girls!* . . . Of course the photos. Are you sure you're all right?"

Jackass again. "Carlotta, I'm a little stressed. Let's talk about what you're up to."

"I've been spending time with my father. He'd like to meet you."

"Really?"

"Sure. He wants to meet this man I keep talking about. Maybe we can visit sometime."

"Anytime, *amore.*"

My mind is flying around. But it isn't free. It is trapped. In some sort of—I don't know what. "Love, can I call you later?"

"Of course. *Amore?*"

"*Sí?*"

"I can't wait to make love to you."

Jackass to the third power. "Me, too . . ."

"*Arrivederci, amore . . .*"

I return it and we hang up.

Rodrigo, you dick . . .

29

HELP ME, RONDA

We touched down in Málaga, and I woke up with a start. I took a private car for the hundred-kilometer ride from the airport to Ronda and arrived around nine in the evening. I almost got sick as we climbed up and up into the Andalusian mountains. I still wasn't feeling well. My thoughts were still splintered. I paid the driver in cash and didn't divulge my name. I couldn't trust anyone.

It was too late to meet the real estate broker, so I stayed the night in a local inn. I had fond memories of the city from when I was a boy, and I was happy to be there again.

I had told Carlotta of my days in Ronda as a young teen, moped-ing around, pursuing youthful crushes, painting, and going to bull-fights. I had told her about Tanya, too, the girl to whom I first made love (or made folly, as it were). Carlotta had been crying with laughter as I recounted the big event in detail. The fact is, I didn't know what I was doing. Once the act began, as I had no problem with erections—I received them spontaneously throughout the day—I just stayed still inside her and thought everything was just supposed to happen. Carlotta bent in half and said, *"Dio mio,* have you come a long way!"

Even that memory didn't raise my spirits. I wondered then about Dr. Abreu's mention of bipolar disorder. I never seemed overly depressed. Usually, the only thing that could sour my mood was a hangover.

I was tired and soon fell asleep. I leaped up from my hotel bed in a panic, sweating profusely, heart pounding. I felt pressure all over. I'd had a nightmare that Desideria had sent me back a text: *Go fuck yourself!*

I quickly searched for my phone and scanned it. There was no text, thankfully.

When was I going to get a firm sense of reality? Or was I ahead of the curve? Was I the one pushing the envelope on the human experience? Perhaps most humans as we knew them weren't sophisticated enough to access a second life. Was everyone else sleeping like dogs, disregarding the richness of a dream life that was just as real? That was how I saw the average man now. A Sleeping Dog. Marching around, eating, shitting, sniffing pussy, looking for the next bone and burying it—in Chase Bank—unaware of the other beautiful universe that, when combined with this one, constituted a unified universe of dreams and consciousness.

Perhaps I should become a Dream Missionary and go to far-off lands and towns and bring dream culture, my specialty, to the masses. To convert them. Maybe I'd become the Dream Messiah. And impart my wisdom to all the Sleeping Dogs and Tech Jockeys.

What the fuck was I talking about?

I had to settle on one or the other. Parallel or Unified. Dream or Reverse Dream. And did they overlap? My mind couldn't decipher what was right or wrong. I couldn't rectify it. I didn't have the capacity. So I settled on it once and for all: the unified universe. Every fucking thing was a part of everything else, and it all blended together. That was easiest on my mind, anyway.

I noticed I was cursing a lot in my thoughts. I wondered where it was coming from.

I WOKE IN THE MORNING and stepped outside the hotel and flamed a cigarette. I didn't remember my dreams from the night before. That hadn't happened in a while, and frankly, it was almost a welcome relief.

First things first. I put a call in to the art supply outlet in Málaga for my shipment of oils and canvases, a chore I'd intended to do when I first arrived in Spain. Salvador, the proprietor, knew me well, and I knew I was in good hands. I preferred some Spanish and French paints, the metallic ones especially, and you couldn't get them as easily in the U.S. This *Unified Universe* was going to pop like there was no tomorrow. I may have not had my mind entirely, but I had my work, and that would be my grounding force.

After that, I simply walked around, though I was still feeling a little muddled.

Ronda is a pretty town with a long and colorful past. I headed toward the Puente Viejo, the Old Bridge, built in Roman times. In more recent times, Hemingway, Rilke, and Orson Welles had lived here, and they all enjoyed hanging out with the bullfighters. At least I remembered something of the town's history, and that was comforting.

I made my way to the middle of the Old Bridge, suspended three hundred feet over the canyon. I contemplated the depths below and thought I'd had worse ideas lately.

I smacked myself to snap out of it. Some people were watching me suspiciously, and though I couldn't be sure if it was because of me, they crossed to the other side of the street. I turned around swiftly to see if I was being followed. That's how you catch them: with a quick swivel. Otherwise they just follow you from fifty yards behind all day.

I didn't want anybody to know I was in Ronda. I had managed to elude Rafaela and her New York posse for several days now, and I knew they had to be looking for me. Creeping.

After meandering the streets a bit longer, I stepped into a vintage clothing shop and bought a Russian admiral's black *ushanka* hat— naturally. From the Commie naval era, with a hammer and sickle on a gold badge, the fur rose high and mightily black, and I could flap the ears down at a moment's notice. I put it on in the heavy August heat and it made me sweat, but it was a bitchin' hat. I didn't like hats, usually. Hats were for baldies. But that *ushanka* hat and my Ray-Ban Meteors kept me under the radar and in disguise. Out of sight.

If one was good, two was better, so I bought a second one. His and hers.

Then, while I was in the same shop, I ordered an embroidered dress worthy of a painting by Goya, and I went into great detail about how it was to be made. They looked at me funny, especially when I designed it with the proper period cut and color scheme of Goya's time. "Don't forget the periwinkle trim! With a touch of coral— somewhere! Anywhere! You know the drill!"

Of course, they had no idea who the dress was really for.

Before I left, they recommended the local gay bar to me—out of politeness for their suspicions that I was a cross-dresser, and respect for the money I'd just poured into their shop. Bless their hearts.

With my *ushanka* hat, I would be known to locals as Vladimir de Valldemossa, the Russian Ronda surf poet. And if we became chums, you could call me Vladdy. *Spasibo* very much. No one would ever find me.

I would go on a *zapoy,* like the ones you read about—a *zapoy* is a drinking holiday, an all-out nonstop binge that can last a week or more. Some end in cirrhosis, some end in death—a favorite pastime of Muscovites for centuries. I was right in step. Just a spiral, some

Stoli, a few stanzas, while watching the swell—a surf poet. *Catching the waves of strife / Total anonymity for life.*

Hang ten, complete Zen.

Ah, the bliss . . .

Gnarly.

I bought a coffee at the bar of a café and downed it. Then I went back to the hotel. Juan Filippo, the real estate broker, was meeting me there. When I'd phoned him from the airport in Madrid and asked him to find me a house in Ronda, I'd told him what I wanted. He said he'd followed my directions perfectly and gotten me a great house that I would surely love.

I checked out of the slow-tel. Juan picked me up and gave me the keys, along with a contemptuous look at my hat. We stopped by a liquor store for some Scotch, no rocks, then climbed up and up to the *finca-villa* estate section. I liked him during the drive, until he got personal.

"Don't you have any baggage, Mr. Shakespeare?"

"*Nyet.*"

"What about clothes?"

"Clothes are for those who haven't found out yet."

Our ten-minute friendship chilled somewhat after that, and his splash-happy questions stopped.

Juan followed me through the front door of the three-story villa, and I had to hand it to him, I liked what I saw: huge sunken living room, dining room, French doors opening to a big terrace and garden and pool beyond, situated in the midst of a wide and deep back lawn. There were seven bedrooms, the master suite on the second floor accessed by a grand semi-spiral staircase. Best of all, there was tons of blank wall space, as I had asked to have all the walls left bare.

I can really make beauty here, I thought.

Juan then became a whish in time, gone.

I was alone.

And I was Vlad Shakespeare.

I recognized that my attitude had changed since Mallorca, and not necessarily for the better. I was snarky and glib and sarcastic and ill mannered. Kind of like the way I acted in New York. I think it was a mental facade I'd erected in self-defense, a self-inflicted mind-fuck, a trick my brain was playing on its more deviant, uncooperative part to compensate for its own fracturing, and to evade and escape its controversial and alternative ways. The only way to handle this was to perform and outwit it. Because if I let my mind roam in introspective ways, in any way, I was sure to get in trouble. I could make sense of the world no longer.

I'd felt so complete and whole and in the moment that day on the beach in Valldemossa—but not now. I was not thinking straight; I was deconstructed. Maybe it was the alcohol, maybe the pills, or maybe just the fallout from my hedonistic life, the "Hey, buddy, not so fast—time to atone for your conduct," and this was the payback biting me in the ass; maybe it was the beginning of a nervous breakdown, or maybe the breakdown was at halftime, awaiting the second-half kick-off; maybe a whole list of things had caused the final fissure. But I was cracked; I needed coping mechanisms by the truckload.

Zapoy.

I was alone and in a big house with no clothes and no food and no blank canvases as yet. What the hell was I going to do now?

The most challenging, terrifying part was the not knowing. Not knowing if I'd already been through the worst of it, or if I was headed further astray—and if that was the case, how far would it go, and could I survive?

Because I could have lucid moments like this, and then I could just go off at any moment with episodes of fantastical thought and be like Heriberto on his good ship.

I went from room to room to find the best place to designate as my studio. Up on the third floor, I found a suitable space, a bedroom with dormer windows looking out over the expansive back lawn and an explosion of afternoon sunshine. That seemed positive.

Zapoy.

I needed to get my mind off itself; I needed to get to work fast.

"Work, Carlotta . . . work, Carlotta . . ." That was my mantra, and I repeated it to myself over and over.

Zapoy.

The surf poetry kept surging through me, too, which was a relief.

Gnarly. Harley.

Did I need a Harley?

Of course I needed a fuckin' Harley!

I couldn't believe I hadn't thought of it sooner. It was the last missing piece to ensure absolute anonymity.

Try to find me now, world!

Zapoy!

part two

DREAM WORLD

30

DREAM BOY

am sitting upright in the middle of the living room floor with my legs extended. Delicate spontaneous tears river down my face. Fresh as a baby's tears and just as effective. This has been happening a lot lately. I think it is late afternoon, and the commodious sunken space is pretty obscured. The curtains are drawn, and the venetians are slatted shut. I am letting the sun go down on the house, too, welcoming the shadows and darkness that will soon envelop it. The last thing I care to do is bring light upon myself. I can't wait until the end of day, when all that obnoxious lighting, as in the bright Spanish sun, will be vanquished by nighttime. I am a cheerleader for the dark team all the way and rooting for the moon's rising.

I have lost track of days, to be perfectly honest.

"Amore."

Through the puddles of my eyes, I can just about make out the form of a person. But how have they gotten in? What kind of security is this?

"*Amore,* what's the matter?"

"What delusionary intruder could this be?" I ask. There is no immediate response. *Shit,* I'm thinking. *They've found me.* "Identify yourself, and how the hell did you get in here?"

"*Amore,* it's me."

"And don't give me that 'I'm the caretaker' crap!" Someone claiming to be the caretaker has tried to get in several times, "to check on the house," he always says, but so far I have been able to catch him and make him leave before he can break in on me.

I wipe my eyes again and my vision clears somewhat . . . Holy heaven! It is Carlotta! "You came!"

"Of course I came! You've been crying." She kneels next to me and hugs me. She kisses my face and my eyes.

"A little. I'm very sensitive, you know," I say, and laugh.

"What's happened to you?"

"Nothing. I've expanded all operations."

"How do you mean?"

"I'm a surf poet now. In a town with no waves."

"Have you been drinking sangria and running with the bulls?"

"That's in Pampy—get your festivals straight!" I smile peacefully. My better wits are being aroused finally. "I have had a thimble or two of Scotch. From what I can recall. It's five o'clock somewhere, and herewhere it's five. Reminds me of a Lorca poem, 'Lament for Ignacio Sánchez Mejías.' Shall I quote it?"

"Please do, *amore.*"

And so I recite, as memorized when I was a boy, the sweet sad images—a boy brings up the white sheet, bones and flutes resounding—all at five in the afternoon.

"Lovely," she says mercifully.

"You see, everything happens at five in the afternoon—even death."

"Why are you thinking such thoughts?"

"It's poetry. Very inspiring. Besides, I'm at the end of my *zapoy*. It's been a long hard road."

"Crazy boy. No wonder I have been worried about you. Have you been getting any work done?"

"Almost. Tangentially. The best way to describe it. Waiting on supplies still. But I've been prepping. I've been waiting for you. Where have you been?"

"I told you I was coming today. Haven't you gotten my message?"

I just look at her stupidly. "Uh, I've kept my phone off. I've been concerned with privacy. Don't want any folk to geolocate me."

"Of course you need your privacy for your work. Why are you so upset?"

"Life of an artist. Garden-variety human-condition doldrums, nothing serious. Missing you, actually. Passion at every pore."

"You sound a little strange. Off-kilter."

"That's what happens when supplies don't show on time. There's nothing to do and nothing to be done about it. Until your Panther comes."

"What are those?" she says, gesturing to my baggie.

"Oh, those help me sleep."

"Do you take them a lot?"

"Only when necessary. Say, you want to come with me?"

"Where?"

"To pick up the Harley."

"Really? You bought a motorcycle? How fun!"

"Of course. It's the last level—"

"Level of what?"

"Security."

"You're pretty tipsy. Why don't we wait a little bit? I love your hat. What a funny hat."

"Know what's funnier? I bought one for you, too."

"You did? I love it!"

"You're officially a member of the Russian navy. I'm Comrade Vlad."

"So poetic, I've been telling you, you *should be* writing poetry."

"No waves. And who will you be?"

"I'm . . . let me see . . . *Verushka!*"

"I love it! Verushka and Vladimir. A twin-V engine!"

"An Eagle and a Panther."

"We've got it all, we're writing our own Russian love story."

"I like that."

"How about *Snore and Peace*? I sleep and dream a lot."

"Dreams are good."

"Dreams are tricky. You may even be a dream."

"That's right. I'm your dream girl."

"I've said that."

"My crazy dream boy. Get up off the floor so I can hug you for real."

I do and we do.

"Does that feel real to you?"

We've jabbered on enough. She leads me upstairs and we make beautiful love and she lets me keep my hat on. Just for grins. It is fun love. A new chapter for us.

I am renewed, and it is Carlotta who has rebooted me. Again. And just in the nick of time. Things were starting to get ugly.

As I lie in bed and the hangover subsides, I watch her put on her *ushanka* hat and settle in and hang her clothes. She has brought a fair number of garments, and that pleases me. It is confirmation that she is going to stay for a while.

Afterward we don our hats and take a taxi up the mountain. There are six Harleys available in the environs, but this one has it all, including two eagles on the gas tank. I pay the young Spanish mechanic as promised. Twice as much as he says the bike is worth.

Then Carlotta and I drive down the mountain together on our new Harley. Wearing our *ushanka* hats. It is the perfect disguise. Me with my Meteor sunglasses and Carlotta with her Prada ovals. No one will ever find us now! We will just dissolve right into the landscape like two sambar deer in the Sariska woods.

The following day, Carlotta goes shopping and I go to work. The supplies arrive that afternoon—pine frames, linen and cotton canvases, da Vinci brushes, and Golden acrylic and Gamblin oil paints. I stretch and prime the canvases, then study all the sketches and categorize them and draw up my list of finalists.

I have conceived of *The Unified Universe* as a veritable explosion of expressionist will. I reclaim my mantle as a creative toreador. And to have Carlotta in proximity to me while painting is the best life I could ever imagine.

I paint, then we make love. I paint, then we have dinner. After we make more love, I paint through the night and am interrupted with a shy, sweet tug on my arm. I look up at her groggy smile and she says, "Rodrigo, come to bed—"

When Carlotta and I come up for air from the all-consuming love-work schedule, we tour the countryside on our twin-eagled Harley. We make trips through the nearby scenic mountains and natural park known as the Sierra de Grazalema. We hike, take pictures of the magnificent views, have wine-and-cheese picnics, and even birdwatch. And this time the photos stay on my camera. We visit many of the beautiful towns—some completely white, known as *pueblos blancos*—enveloped by the range on both the Cádiz and the Málaga sides. We venture even farther and rent a boat in Puerto Banús for an overnight and go to a masquerade party at the glamorous Costa del Sol hot spot Olivia Valère, which is situated in a Moorish castle. Though it's a famous spot, without the mandatory mask requirement we would not have attended. All anonymity has been preserved.

One bright sunny afternoon, Carlotta sports butterfly oval sunglasses, and they make me think of Desideria—but only as a dreamland friend and artistic muse in a far-off dimension. As there were no corroborating photos on the Valldemossa camera, I still don't know for sure if we spent that afternoon on the beach or if I only imagined it. But I am no longer unglued or splitting and protruding at the seams. I am stable again. My crack has been sealed or cemented over. And my life's angel, my Panther, has nourished me once more and offered that adhesive cement and stability to me, my life, and my work.

The art itself—the canvases conceptualized, sketched, painted, and refined—is a reflection of me at my best. The canvases are large, they are ambitious, the whole series is an enormous undertaking. But I am more than up to the task. I feel spiritually realigned, artistically bold, and at my peak, and I am—we are—very much in love. I feel that completeness again, that wholeness of a life in harmony with the unified universe.

I have traveled through the gamut of experiences to capture *The Universe,* and I paint them all—the lovely Akira; Heriberto's ship of clay, and young and old portraits of the Maestro himself; the church at Valldemossa, the monastery, George Sand at her desk and Frédéric Chopin at his piano in their apartment there, the Technicolor gardens; there is the white-sand crescent beach, Platja des Coll Baix; the Hummingbird and the Butterfly, dancing in the air together; two lost flip-flops; the iris flowers, the alpine trees; there is Dr. Abreu caught between two universes; there is even one self-portrait of me presiding over one unified universe.

There is the battle between the two universes, beautiful nudes of Desideria and Ana Paola on the beach, in the water, in the jungle woods; there is the butterfly kiss on the napkin; there is an eagle series—soaring over Cap de Formentor, perched on the monastery, flying alongside the Hummingbird and the Butterfly; there is the Panther sprinting at gazelle speed, providing a whish of wind beneath the wings of the Eagle.

There is even a *Brain* series, showing the organ in two dimensions, then one; some collaged, some not, using the actual fMRI brain-imaging scans. There is *The Unified Universe* contained within the brain.

I paint spontaneously, too, of the beautiful life we are living: some classic still lifes of the produce that goes into Carlotta's Tuscan dishes, the dishes themselves, pastas, meats, and salads. There is the Harley series of the two of us speeding and slashing through the Andalusian hills.

Then there is the Carlotta installment: in a sundress with one shoulder strap released, exposing her perky breast. I paint her every which way. Every way. Innumerable poses. With love and affection. I paint her with the subtext of making love to her. I have a special appreciation for the series. Because I know then, as I've known for a while, that I will spend the rest of my life with her, that she is going to be my wife. It is just a question of when and where I will ask her. But it is on my mind.

My new *Unified Universe* has been jump-started like the Harley, and I am zooming down the highway at racetrack time-clock speed. I let Carlotta critique my creations. Not only does she view their progress on a daily basis, I welcome her perceptions and viewpoints, from conception to color palette. I am ecstatic to have her so close and becoming a part of my work. I've never listened to anyone before, but I listen to her. In this way, we've become collaborators. In love. In life. And in my art.

And the series is becoming a bomb. An explosion. Of form and content and brought to life and enlivened with an electric palette.

But it is not all about art, obviously. It is Carlotta and me being free, sprinting and soaring, on the double-eagled Harley with our *zapoy* hats. The *zapoy* is over, but the zest is not. We road-trip in tandem to local flamenco guitar concerts, Spanish carnivals, wine tasting and food festivals and fairs, and we attend poetry readings. I even contribute, at Carlotta's behest, and read aloud my surf poetry. I am introduced as Vladimir de Valldemossa, and we pass out a small booklet of my poems that I've been writing in the backyard whenever something hits me while painting. I scribe always in the shade beneath a sky-high lazy Spanish fir "poet-tree." I even leave my spiral notebook in the convergence of the limbs. And after I finish reading to my Panther, we make more Panther-Eagle love. Then skinny-dip in the pool, the same way we find an excuse to do every day.

I am expanding myself, becoming enamored with words and language, and it feeds my art, too. In a word, I am *soaring*.

31

A TOUCH OF BLISS

All is good in Ronda in August. All is better than good.

Carlotta and I continue to grow together. I learn from Carlotta and she learns from me. In particular, she introduces me to the freshly revitalized Catholic Church, more modern and less judgmental than I remembered. I was brought up Catholic, and as a result I often felt guilt and was judgmental, especially toward women; that was how Catholic boys were taught. Carlotta and I attend some Sunday masses, even, and I'm impressed with the thoughtfulness of the sermons. That prompts me to do a series of twenty-first-century neoreligious paintings, which I finish off with an enormous canvas of my interpretation of the gods of all religions combined. I have the representatives—Christ, Buddha, Hindu Brahma, Muhammad, and the Great Spirit—all seated, having a "Heads of the Unified Universe" dinner. I call it *The First Supper.* I've never soared so close to the sun creatively, skimming the sky and in touch with the divine.

Carlotta nourishes me with her Florentine culinary traditions and introduces me to Italian cuisines from Liguria, Tuscany, Genoa, and Bologna. We shop the local markets for fresh ingredients, prepare and cook numerous meals together, and often eat on the terrace, bathed in daytime sunshine or evening candlelight. We serve Ligurian seafood dishes, Venetian risottos, white truffle *pici* pastas from Tuscany, and sweet authentic meat and pork ragù, Bolognese-style. The dishes are decidedly Italian-made-from-Spanish products, a perfect blend of our cultures.

I bring some traditions of Spain to my beloved Carlotta as well. We tour Spanish vineyards so she can familiarize herself with indigenous wines. We make special sangrias for lunches and sunny afternoons. We eat *jamón ibérico,* or *pata negra,* the black hoof ham, and we slice it right off the furry leg held in a *jamonero* clamp. We tour Andalusian tapas taverns, sampling the traditional sherries and enjoying tapas appetizer tastings: chorizo, Spanish cheeses, olive tapenades, *chopitos* or fried bay squid, almonds, and citrus fruits, all dusted with fragrant spices.

Mostly, however, for Carlotta's full introduction to the traditions of Spain, I am very excited about the upcoming Corrida Goyesca, a huge annual festival that for some sixty years has been a celebration of Ronda's greatest bullfighters. I went to it every September as a boy, and I am even more elated that Carlotta intends to go with me this time. She has never been to a bullfight, and I'm not exactly sure how she will react.

She says her father is a big fan of bullfighting and has traveled to Barcelona and Madrid several times to see the *corridas.* He always dreamed of becoming a matador like Joselito or Belmonte; either that or a black-tie smoky-lounge stage crooner like Sinatra or Vic Damone or Dean Martin. But of course Carlotta processes her father's lounge-lizard dreams as merely unevolved idolizations of legendary international playboys, vehicles for him to seduce more women—not because he holds passions for the art of song or the skill required to be a bullfighter. And her suspicions are most likely justified.

More than this, though, the Spanish *fiesta nacional* goes completely against her natural instincts and her immense respect for animals and their spirits. For these reasons, I am wary of taking her to the bullfight, but Carlotta decides she will meet the challenge head-on with an open mind. She even claims to admire me for not turning my back on the Spanish traditions I grew up with. And I believe that is her interest, really: to better acquaint herself with the Spanish in me, to better understand me so she can meld her way of life with mine—another testament to the undying love and respect we have for each other.

I buy a copy of Hemingway's *Death in the Afternoon*, his famous treatise that describes in detail the ritualized, almost religious art of bullfighting as seen by an expatriate American. She reads the entire text over the course of two days and feels prepared for the ordeal. I am proud of her for leaping forth this way and admire her once again.

But the Ronda days are not without their sketchy moments. The mysterious "caretaker," the one I keep sending away, continues to try to enter the grounds and even the house without any warning. I think he must climb over the stone walls. Since he can't get inside the house, I often catch him trying to look through the windows. But it doesn't do him any good—I keep the curtains and venetians closed on the ground floor, to protect our privacy. I figure he is some kind of spy for the people I left behind in New York, but he always claims he works for the owner of the house.

Another time, Juan, the real estate broker, stops by to talk with me. He says the owner of the house is complaining that all the flowers in the garden have been mauled or eaten by rabbits or deer—even though the villa's stone walls are secure and animal-proof. I tell him,

"I remember eating the petals of one flower during a poetry recital to Carlotta, and we've used several single stems for table decor, but that is it." After a few more verbal skirmishes, thankfully, he goes away.

None of this really matters, though, as long as I have Carlotta with me and I can continue to paint.

32

DEATH IN THE PLAZA

The Feria de Pedro Romero y Corrida Goyesca is pure spectacle, a colorful festival held in Ronda during the first week of September every year, and people attend from all over the world. The *feria* honors the memory of Ronda's greatest bullfighters and celebrates the legacy of the Spanish painter Francisco de la Goya, who sketched and painted bullfighting, matadors, and all the tradition and ceremony that accompanied them.

As I've described it to Carlotta, on the first day there is a parade of richly decorated horse-drawn carriages, and everyone dresses in ornate costumes inspired by Goya's paintings. There is music, dancing in the streets, and special concerts. The highlight of the festival is the Corrida Goyesca at Ronda's bullring, one of the oldest in Spain.

We attend the opening parade enthusiastically. Besides the horse-drawn carriages carrying the matadors and *Damas Goyescas*, or Goya Ladies, there are dancers, musicians, trumpets blaring, and drums and cymbals crashing. I must say that since we have on our Russian hats as disguise, we blend in with the crowd, and no one gives us a second glance. Still, I keep an eye out for anyone who might be trying to sneak up on us.

"And today matadors are like celebrities?" Carlotta inquires as we watch the procession roll past.

"Movie stars. And *amore,* I will not sugarcoat it for you, the greatest *torero* of them all was Pedro Romero, who—" I hesitate.

"Killed?"

"Yes, killed, over six thousand bulls without receiving a single *cornada,* or injury from a horn. He performed his last *corrida* when he was eighty years old. Goya painted the best-known portrait of him and even designed some of his fancy matador suits. They were intricately decorated but very sophisticated, and the design holds up even now."

On the afternoon of the bullfight at the Plaza de Toros, we gas up the bike and go to Alameda Park so Carlotta can see the bronze statues of the *Dama Goyesca* and Pedro Romero himself. Then we motor onward and park near the plaza.

Thousands jam the streets and parks outside. We enter the Plaza de Toros around five-fifteen in the afternoon and settle onto the long shared benches of the arena. The crowd is at a fever pitch, awaiting Sebastian Manuel Orosco, the featured matador. Sebastian is a dear friend from my youth. I did several portraits of him when I was younger, when he took me to his house in one of the charming *pueblos blancos* in the Ronda mountain range to demonstrate matador poses—with and without the *toro.* I got word to him that we hoped to attend this *corrida,* and he provided the tickets. He even invited us to his dressing room, but I prefer to avoid a high-profile setting with press, so we decide instead to dine later at a flamenco *tablao,* a cozy supper club in the old city.

Carlotta is impressed by the uproarious crowds dressed in their Goya-themed outfits. She especially enjoys the procession into the

ring of the chosen young ladies of Ronda, the *Damas Goyesca*, shining resplendently in their hand-sewn *feria* dresses and mantilla head-
dresses. "The Lady Goyas are like a welcoming committee for the
city," I explain to Carlotta. "One highly respected woman is chosen
to be president, and fourteen teenagers assist her. It is a huge honor.
Some of their clothing and accessories are similar to what the noble-
women in Goya's paintings wore, but if you look at the shoulders
and the complex designs, you'll see some of them are influenced by
the matador costumes. And everything is custom-made, including the
shoes."

Carlotta seems transfixed. "I would love to be chosen as a Lady
Goya." She smiles and kisses me. "Thank you, Rodrigo, for sharing
this with me. I'm having a fantastic time. Have I ever told you that I
love you?"

"Have I ever told you that I love you more, *amore*? And you will
be—"

"I will be what?"

"A *Dama Goyesca*. I will paint you right into the pageant."

She squeezes my hand. "But I need a dress!"

"I had one specially made for you."

"You mean you have one? There's a dress?"

"You'll see. I just hope it fits! You Italians!"

We both laugh. But her face is lit up like a holiday tree. "What
color is it? You have to tell me—"

"Cream base, off-white background. For trim, seafoam. Turquoise.
Mint. Periwinkle."

"Oooooh . . . the pastel greens will bring out my eyes . . ."

"You know me and my colors," I say. "Low-cut. Tight to the arm.
Ruffled at the wrists. Tightly curved to the hip and knee. Then blossomed out in ruffles again at the bottom. Periwinkle headdress to top
your head and matching flowers for your hair."

This warrants an even more prolonged kiss.

Just then the crowd goes ballistic. Sebastian is entering the ring, wearing his elegant three-piece matador suit—the jacket, form-fitting trousers, and cloak are covered with sequins, small glittering stones, and elaborate embroidery, all matching the royal blue background fabric.

The trumpet blares, announcing the first stage of the bullfight, and Carlotta grips my hand firmly. She doesn't let go for the next hour.

The bull enters the ring snorting aggressively, its magnificent muscles rippling in the sun, and the crowd goes wild again. Then the noble beast breaks into a quick trot and is ready for war. Three *banderilleros* taunt the bull and Sebastian assesses his foe, observing how the bull moves and how fierce he is, looking for any flaw or weakness that he can use to protect himself and to defeat the bull.

Now two *picadores* enter the ring, carrying long, sharp lances and riding heavily padded blindfolded horses, and the ritual proceeds. I explain to Carlotta, "See how huge the *toro*'s neck and shoulder muscles are? The *picadores* must use their lances a certain number of times, set by the plaza judge, to cut into those muscles. This makes the bull lose a lot of blood and eventually weakens him. He is supposed to respond to the cuts by attacking the horses, and this causes additional bleeding and weakness in his neck."

Carlotta is crushing my hand, but she doesn't turn away. She is struck by how patient the blindfolded horses are while they endure attacks violent enough to lift them off the ground. "Until eighty or ninety years ago, the horses were not given any padding, and many of them were gored and killed in the ring," I tell her. We can see the bull becoming weaker. His posture has changed; his enormous shoulders and head and horns are no longer held high, as his lifeblood slowly seeps away. Sebastian walks to the side of the arena and stands apart so the others can do what they have to do.

The trumpeters toot once again, to initiate the second part of the bullfight.

The three *banderilleros* stick colorful barbed *banderillas* deep into the *toro*'s neck and shoulder muscles to drain even more of his blood and weaken him further. The bull makes ferocious charges at the *banderilleros*, over and over, and we marvel at their courage. The crowd goes wild again when Sebastian returns to the ring with his cape and sword. He provokes the enraged bull into new charges and tires him even more. Then Sebastian goes to the edge of the ring and waits.

The trumpets sound a third and final time, for the last act of the bullfight.

Now Sebastian enters the ring alone, carrying a small red cape—the *muleta*—stretched over a sword.

"It's a myth that the bull sees the red. He's color-blind," I tell Carlotta.

"Why is the cape red if the bull can't see the color?" Carlotta asks.

"Bloodstains will be less noticeable that way," I say. Carlotta shudders.

Sebastian taunts the *toro* with the *muleta*. He demonstrates his bravery, his skill, and his control over the enormous beast by standing terrifyingly close while he conducts a series of highly ritualized passes with the *muleta*. The crowd cheers these spectacular passes and urges him on with shouts of *"¡Olé!"* Sebastian maneuvers the bull into the final standing position. The bull is spent, his great head and horns hanging low. A hush descends over the arena.

Carlotta begins to turn away, but she holds off averting her eyes and continues to watch. And strangle my hand.

Sebastian approaches the *toro* head-on, in a quick dash forward. With both hands, he raises the sword above his head and plunges it straight down between the bull's shoulder blades and through the aorta and heart—a clean *estocada*. The huge beast falls to his knees and then flops over.

Even some of the Lady Goyas join in when the passionately cheering spectators raise white handkerchiefs—which is their way of requesting that the president award Sebastian an ear cut from the bull as a trophy. Then the *toro*'s body is dragged out of the arena by a team of mules.

My *amore* looks my way with a shy, wry smile. *"Olé,"* she whispers to me. We interlock fingers with the same hands that gripped so very tensely only moments before.

"Gracias," I say appreciatively, "for having joined me."

Carlotta has endured death in the late afternoon amid much pageantry. We do not speak again until we are outside the plaza. We make only small talk, deciding to take a walk and come back to retrieve the bike later.

33

FLAMENCO NIGHT

After the bullfight, we have some time to kill before we are to meet Sebastian for dinner—first he must shower, give a few words to the press, accommodate selfies with adoring fans, and sign autographs—and Carlotta wants me to show her some of the places I like in Ronda.

When she first arrived, I was on the very edge of survival, mentally and physically, with nothing in the house to eat but the contents of my baggie, and nothing to drink but alcohol. She has brought me back from the brink with her kindness, gentle understanding, and love, and I am pleased that she is interested in knowing people and places from my formative years.

First we walk to La Ciudad, the old part of Ronda, with its cobbled streets and mansions and palaces from long ago. We eye the impressive Casa de Don Bosco and then walk to the magnificent Palacio de Mondragón. It is still open, and I especially want to show Carlotta the exquisite miniature water gardens dating from medieval times, when it was a Moorish palace.

"There is an ancient legend"—and here I pause for effect—"that proclaims if you kiss your beloved beneath this very arch at eight-oh-seven on a Saturday night with all the sense of hope, dignity, mutual trust, shared integrity, and passion that reflects your deep abiding love in every sense, you are permitted to make a wish of your choice." I point to the grand arch just above our heads.

Carlotta checks her iPhone and confirms the time. "Is that true?"

I smile wide. "No. Does it have to be?" And we both laugh.

"You're so much more than a surf poet in a town where there are no waves."

"I know." I blast it boastfully aloud. "I'm Rodrigo Concepción de Ronda, *legend maker!*" A few annoyed stares are aimed in our direction from the gallery.

The cobbled alley from the Mondragón takes us to the Plaza Duquesa de Parcent, a beautiful public space surrounded by some of the antique architecture I think Carlotta will enjoy seeing—a sixteenth-century convent, the arched council building, and the Iglesia Santa María de Mayor, with its intricate Renaissance bell tower on a minaret base.

A flicker of worry nags at me while we walk around. For a second, I think I see someone I know peeking at us from behind one of the arches of the council building, and I panic, but I look again and no one is there. We are to meet Sebastian at the *tablao*, but I could be spotted in such a place, dining with the festival's star toreador. It is important to maintain my anonymity, to keep from being discovered by those who would try to take me captive again.

"I want to talk to you about the bullfight," Carlotta says.

"You don't have to—"

"It's very simple, actually. I see both sides of the argument," she says.

I light up a cigarette. "And I do, too. More than ever. Since I met you."

That is true. It has to be. I am no longer the bold, brash, egocentric, reckless, and arrogant *toro* of my youth, with two horns. It isn't that I've been made soft. I've been made more receptive. And more aware. My sensibilities have been realigned, even politically, and of course spiritually. Amen.

"Rodrigo? I'd like to wear the dress."

"Tonight?"

She nods exaggeratedly, like a young girl. I am filled with such joy at her excitement. I tell her, "We still have enough time."

We hurry back to the Harley and motor back to the house and get to work. I open the closet door, and Carlotta almost cries. She plays the role of beautiful body, and I play the role of stylist. I slip the elaborate garment over her head. The dress is tight to perfection.

"Should I wear the headdress?"

"No, too much for the night. It's for the portrait," I say.

"It's the most beautiful dress I've ever seen. Did you design it?"

I smile, remembering my visit to the vintage clothing shop where I did indeed design it. "You may not be able to eat."

"With a dress like this, food can wait, *amore,*" Carlotta says.

When I show her the matching shoes, she almost dies.

I do my part and slick back my hair into a ponytail and wear thick-rimmed prescription glasses, all topped off with a fedora, as a disguise and a deterrent to being recognized.

We get out of the taxi, and I follow Carlotta as she steps gingerly inside the lively establishment. The flamenco *tablao* consists of a main room with tables for dining, with the stage in back. The walls are adorned with bullfighting posters and mirrors. As Carlotta makes her way through, she receives applause from appreciative patrons also in *feria* dress. She dazzles. She is a dead ringer for the finest gypsy *Dama Goyesca* ever to meet the eye—and a subject Francisco Goya undoubtedly would have felt privileged to paint. With all eyes upon us, we are led to a booth deep to the side of the stage, the spot reserved for royalty, movie stars, and celebrated toreadors.

We order some light tapas and champagne, and a commotion erupts around us. I look up and see two matadors carving their way to their tables, trailed by Sebastian. My friend shakes some hands through the boisterous cheers and shouts of "¡Olé!" and then spots us. Sebastian and I exchange a warm embrace, and I introduce him to Carlotta. He bows slightly and kisses her hand.

"*Piacere*," she says. "I am an Italian gypsy."

"I see. Your charms do not escape the eye. Marvelous. Always in the best company, Rodrigo."

I concur.

We all settle into the booth as another bottle is dutifully placed in our standing champagne basket.

"Masterful performance," I say.

"I hope my brother died with honor. He was a worthy adversary," Sebastian says.

I whisper to Carlotta, "Sebastian is referring to the bull—he talks that way."

"How did you become a toreador?" Carlotta asks.

"It was all I knew. My father was a rancher on a bull farm. Still is."

"I understand that. I have taken over my family business."

"Carlotta is a wine aficionado."

"We do what we know, yes. And if we are fortunate, we add our own creativity along the way," Sebastian says.

I pour for Carlotta and Sebastian and take a slow sip myself.

"Creativity lives within all of us," I add. "But in some it remains dead. Because some are afraid to put themselves out there, to enter the ring. It doesn't matter if the talent is not appreciated by others. The important thing is to try. And not be overcome by fear. Otherwise you will never know. And part of one's soul stays dim."

"I tried to sketch a horse one time," Sebastian admits. "It was a disaster."

We laugh, of course, and I say, "But you tried. You put yourself through it, and now you know what it is to have tried. Before we die, we must try everything possible. To drink the cup of life, the whole cup, not half."

To this we toast, and the waiter brings another bottle.

The stage lights dim, and the flamenco performers take the stage to resounding applause. They break into a whirlwind of a spectacle, performing a *fandango de Málaga*. The audience applauds wildly at the conclusion of the dance.

"The performers all seem so—how do I say it?—almost sick with passion," Carlotta remarks.

"They are gypsies," Sebastian adds.

"That's true. And there is something unique to the gypsy persona," I say. "It is special, profound to their core, deep within their being. It is called *duende*."

"Another word for 'soul,'" Sebastian adds.

I am sufficiently saturated with champagne to be light-headed and to need to choose my phrases carefully. So I pause and wait for the words to flow to me, perhaps through me. There are moments you must seize. This is one.

"Yes. But *duende* is more than that. It's a heightened state of emotion. And expression. And authenticity. And it is connected to flamenco. It comes from Spanish mythology. In the stomach of a gypsy resides a fairy. And it flies freely within the ribs, up and down. It is *duende,* the passion of the soul, that responds physically and emotionally to an artistic performance that is particularly powerful and expressive.

"The *duende* fairy inside helps the flamenco artist see the cruel limitations of human existence, and to understand that death is always there. One heartbeat away. It makes the artist confront death. And that death-in-the-face contest helps an artist create memorable, spine-chilling art.

"*Duende* is virtuosity. God-given grace. And charm. The artist must use the power of *duende* skillfully. Work with it. Attempt to control it. The energy of *duende* must be channeled and tamed. Otherwise the performance is dissipated, scattered. You see, the audience, whether rich or poor, crude or educated, they feel the *duende* of an artist. As the great poet Federico García Lorca said, *duende* is 'a sort of corkscrew that can get art into the sensibility of an audience . . . the very dearest thing that life can offer the intellectual.'"

I watch my tablemates, who seem to be reflecting on my words.

"I am not an intellectual. I am a simple man," Sebastian proclaims. "This discussion is perhaps over my head. But you have summoned your own *duende* in speaking of this cultural mystery, and that I recognize."

"On the contrary, my friend. You are an artist. You have *duende*. You look at the face of death every time you step into the ring. And you *tame* that *duende* fairy within—as you tame your brother, the *toro*. With virtuosity. And grace. You provide that 'corkscrew' for forty thousand people. You have it, Sebastian. And you use it well."

I raise my glass, and my tablemates are inspired to raise theirs, too. *"Olé,"* I toast in a whisper.

"Olé," Carlotta and Sebastian echo in tandem.

Carlotta leans in and kisses my neck. I sense she is proud to hear me speak this way. I never would have before. I never could have before. I behold then the sheer beauty of a great woman by one's side, and I propose my own toast to that silently but gratefully and so very deferentially.

"Rodrigo, *mi amigo,* since you just mentioned the great Federico Lorca . . ." Sebastian begins, and he withdraws his wallet and teases from it a small square of yellowed antique paper. "I carry this next to my heart. For every contest. It belonged to my grandfather, an Andalusian matador. He kept it with him for all his *corridas.* When he died in the ring over fifty years ago, it was found in the breast pocket of his satin suit. It is a short quote by Lorca: 'I want to sleep for half a second, a second, a minute, a century, but I want everyone to know that I'm still alive . . .'"

"Bravo," Carlotta praises.

We all clink glasses, albeit somewhat clumsily.

"Now, Sebastian, maestro of the Plaza de Toros," I say. "From the lessons we've learned tonight, it would appear that all you have to do to achieve immortality is to die in the arena."

The humble toreador, my friend, states nobly with an emerging smile, "I'll do my best."

34

TOSCANA CLASSICA

Carlotta and I are in Tuscany at last, to visit her family. She needs to be here for the Chianti Classico festival, to play hostess and to present her selections. Also, her parents are eager to meet me, and I want to meet them. I am a little apprehensive about meeting Carlotta's mother, in part because she is such a strong influence in Carlotta's life and, by extension, mine: Carlotta would break up with me rather than live with the kind of betrayal her mother has put up with throughout her marriage. And Carlotta's father—he will expect me to live by a different standard than he did, if I am to be with his daughter.

So, immediately after the bullfight in Ronda, we have come to Gaiole, where Carlotta's parents have a house near their winery. Her father is at the Ballerini factory when we arrive, but her mother is home and welcomes us warmly. She is gracious and soon puts me at ease, and my preconceived notions begin to evaporate.

I see at once that Giuliana is a gentle soul with kind, mournful eyes, a beautiful countenance, and an air of dignity. She must have been a classic beauty in her younger days, but now her face reveals something of her age and the disappointments she has endured.

Carlotta has responsibilities connected with the festival, and she wants me to see the breathtaking Tuscan landscape, so we set out on bicycle to visit some of the vineyards participating in the festival. The famous white gravel roads of the Province of Siena are bumpy, especially on a bicycle. We pass endless sweeps of olive groves covering the soft, undulating hills, and where the groves disappear, they are replaced by vineyards as far as the eye can see, featuring the region's legendary Sangiovese grape.

It is a long ride back to Gaiole. The exercise revitalizes me, as lately, I have been making a strong push on my *Unified Universe*. There are so many canvases I've planned, but it is the unplanned ones that I'm now fervently trying to put to paint—canvases inspired by my lady love—and there are portrait concepts flourishing all around me. All I have to do is stop a second and seize them out of the air.

We arrive at her parents' house just in time for *pranzo*—an afternoon meal that could be either lunch or dinner, depending on the time and circumstances; today it's lunch—and I meet her father at last.

Salvatore Ballerini, Carlotta's father, is Mediterranean matinee-idol handsome, with a sharp, silvered hairline that is sliced back at the temples. He is tanned, with piercing brown bordello eyes that glint in the sun, and the creases in his face show ever-present traces of his charming smile. The man is brash, energetic, and charismatic, and he has a full tank of testosterone and isn't afraid to step on the gas. Given Carlotta's profile of him, it is easy to see how he could be a formidable force in the mistress arena.

Pranzo is already on the table, so we hurriedly wash up and sit down.

It is evident that the Ballerinis take full advantage of their location in Tuscany when it comes to their food. There is spicy bruschetta with the freshest tomato, garlic, onions, and basil; *ribollita* soup with cannellini beans and vegetables; locally harvested black-and-white shaved truffle ravioli filled with spinach and cheese; a seasoned pork roast with terra-cotta–colored crackling from a prized Tuscan Cinta Senese pig; for dessert, there's *panforte* stuffed with fruits and nuts and *ricciarelli* almond cookies. And yes, we all have our fair share of the Ballerini red Chianti Classico.

Conversation begins with a direct and somewhat provocative missile from the fearless and irreverent patriarch, aimed at me: "So, Romeo—"

"His name's Rodrigo—"

"*Scusi.* So I hear you took Tes to a bullfight—?" "Tes" is his pet name for Carlotta, short for *tesoro,* or "treasure."

"*Sí.* I was happy she came."

"How did that go?"

"Papà," Carlotta objects.

"She didn't jump in the arena and try to save the bull, did she?" I smile. "No."

"Don't mind him, he's always this way," Carlotta says.

"What way? I've tried to get you to go a million times," Salvatore persists.

"Going with you and going with Rodrigo are two different experiences."

"Where did you see a *corrida*?" I ask.

"Where did I not go? I went to Barcelona, Madrid, Seville, where else? Pamplona. Never saw a goring, though—my one regret."

I take a good drink of Giuliana's eyes and can see what *she* is hearing when her husband talks about his trips to the bullrings: opportunities for him to spend time with his mistresses.

"And I hear you're an artist. What kind?" Salvatore asks.

"You know what kind," Carlotta says. "I showed you on the computer."

"*Per favore,* can I have a conversation with this young man? Actually, not so young. How old are you?"

"Forty-nine."

"When I was forty-nine, Giuliana and I had been married for over twenty-five years already. You making good money?"

I nod.

"That's good, that's good. The last guy Carlotta brought home—"

"Salvatore!" Giuliana spits.

"Papà!"

"What? What was he, an undertaker?"

"He's an arborist."

"Arborist? More like a florist. Well, I think he was a little—" He flutters his hand, indicating a homosexual.

"Was not! *You're* a little—" Carlotta says, fluttering her hand back at him, and everyone laughs.

"I mean, *mi dispiace,* but who does flowers for one's lifework? Tell me that!"

"Could you be more embarrassing?" Giuliana asks.

I can tell Carlotta is her mamma's pride and joy. Giuliana must have stuck up for her all these years; it is obvious that she admires Carlotta for her courage, feistiness, and independence—everything she wishes she had been and might have been if the times had been different. It is etched all over Giuliana's face. I've never seen a woman's eyes so connected to her soul.

"Now let me tell you about this guy—"

"You think Rodrigo cares about him?"

"Well, I would. I'd want to know where my girl had been."

Fed up, Carlotta tosses her napkin on the table and leaves the room.

"Let me tell you, this guy comes here, takes me for a walk, and tells me about the disease in all my trees and what I'm doing wrong and all the brainy tree arguments and all my violations and— I'd just fed him for a month and made his bed! I wanted to kick him in the ass, hoist him up and hang him by his slippers, and say, 'How rotten do you think my trees are now, you snotty jackass!'"

"He didn't wear slippers, they were espadrilles!" Carlotta yells from the other room, and I can hear her breaking up ebulliently.

"See? She knows. What a joke." Then Salvatore lifts the table-cloth to look at *my* shoes.

I'm laughing now. This guy is hysterical. He is entertaining. And I can tell he cares. He loves his family. And he loves his daughter. They are both alphas and bound to collide. There is no give. He is every-thing in that old-school-machismo way. He has a good heart, within the confines of the house, his castle. But, like a king, he wants his perks, too—and it is his wife who has paid the price.

It is time for me to have a second glass; Giuliana instinctively notices and gets up and pours it for me. Carlotta reclaims her seat at the table.

"So how's the art business?" Salvatore asks me.

"It's okay. I love the painting, not so much the business."

"But you're a famous guy, you do well."

"I've had my moments."

"A lot of nudes?"

"Here he goes again," Carlotta complains.

"What? If I were a painter, I'd do nudes. What's wrong with that?"

I remain silent, which is a mistake, and drain my glass quickly. I pour myself a third.

"Unless you prefer the male form," Salvatore tosses with purpose. "Imagine how many fruit flies are in town for the festival. I mean, like shooting fish in a barrel!" He is laughing so hard he has tears in his eyes.

"That's enough!" Giuliana says.

"Let's end this conversation right here," Carlotta adds.

"What? We're all family here! Okay. So, Romeo, you know any-thing about Chianti?"

" 'Traditionally, Chianti is a light wine of high acidity with a slightly bitter but fruity taste and berry aromas,' " I quote.

"*Ma che!* What have you been doing, reading the Michelin Guide? 'Traditionally'—you sound like that gay florist now!"

Even Carlotta has to laugh at that.

"I confess. I checked Google."

They laugh even louder.

I stand up then, and I am pleasantly soused enough to take liberties. "Say, Sal, I'm a little bushed. You mind if Carlotta and I take the master bedroom upstairs, and you can take the couch? I'll fetch you a blanket. Oh, and you got any PJs?"

The table erupts. Salvatore tosses his napkin and then Carlotta's, and both splat me in the chest. Even Giuliana is crying with laughter, and she and Carlotta break out in supportive applause.

I am happy to be with Carlotta in her home, and it feels like exactly where I should be. I could envision this kind of family interaction going on forever.

35

THE GRAPES OF ROMANCE

stay in the small stone house reserved for guests. Carlotta is somewhere preparing for the festival. After that long bike ride and then the wine, I welcome some repose. Around six in the evening, I hear a knock on the door.

"Rodrigo?" It is the voice of Salvatore, and it is the first time he has called me by my name. "You up?"

"Yes. Be right down."

"I want to show you around."

"Great."

Salvatore and I take a stroll through the vineyard. Once he gets out of eyeshot from the main house, he lights up a cigarette and gives one to me. "Mamma doesn't like me smoking."

We walk down a corridor with grapevines piled high on either side. The corridor seems to go on for miles.

Salvatore reaches over and pulls on a bunch, and he hands me the entire bunch, pregnant with grapes. "We're harvesting next week. Sangiovese—the blood of Jove."

I pick one, rub it in my palm, and chew on the deep blue-purple grape.

"They're ready. Are you?" he says.

"Sir?"

"I know why you're here."

"You do?"

"*Sì.*"

"How do you know?" I stop chewing. I have the self-conscious image of myself eating his fruit. And all it implies.

"I'm a lot of things, Rodrigo, and not all of them good. I have gotten along on my wits and my ability to read people. There's a reason Machiavelli is from Tuscany. I'm all that. Maybe more, maybe less. But I see it in your eyes. And more important, I see it in hers."

I realize then that he wanted me to taste the grape. With intent. I gaze deeply into his irises, and there is a hint of desperation. And I don't know why.

"So—are you ready?"

"I am, Salvatore."

"You know, I've been a provider, maybe even a good one. I've been a good father. I instilled my daughter with a work ethic. And drive. But I haven't been a good husband. There are some things I wish I could take back. I've hurt people. And I've hurt myself. It's no one's fault but my own. Carlotta's mother is the salt of the earth. There's never been any other woman for me. And that's what has saved my marriage more than anything else.

"I did my research on you, as much as one can, sitting on fields of dirt in the middle of nowhere. But I know you are a man, or were a man, who liked to have a good time. I've seen all the photos of you globe-trotting around with all those beautiful ladies next to you. You have great taste, I might add. In that way, I'm not a whole lot different than you. I understand all that. Takes one, as they say. Which puts me in an awkward position. My instinct is to—has always been to—"

"Protect your daughter."

"Correct."

"But I have a good feeling about you. You had an advantage over me."

"How so?"

"The times. Nowadays you can sow your oats to kingdom come before settling down. Men marry in their forties and fifties. Women marry in their thirties and forties. We were kids compared to that. Babies. *Bambini.* And me being me—again, no excuses—I was too young, too weak, that way. And too damned selfish. It was something deep within me burning. And I couldn't stop myself. I hadn't lived enough life to my selfish specifications.

"But I think you have, Rodrigo. You've been able to let it all hang out for years. And I know it does get empty. And lonely. For a while you're thinking, *Hey, isn't this great, I can fuck whom I want whenever I want, and no strings attached.* And you think you're the freest guy on the planet, to the point where you're really not free anymore. Much less happy, because you're *not* free. You're trapped. It becomes another cage."

"Yes, it does."

"You've avoided one cage but found another."

"*Ecco.*"

"And that's when you pay the piper. Because the piper always gets back more than you took. And you're given a life sentence and waltz around homeless for the next fifty years. Unless you're lucky. And you're lucky. You found a gem. Oh, that Carlotta, she is a gem."

I can see the tears rush to the man's eyes. But he doesn't blink. "And perhaps she's found one, too."

"I'd like to think so," I say. I bend down and respectfully place the bunch of grapes I'm holding in my hand flat to the earth. Then I rise back up.

"I thought you liked my fruit."

"I do."

"So, you have anything you want to say to me?" he asks, and that charming grin breaks hopefully across his face.

"Everything you've said is absolutely true. I did the dance. I did it hard. But I'm over it. The music plays for one person now. Carlotta. She has made me a better man. In many ways. In every way. And I thank the gods of all religions that she came into my life. And therefore, I thank you. Salvatore, I would like to marry Carlotta. And I would like your blessing. And Giuliana's."

The man stands there with tears streaming down his face. "I never thought of it until now."

"What's that?"

"I'm saying good-bye to Carlotta."

"You're wrong, Salvatore. Where I come from, you're saying *hola*."

We embrace warmly, and the man cries into my shoulder, softly weeping at first, but then he ruptures into deep heaves. Not for the symbolic departure of his daughter but for the many things he has done in his life that hurt people. And I can tell that he is sorry. Whatever this man has in his soul, he has revealed it to me. There is honor and dignity in that. And I appreciate it more than he could ever imagine.

He pulls away from me and stumbles sideways, then pivots around and walks back down the corridor of grapes beneath a sky bathed in fuchsia-orange by the setting Tuscan sun. It is an image I know I will paint.

I stay there awhile and count my blessings and give thanks.

I hear him yell to me, deep in the distance, *"You have my blessing!"*

"Grazie!" I shout back.

"But no slippers!"

"Flip-flops?"

"Get outta here!"

36

NEW BRIDGE

We are back in Ronda, having breakfast on the terrace, with a single purple-blue iris stem in a vase between us. I snap a photo of the iris in my mind to use for another portrait. An homage to Vincent, of course. I have always loved his iris paintings. Carlotta is going over the recent rush of orders for the new vintage that have piled in as a result of the successful tastings at the Chianti Classico festival. I got up early to do one of the *Damas Goyesca* portraits. Carlotta's. I have not let her see it yet. It is the only one I haven't allowed her to see ahead of time.

"Let's go into town," I say.

"What for?"

"I want to go to the market, pick up a few things."

"I just went shopping."

"I feel like taking a break. Will you come with me?"

She angles up from her paperwork. *"Certo, amore."*

We wind down the hill and motor toward town. I downshift just before we cross the old bridge that connects the old and new towns.

The bridge, Puente Nuevo, was built in the 1700s on top of the four-hundred-foot cliffs of El Tajo gorge and the Rio Guadalevín. Hemingway used the cliffs and the bridge—and events that really happened there—as the basis for a scene in *For Whom the Bell Tolls*. In the novel, set during the Spanish Civil War, fascists in a small town were rounded up, clubbed, forced to walk a gauntlet of townspeople, and thrown from cliffs to the jagged rocks far below. But that horrifying fact is not the reason I have parked the bike and gone for a stroll across the bridge with Carlotta.

Bridges have always had significant meaning for Carlotta and me; I often recall our meeting at the Old Bridge, the Ponte Vecchio in Florence, where I first observed her attraction to the panther as she looked at the one in the silversmith's window, and where I presented her that morning's sketch of the flower. The Ponte Vecchio was also where our relationship, after a disastrous beginning, turned for the better.

On this "new bridge," the Puente Nuevo in Ronda, I hope our relationship will take yet another turn. We hold hands while striding to the middle of the bridge. We stand by the cement wall and peer over the edge into the chasm and the river far below, flourishing deep in the bottom of the canyon. Beyond, we can see a verdant valley smothered in Spanish firs, and behind that, the magnificent sweeping view of the untamed and majestic Serranía de Ronda mountain range.

I stand before *mi amore* and extend another iris stem. The three large outer blue-purple petals, the falls, have soft hairs along the centers, forming a crested ridge. Atop the three inner upright petals, the standards, lies a diamond ring.

"*Per te,*" I say, indicating that the ornate silver band is for her.

She gasps, bringing her hands to her face. "Rodrigo, *amore! Dio mio! Incredibile!*"

I extend the stem to her, and she softly teases the ring from the flower petals. There is a small eagle on one side of the silver band and a panther on the other, with a diamond stone set high in between, firing shards of reflected sunlight in all directions.

I drop to one knee. "Carlotta, will you marry me?"

Her face is radiant and her smile dazzles across it, but in an instant her expression changes. It is in her emerald eyes, a hint of confusion, even disorientation.

"Yes, I think so . . . But I need time . . . to be sure."

I rise up. It is not what I expected. But it's close. For now, that will have to do—at least it wasn't an outright no.

"Will you do me the honor of accepting the ring until you decide?"

"*Sì, amore.* I will."

We kiss then, in the midday sun, high up on the New Bridge.

part three

DREAM NO MORE

37

ROME TO NEW YORK

think I found him."

"Where?"

"I'm in Rome on a photo shoot and saw a picture of him in a magazine. It must be him."

"What magazine?"

"¡Hola! The European gossip rag, Spanish version."

"Where is he?"

"I think it was him, in the stands of a bullfight in Ronda, Spain."

"How come you're not sure?"

"He was wearing a freaky hat. One of those Russian military hats. And he had on Ray-Ban sunglasses. And an eighteenth-century something-or-other jacket. Almost like he was trying to be in disguise. But it wasn't a disguise at all, because with those crazy clothes, he stood out even more! Everyone in the stands was dressed up . . . but not like him . . ."

"But didn't they mention his name?"

"No! He was in the background, in the audience. The photo was of the matador and the bull in the ring."

"Ronda makes sense. He used to go there as a boy. And we've traced him as far as Madrid. No wonder we couldn't find him."

"Did you contact law enforcement yet?"

"No. Private investigator."

"Smart. Are you going to fly over?"

"I'd like to. But by the way he was acting the last time I saw him, I think he'd resist me."

"What are you going to do?"

"I don't know. There's so much riding on this . . . Julia, you may have an easier time of it. You might be able to persuade him. He listens to you. Would it be possible for you to go there?"

"Damn. I don't know, Rafaela. If I get involved . . . I mean . . . how do we even know he's there?"

"We don't. But it's a start."

After a long pause and a huff: "Okay, of course I will . . . but I won't be finished here for several days . . . But—I could maybe take a flight from Rome to where—Madrid . . . ?"

"I'm checking now . . . no, Málaga."

". . . on Monday. And then what? Bring him to New York?"

"Yes. He has to come back."

"This is so freaky . . ."

"I'd be so appreciative if you'd go and collect him. But please don't tell anyone."

"Why would I ever say anything? I don't want to be mixed up in this mess, either!"

"I know. I'm sorry . . . I know you'd never say anything. I'm not thinking straight."

"It's okay. You'll get through it. What will you do with him once he's back?"

"Depends on what condition we find him in."

38

COME IN, RONDA

You're not going to believe this—"

"You found him?"

"Well, no. He's gone."

"No!"

"But he was here."

"Where?"

"I found his house. I'm in it now. And this is the insane part. The walls are filled with his new paintings, and I have to tell you, Rafaela, they're incredible! For as much as I know art, and it may not be that much, but—these look like masterpieces."

"How did you find where he lives?"

"I checked with some real estate brokers in town to see if anyone had rented an apartment with his description. The third broker I spoke to said finally, 'You mean the poet? Vladimir? The fool on the hill?' And he laughed, because that's what they called him, and they'd been singing the Beatles song. He's been the talk of the town all August—"

"*Did he do anything bad?*"

"*No, I don't think so. They didn't say so, anyway. I mean, no cops or anything.*"

"*Good.*"

"*But the owner wants to break the lease. He wants him out. They think he's been eating all the flowers. And he lives on churros and bocadillos. They're all over the kitchen. And coffee. The place is a total mess. It looks like it hasn't been cleaned once. There's stuff everywhere. And where there are no canvases hanging, he painted—*"

"*The walls?*"

"*Yes. And the grass is high. Apparently, he fired the grounds-keeper. Thought he was . . . what did the guy say? A 'spy.' Oh, and get this—he rides around on a Harley—he bought it from a teenager. It's a small town, everyone knows everything.*"

"*What's this about being a poet?*"

"*He introduces himself around town as 'Comrade Vladimir, the surf poet. In a town where there are no waves.' He crashed a poetry reading and got thrown out. And he talks to himself, and he has an imaginary girlfriend named Verushka. And he wears that crazy Russian hat, the one I was telling you about.*"

"*I saw online.*"

"*And he rarely goes out. But, Rafaela, I'm telling you, these works are so good. And it's not just a few. They're all over! Upstairs. Downstairs. The stairwell, the kitchen, in all the bedrooms. There must be forty or fifty, I'm not kidding, each one more amazing than the last—*"

"*Here's what to do. Can you stay in a hotel tonight? Or better yet, stay there tonight?*"

"*I booked a room already, but sure, though it's a little creepy. These paintings are intense. They glare at you.*"

"*Just wait a day. Or a couple days if you can. Until he returns.*"

"*If—*"

"*He has to be around somewhere. No matter how far off the deep end he is, he'd never leave his art. Take pictures.*"

"*I will. Maybe something happened to him.*"

"*My God, this is so crazy.*"

"*I did see the motorcycle.*"

"*You did?*"

"*It's on its side on the grass.*"

"*How did you locate the house?*"

"*The broker drove me. They could tell I knew him. And he recognized me, too, from my modeling work.*"

Julia gave herself another tour of the house and private showing of the art. She took some pictures with her digital camera, then walked down the main staircase and passed through the sunken living room. The French doors were flung open, and she moved out to the terrace, where the dining table and chairs, as well as the pool furniture, were toppled and haphazardly angled.

She stepped into the backyard, past the devastated garden, and spotted a lone flip-flop lying in the grass. She looked deeper into the backyard expanse and saw a leg extending out from behind the towering Spanish fir tree. She made a quick dash and saw the notorious surf poet lying flat on his back, his spiral notebook and ushanka hat lying beside him.

"*Oh my God! Rodrigo!*"

She rushed to him and, falling to her knees beside him, checked for his vital signs. He seemed comatose, but after she prodded him aggressively, he emitted several groans. He looked terribly unwashed, and it appeared he'd been wearing the same jeans and T-shirt for a considerable amount of time—they were paint-splattered, soiled, and form-fitted to his body.

"*Rodrigo—?*"

39

TOKYO IN '20

heard it from far off. It was a voice I knew. Was I dreaming? Then I felt hassled and pulled and bothered. My mood at best was cranky and getting crustier by the second.

"Hey, get off me!"

"Rodrigo! Wake up!"

"What—?"

"It's Julia! Please!"

"Who—?"

My eyes slowly unsealed and someone was in my face. I jerked backward as if struck with a lot of voltage. I spun away from her and rolled over on my stomach. I lifted my head up like a turtle and took a better look at her.

"Shit! Julia—"

"Rodrigo!"

"What the *fu*—? How did—?"

"We have been so worried about you!"

Nothing to say to that.

"You totally disappeared!"

"Julia, I need to know. Do you have scabies?"

"What—?"

"Be honest. You have to be honest with me!"

"I don't know what you're talking about."

"Do you or don't you?" I think I yelled.

That calmed her. She spoke softly, as meek as a mouse. "No, I don't."

"You don't what?"

"I don't have scabies."

"Good."

She was still whispering. She might have had a tear in her eye. "Are you okay, Rodrigo?"

I jumped to my feet and did a tennis hop like I was about to return serve. "I'm fine. Never better."

She seemed surprised at my sudden display of physical fitness.

"Feel like an Olympic champ. Training for Tokyo. It's in 2020."

"What's in 2020?"

"Games of the Thirty-second Olympiad. Tokyo, baby. Either wind-surfing. Or sailing. But don't tell anyone that's our move."

"Who's *we*?"

"Carlotta and me."

"Carlotta . . ." She uttered it so deadpan that even the letters were dead.

I wondered then if I should have them meet. But maybe that wasn't such a good idea. Julia never liked being second fiddle. So I gave it the noncommittal "You'll really like her" without giving her a full invitation, as in time and place.

I mean, I didn't trust Julia, either. I mean, I knew I was spiritually reconnected, but I knew she was not. So much work to be done. Real heavy lifting. And she didn't know enough to know there was even a problem. But she would, and then she'd have to pay the piper, and the piper always asks for more than you took. You can't take, take, take forever and not create a mini–black hole in the universe that rides at your hip; eventually, it will suck you right back through the hole you created at pretty much magnum force, and then: *Ta-da!* Justice for the unified universe. And everything goes back to an equilibrium. I knew that now. She had a Niagara Falls' worth of tears coming. And then I felt bad for her.

I took down a note in my spiral notebook. "So how are you, baby?" I said it softly, so as not to tip her off. So she wouldn't think I was being judgmental or trying to mine her psychological quarries.

"What are you writing?"

"A note." I flipped it so she could see.

She read: " 'The Revenge of the Piper' . . . What's that?"

"Poem. I'm going to write." I shuffled one end of the spiral like a deck of cards. "Pick a card, any card—"

"You've been writing a lot."

"Writing and painting go hand in hand."

She read the cover, too. No big deal. It said: *No Waves.*

She sighed then, a huge release from her lungs. She was already feeling the pressure. I could tell. *Let it out, let it all out,* I said in a self-help way for her, but to myself.

"I saw the new work. Astonishing."

"You did? Do. Not. Tell. A. Fucking. Soul. You hear me?"

She didn't say anything. Now I knew I'd been right not to trust her.

"How did you get in, anyway? That spy?"

"The door was open."

I was about to toss her out on her ear if she said someone let her in. That meant more eyes on me. She was lucky. Though she may have been lying. Not to worry. I'd set a trap for her in a few. Maybe now.

"Want to ride the bike? Go check out the White Villages?"

"No, thank you."

That didn't work. That was like a dropped egg. *Splat! Way to go, Rodrigo.* I should have saved it for later, because I could tell: she was going to stick to me, stay with me, spy on me.

"You hungry?"

She shook her head.

"I'm famished." I sprinted up to the house—sprints are good for '20—and spun back around on the terrace. "Join me for—what time is it? *Pranzo?* Just pick up a chair, I'll meet you at the table in five."

I had plans for her.

I knew how to work her now. It was game on.

40

FRENCH LUNCH TÊTE-À-TÊTE

was chomping on a *bocadillo* and employing the tactic of appearing to listen politely to Julia while at the same time ignoring her. She sat across from me at the outdoor table, the place of so many lunches and dinners with my beloved.

Then I spoke to her of my spiritual reawakening and fresh enlightenments. She did not respond in kind. Go figure.

"Have you been eating well?" she asked.

"The best. *Bocadillos, churros,* and the best Spanish coffee, *café con leche.* Minus the *leche.*"

She looked at me with heavily weighted, sharpened eyes. "Rodrigo, look at you. You look terrible. You haven't showered. Your hair is filthy-greasy. The place is in shambles. And I saw an eviction notice on the door—"

"Really? How come?"

"How come? You've painted all over the house."

"Those are murals. They're supposed to be on the walls. 'Mural' comes from the Latin word *mura*"—and I spelled it—"m-u-r-a. It means 'wall.' Duh!"

"But they're not *your* walls! You claim you're spiritually realigned. Is that spiritually aligned? You're getting a reputation around here. A bad one. They call you 'The Fool on the Hill.'"

The optics of the situation likely didn't look good from the outside, admittedly. "I've dealt with jealousies all my life."

"This is not jealousy! This is destruction of property. Look at the gardens. What did you do to the gardens?"

"They nourish me."

"You mean you ate the plants?"

"Roots, mostly, no nutrition in the flowers. It's the only way to taste the Spanish earth. Good for poetry. Stems, branches, that sort of thing."

"And what about the living room furniture?"

"What about it?"

"It's gone. Where is it?"

"Those ugly chairs? At night it gets very chilly. I needed it."

"What? For *firewood*?"

"Those chairs were eyesores. They didn't go with the decor, the paintings, nothing. I did the owner a favor."

"You torched his furniture in the fireplace?"

I looked at her a moment. My face was pleading the Fifth. "Just kidding."

"Because I see a lot of ashes and soot on the floor."

"I have to come clean with you. I'm not training for the Olympics."

"Thanks for leveling with me."

"I hear the sarcasm. Be careful. Sarcasm is like hepatitis C. It comes from dark places, and it can infect the soul. The negative complex. You want to know why I've stopped training?"

"Sure, Rodrigo. Enlighten me."

"The radiation."

"What radiation?"

"It's still in the water around Tokyo. Around all of Japan. From the Fukushima power plant. So, sailors, windsurfers, beware. Carlotta and I decided to pull out of the games."

"Rodrigo, this is crazy talk!"

"Like Picasso said, 'If you want to paint a table, paint a chair.'" I lit up a cigarette for grins, and contemplated the smoke through my nostrils. "Maybe I'm doing it on purpose."

"Why?"

"So you'll leave. So everyone will leave. And leave me alone. And leave us alone! And let me finish *The Unified Universe*! In peace!"

"I'm here to help you."

"Did you receive a call for help? Have I ever telephoned you once?"

"I spoke to Rafaela. She loves you. And is concerned for you."

"She's concerned about the money train. Slipping away. Because I don't sell anymore. I'm out of the art business. The best thing I ever did, by the way. And that's in direct conflict with her agenda. And everyone else's agenda."

"Not mine."

"Look, Julia, just because we had sex a few times doesn't give you the right to interfere with my life. Why are you here?"

"I care for you. And your well-being."

"That's horseshit."

"Have I ever asked you for money?"

I took a puff instead of answering her.

"Have I ever been on your payroll? Have I ever taken anything from you other than your friendship and affection? Have I ever made or tried to make a dime off of you?"

"I would have to say no."

"I'm here for one reason and one reason only. Because I love you, Rodrigo. That's all. But it's enough for me. To be here."

"Too late."

"Too late what?"

"I'm getting married."

"To whom?"

"Whom do you think?"

"Carlotta doesn't exist!"

"I've already proposed. On the bridge you and that traitor real estate broker crossed to get up here." Just then I realized spies were everywhere. They were international.

She rose and brushed off the dust from her jeans. "Will you come with me?" she asked.

"Where?"

"I want to show you something in the house."

"What?"

"Trust me."

I considered that a funny phrase for her to use, but I followed her anyway, and she guided me right up the stairs to my bedroom.

"I can't do this—"

"Come."

She led me into the bathroom and stood before the mirror. She positioned me next to her. "Do you see me here?"

I said I did.

"Do you see yourself?"

"Yes."

"We are both here. In the same space. At the same time. Agreed?"

"Agreed."

"Do you see Carlotta here?"

"How could she be here? She's handling everything in Gaiole. We're going to have a big-ass Tuscan wedding."

"Carlotta does not exist! If you don't believe me, call her right now. *Call her.*"

We went back downstairs into the kitchen and retrieved my phone from the top shelf of the pantry closet. And placed the call.

"She's not picking up."

"Of course she's not picking up. Because there is no Carlotta. She's in your mind, yes. But she is not made of flesh and bone. She exists in your dreams. And only in your dreams."

"But this is a dream. You here. With me. You see, what you think is a dream is because you're *in* a dream. You're in my dream. You have it backward. In reverse. In real life, she picks up the phone."

"Rodrigo, wake up! Snap out of it! Did you attend the bullfight a couple weeks ago?"

"Yes."

"With Carlotta?"

"Yes."

"Did she sit next to you?"

"Of course."

"Did you have a Russian hat?"

"We both did."

"Okay—look." She produced from her bag and held up a magazine and flipped it open to a picture of me in the stands in the Plaza de Toros.

"Okay, so what? They got me."

"Carlotta is not there! That's you in your Russian hat, and you're alone. Totally alone! Carlotta was not there. She never was there. She never was with you. Only in your mind."

I must say, she had pretty good evidentiary proof. I was about to tell her Carlotta had gone on a beer run, but that would have been lying. Carlotta never left her seat on the bench beside me in the stands. Lying would have been self-serving, which is something Salvatore would say.

"Dreams are tricky, though. You're pulling out magazine articles in my dream. In my mind. *You're* in my mind. You don't exist, Julia. I'm creating you right now. While I sleep."

"I don't exist?" she asked, irked.

"And if you don't stop this, I am going to wake up!"

"Go ahead, wake up—"

"And you'll be gone! I'm warning you—"

"I want you to come to New York with me. Take some tests—"

"I'm going to erase you! I'm going to wake up now!" But I couldn't erase her. She wasn't going away. "Wake up, Rodrigo!" I yelled at myself. "Somebody! Carlotta! Akira! Desideria! Wake me up! Now!"

"Some basic tests, no big deal—"

I avoided her now and moved into the living room and plunked down on the remaining stool. Julia stuck to me like a remora fish and followed right beneath my gills, nibbling the plankton and algae off my neck. "I took tests already."

"Where?"

"In Valldemossa. I had brain-imaging scans. They didn't find anything. I'm fine."

"You were never in Valldemossa. You flew to Madrid directly."

"Then I flew to Palma!"

"There is no record of you on another flight!"

"Because I paid in cash!" I jumped out of the chair. "Come here—now *you* look." I showed her the *Butterfly Triptych* and, next to it, a nude portrait. "That's Desideria."

"That's wonderful. She's very beautiful. But that's your mind. Your beautiful, beautiful mind that imagined this splendid creature. It's the beauty in your mind . . . such a beautiful mind."

"Then respect it! She's a doctor at the sanitarium. She's very real." I grabbed Julia by the hand and brought her into the dining room. "Here, look at the *Brain* series, there's an fMRI scan, a real one I collaged into it."

"Where?" she asked. "I don't see anything. Where's the scan?"

"I collaged it in, I swear! Someone must have taken it, that spy! That caretaker spy! Or this is a dream, a damned dream, and the scan can't be in the dream because that's in the other part of the universe. When I wake up, the brain image will be here, and you'll be gone!"

"I want you to have some tests at Columbia Presbyterian."

"I've heard that before—in my dreams."

"No—you heard Cornell Med, right? Remember, at the intervention? You agreed to go there. How could I know that if I'm not real? How could I pull that out of your mind? We have an entire long-standing history together. How could we have that if I don't exist? How could you have memories of me, painting and collaging in your Beverly Hills bungalow, calling me a 'passion accelerator,' making love to me eight times in one day? How could I know that? You just confirmed we had sex 'a few times' five minutes ago."

And then she grabbed me by the collar of my T-shirt almost violently, and all up in my face, she whispered it to me, harshly so. "How could you have memories of me, fucking me in the ass in the Ritz-Carlton? In July! You remember that? How could I know that? Well, *I remember.* You know how? No one has fucked me in the ass since! And you were thinking about someone else while you did it! *Her.* Carlotta. Someone who doesn't exist. And you used *my asshole* to do it! And I gimped and limped around all day long! How the hell could I have experienced that, Rodrigo?"

My hair was now standing on end, and chills rippled up the length of my spine.

"We have history," she continued. "Where did that history come from? Years and years of recurring dreams with me? No. Because we did things on and off together for a few years. In the flesh. Sharing flesh. Shrieking ecstasy in each other's ears. With our lips attached. Want me to describe your cock to you? You're circumcised, the shaft is long and thick, and it curves to the right! How could I know that if I'm merely a figment of your mind?"

"That's the everyman cock."

"No, it's *not*! Trust me!"

"Cock Classico—" I sighed and looked away and paused to dwell on things. "I have history with Carlotta, too."

"A few months?"

"Yep."

"You have recurring dreams with Carlotta! You want to see the hotel tapes? Of you entering the Ritz-Carlton with me? I'm the one who was getting fucked—not her!" She approached me again and squared before me; she toned down her voice, appealing to me. "I'm doing this on my own. Without Rafaela. Without Jean Paul. Without Rachel or Tex or The Raven. Without any of them. Do you hear me, Rodrigo? I have a doctor friend at Columbia Presbyterian. I want you to come with me and—"

"And what?"

"Bring Carlotta if you want!"

Julia left me then and went back out to the terrace and on to the pool. I followed her twenty paces behind so she wouldn't know. I stayed out of sight at the French doors and peered out. I felt like a little boy.

She took off her jeans and pulled off her top. She unsnapped her bra, and her ample breasts poured forth. And then she slid off her peach panties, revealing the trimmed little bar. And she stood there. Naked.

"Rodrigo! Come here!" she yelled almost angrily, in a scolding tone.

I took small steps like a kindergartner. I felt like a kindergartner. I felt like I was six years old again. I stepped onto the terrace.

She was standing erect and naked by the pool. "Come closer."

I did. A few more short steps. Then I stopped.

"Closer . . ."

A few more . . .

"Closer still . . ."

"I see your pee-pee." I don't know if I said it or thought it. I was getting confused.

"Come here, Rodrigo." She was talking to me like I was a little boy. I was a little boy. And I was getting a boner looking at her.

"Closer."

I did until I was really close. I felt embarrassed, and I might have been blushing. My face was very hot and prickly.

"Now touch me."

I wouldn't, so she placed my hand on her shoulder. "Do you feel the flesh?"

I nodded. Like a little boy would.

She knelt down and dipped a hand in the pool. And splashed me.

"Hey!"

"Did you feel the water? The real water?"

I rubbed my wet arm.

"Feel the wetness?"

I nodded again.

"I have always loved you, Rodrigo," she said.

Then she plunged into the pool. It was a graceful dive. I saw her swimming underwater, doing the breaststroke to the deep end, and she dove farther down near the drain. A bubble came up. She was at the bottom of the pool. But not really swimming now. She was down there hovering. Floating. She was holding her breath. She stayed down awhile. Testing her lungs. And her breath.

She'd stayed down there over a minute by now. She looked like she was really floating, almost like a rag doll. Ten more seconds . . . I started to have other thoughts. Like nervous thoughts. She was hovering below somewhat lifelessly. Not really moving.

. . . Another fifteen seconds . . .

A few more damned bubbles came to the surface. They came from her. I started to get really nervous. Was she drowning? How could she still be down there? *Come up, Julia! Come up!* I thought. What was she doing? She'd always had a flair for the dramatic, but . . .

Another half-minute . . .

Was she losing precious seconds? Was *I* losing precious seconds? She'd been down there too long! Too damned long!

I started yelling. "Come up! Julia, come up!"

But her body wasn't moving. Not at all. Dammit! Dammitall! This was terrible. This was no dream.

"Come up! Please, come up!" I was sobbing, then crying. "Gods, please make her come up! I'll do anything, anything at all! I'll go to New York if you just get her to come up! She doesn't deserve to die! She deserves to live! She's worked too hard! She's too young! Gods! All of you! Please!"

I could not stand it anymore. Even if it was a dream. A very bad dream. And what if it wasn't a dream? What if I was wrong? What if it wasn't a unified universe? It wasn't worth proving her wrong! It wasn't worth being right! And maybe I *wasn't right!*

I vaulted into the water and duck-dived to the bottom and clutched her arm, and kicked wildly, and hauled her body, and pulled her up, up to the surface. I got her head above water, and she didn't seem to be breathing. I swam her to the shallow end and pulled her up the steps. She was deadweight, and it took all I had to get her up and over and onto the granite on her back. I bawled as I pumped on her chest, on her lungs hard, very hard, and I turned her head to the side and water came out and then she coughed and coughed and her eyes opened and I was crying my eyes out.

She opened her eyes all the way, and a faint smile came to her mouth. She whispered, "Rodrigo . . ."

She was squinting, and she had a dazed, weak smile. I clasped her hand. And I held her head up.

"What, baby?"

"Rodrigo . . ."

"Tell me. Speak to me, Julia, please."

"Try . . . and . . . get someone . . . in your . . . dreams . . . to die for . . . you . . ."

I clutched her head and held her so close and cried like a baby for the next hour. And I got clothes for her and we stayed there by the pool a long while. I was happy to watch the sunset and we gazed at the sky for a long, long time.

That night I called Carlotta and told her I needed to do some errands in New York, and I invited her to join me. She said she would come, and we planned to go shopping and spend a weekend in Montauk and Shelter Island, doing some wine tasting on the North Fork. We were looking forward to it. I was relieved she was coming, because I hadn't been to New York in a while and my memories of it weren't so hot and it would be good to have her with me. I would need her support to go through the tests I had promised Julia and all the gods that I would take. And if Carlotta was there, it would prove she was real, and not someone who existed only in my dreams—and Julia would see that she was wrong.

41

TAXI BLAST

woke up in the middle of the night, disoriented. I saw a big black box ogling down at me. I looked left and there was a door. Though it was dark, there was an amber night-light plugged into the wall. The room was white, totally white. The black box was a television, angled up high, staring at me. I had gadgetry on my bed. Remotes. I pushed a button and the bed started moving. My arm was attached to something. An IV hookup. Everything I spied was in English. And the wall sockets were American. Then I heard a signature taxi sound below. That irrepressible New York taxi blast.

Fuck. I was in a hospital.

"Rodrigo?"

The voice startled me. Deep in the corner I saw Julia, slumped in a chair. She'd been sleeping.

"Man, am I glad it's you. Did you sleep here, too?"

"Yes."

"Am I okay?"

"You haven't had any tests yet. Other than blood."

"How long have we been here?"

"Two days. You've been sleeping a lot."

I motored the backrest up to see her better. "I feel so groggy . . . foggy."

"They gave you sedatives. You needed rest. They didn't think you were in the best of health from a nutritional perspective. Your cholesterol levels were very high."

Then a shot of pure panic and terror hit me. "Where's *The Universe*?"

"What?"

"All my work!"

"Packed up. I personally saw to it. Everything was sent to a warehouse in Brooklyn. Only you have a key and access to it, no one else. I took photos of each."

"Perfect. How many pieces?"

"One hundred and six."

"Sounds right. Was *Salvatore* there? In the Tuscan vineyard sunset? 'Cause that's a gift . . ."

"I think so."

I tried to organize my thoughts, but one predominated. "What . . . Why are you doing all this for me?"

"Why do you think?"

"You know, I dreamed you almost drowned. It was a nightmare. But there was something very beautiful about the way you hovered in the water there, deep down. I thought to put it to canvas—if you don't mind."

"I do mind. Very much. And I *did* almost drown."

I laid back then, and some wind was released from my chest. "I'm sorry. I'm so, so sorry."

She approached the bed and looked down at me. She wore no makeup and the night-light exposed her weariness. I extended my hand and she clasped it. Then she handed me my spiral notebook. "And here are your poems."

I smiled lovingly at her.

"And your key. The only one. So don't lose it."

"You're an angel."

"No. I'm just a friend."

"I love you."

"I love you, too. But if you don't mind, I have some things to do. You'll be okay here. No visitors for now, then you can provide a list of names. Dr. Jeffrey Wincott is your doctor. Highly reputable. He's a colleague of my friend. He'll be seeing you later today, after your tests."

I hesitated a long while, and we gazed deep into each other's eyes. "Thank you."

She kissed me on the forehead and turned around and headed toward the door.

"Did you read any?"

She nodded. "I hope it's okay."

"What do you think?"

She sighed. "I think they're beautiful, Rodrigo. There *are* 'waves.' Of brilliance."

I could see a glint of tears in her eyes. Then she walked out. I'd put her through hell. More than hell. Turbo hell. With a boost.

Julia's sudden appearance in my life was something I could build on while I was in New York. I could feel it running through my system. Julia had given me a lead on something so very precious.

Hope.

42

WARHOLIAN MIND

They tested me for days. Scans, scans, and more scans with the most colorful wires and electrodes, a veritable high-wire circus act of technological receptors. And lab samples. And blood. And I must say, with the IV hookups, I was getting stronger. They wouldn't let me walk in the park or even go outside. But I was buzzing about, scampering around the room like a meerkat, collecting all sorts of medical paraphernalia, IV tubes, sanitary bags, food packets, clipboard forms, plastic gloves like Francis Bacon used, plastic hospital bracelets, anything I could get my hands on. Every day Josie the Caribbean nurse from St. Vincent asked me where my identification bracelet had gone. I slyly smiled. And she smiled back. She knew. She thought I was a French *collecteur* and *collagiste* and I needed the items for my new art. For this hospital series, I was using the bracelets instead of my signature to sign the works. I gave Josie a sketch of herself to hold fast our oath of secrecy.

Carlotta had delayed her trip to the States. I had let her know I had appointments and such, dental and medical. And she had so much to do, with the planning, the invitations, and the guest list, I suspected. Even though she hadn't officially accepted my proposal. I hoped she would select one of those cool churches in the Chianti Classico subregion. She had such good taste, I'd let her do it with her own unique Tuscan panache and charm—with a dash of Panther nobility and fearlessness.

After one week of tests, I was allowed to have visitors. I chose only one. Alfonso. It was good to see the dutiful man. And Alfonso brought me my art supplies from Ronda and New York. I initiated some small canvases—sketches first, then the oils.

I was so tempted by the walls. The wide, flat, white, white walls. They were all so virgin-pure and clean, tantalizing me, and I wanted to deflower them all. But I was advised not to. So I held off, but, man, were those walls calling me. If only . . . Whether sitting up in my retractable bed or standing nose-to-nose with their whiteness, I was licking my chops, wide-eyed and unblinking like a spotted big-eyed Bengal cat patiently eyeballing a plump canary in a cage. I felt sad for the walls. *They* were in a cage. If only they would let me liberate them.

I was eating the hospital slop, but the meals could have been worse. I'd met Dr. Wincott, and he seemed pretty okay—John Lennon round-rims, forties, and preppy handsome. He was scholarly and amicable, and he seemed to understand me. I told him a lot of things, mostly everything, about my two competing but melded worlds and the friends who inhabited them, including my lovely wife-to-be. He gave me some meds, and I seemed to have a pause in unified universe thoughts and brain activity.

Dr. Wincott was very twenty-first-century, a cutting-edge full representative of the technological age, as well as a proactive contributor to the leapfrogging in progressive theories and treatment advancements in his field of neuroscience. I learned from Dr. Craig Olsen,

Julia's friend, as well as other colleagues with their clipboards, polite smiles, and subtle probing interrogatives, how Wincott had written extensively in medical journals on his fields of study: brain abnormalities and personality disorders, for the most part—including Alzheimer's, Parkinson's, and schizophrenia, with the sidecars of obsessive compulsivity, bipolarity, avoidant personality, and hypersexuality.

Dr. Wincott couldn't give me the full-blast or even petty diagnosis on whether I had a condition—and if I did, what it was—until he had the full measure of tests. The festival of electrodes and hookups marched on, eventually concluding days later with a simple tap-dance on the scale indicating that my weight was appreciably up for the better.

And then he did have a diagnosis.

He stepped in midmorning with a flock of other white-coated and -winged doctors. I asked if we could go one-on-one for this initial conference, for privacy, and the good doc complied. The accompanying squadron lingered a bit to give themselves their own private showing of the *Uptown Hospital* series of collaged art. Then they raised their proud clinical beaks and flapped off.

"Rodrigo, what I'm detecting in the numerous fMRI scans is a considerable loss of gray matter in the frontal and temporal lobes. The damage started in the outer or parietal region and spread beyond. You have enlarged ventricles, increased CSF indicating enhanced neurological abnormalities, and there have been decreased prefrontal brain functions as we tested those brain waves . . ."

"No waves," I said with intent.

"Fewer waves. But the cause for concern is the pervasive, unrelenting wave of tissue loss that can sweep forward like a forest fire. It likely started in your teens. Average teens undergo extensive pruning in which one percent of gray matter disappears each year. That's normal. Schizophrenia strikes at this time and causes an exaggeration of normal pruning, like a gardener gone wild. And those afflicted can lose twenty-five percent of their gray matter in certain areas by the time they're eighteen. And how old are you, let me check—?"

"Forty-nine."

"But the acceleration of brain tissue loss appears mostly at the beginning of the illness, and less so over time—for you, a while back—and it would appear an all-out forest fire never happened. This explains why the damage to your brain is not more extensive."

"*Bravo.*"

He showed me from his stacked clipboard a slice image of two brains in black-and-white, the normal one and mine at right. The enlarged ventricles were clearly apparent. Then he showed me another PET scan image of two comparative brains, black with electric yellow and fiery red trim: the normal and mine. The enhanced bright red and yellow areas on mine indicated the abnormalities he was speaking of.

"My God, they look Warholian. So colorful. I actually like my image more than the 'normal' one. Can I get copies?"

The doctor nodded and smiled. "Sure. The PET scans are rather colorful. But color can be deceiving in this case."

Then he showed me more black-and-whites, X-ray–style, accentuated with more red and red-only amoeba-like shapes. "These correspond to the PET scans and show the results of decreased brain activity as compared to the normative."

"You mean less red means less brain activity in mine at right?"

"Yes."

"I like the normal patient image better in that one."

"And this last one is a three-dimensional profile of gray-matter loss using image analysis algorithms."

It was the full 3-D brain image in brilliant, electrified sapphire, turquoise, aqua, lime green, yellow, and red on top—which indicated the damage.

"*Dios mío,* that's a masterpiece! Can you provide me digital copies of all of these?"

"Rodrigo, I appreciate your creative and visual analysis, and I find it refreshing. But I must say, the neuropsychological abnormalities caused by this gray-matter loss result in considerable deviations: compromised cognitive function, information processing, verbal memory, planning, introspective and self-reflective capacities, and impaired awareness, especially when it comes to belief of any illness. Denial. Closely associated are paranoia, distrust, avoidant social drives, a dependency on drugs and alcohol, hypersexuality if not sexual deviancy—"

Here we go, I thought. So I figured I would quell his enthusiasm. "That's me," I confessed. "But can we please leave my sex life out of this?"

"I'm speaking in general terms, but—"

"As for paranoia, you know what the Beat poet William S. Burroughs said: 'Sometimes paranoia's just having all the facts.' I've always thought my paranoia is reality on a finer scale. Or greater detail. Perfect paranoia is perfect awareness. I've often wondered, am I paranoid *enough*? There's a hidden order behind the visible. I believe that. Paranoia's a gift. And the truly paranoid are rarely hustled."

"Perhaps," he deflected. "But there may be an element of fantasy-prone and maladaptive daydreaming that *is* personal to you."

"How so?"

"A person who is prone to intense schizophrenic fantasies can also have paranormal and religious experiences, and be susceptible to false memories. Extreme or compulsive fantasizers cannot distinguish the difference between what's real and what's not, and they may experience hallucinations. They create paracosms: extremely detailed, highly structured, and immersive fantasy worlds that may be dissociative, or out-of-body, or sexual. They become absorbed in their vivid and realistic mental imagery, have intense sensory perceptions, and experience imagined sensations as real. The fantasies include the perception that the world at large is unreal—prompting the assumption of a new identity or self—and the fragmentation of identity or self initiates, if not forces, separate streams of consciousness."

"And why would one do that?"

"To escape the harshness of reality. To create a happier world to reside in that's positive and survivable. Or because they're exposed to abuse from which fantasizing provides a similar flight; or they've endured severe loneliness and isolation, and fantasy alleviates the boredom. From what you've told me about your life in New York, it's clear that you felt the alienation romantically, socially, and professionally. And if you were feeling surrounded by duplicitous and greedy people, you could have constructed a paracosm to escape all that—one that made you happy, spiritually connected, in love, sexually satisfied, creatively inspired, fulfilled in all ways—essentially, your perfect world."

"Carlotta is real, Doctor. There's too much detail. Perhaps you're a dream."

"The creative mind does have this openness, yes. And coupled with your condition, anything seems possible. Perhaps we exist in another dimension and multiple realities. In that school of thought, I'm out of my league. And we have no way of testing its veracity." He smiled.

"Thank you," I said, even though I knew he was indulging me. "So much for twenty-first-century tech."

"But harnessing the best science of the day, from a medical standpoint, dynamic brain imaging has helped identify some of the faulty genes that predispose people to schizophrenia. The enzyme calcineurin is involved in memory, and if that enzyme is hampered or deleted by a faulty gene or a risk gene, the likelihood of not only memory loss but also the advent of schizophrenia is much greater. You have one of the four risk genes that encode calcineurin."

I processed it like a narcissist would. "With all this going on, Doctor, I may well be at my absolute creative peak. I mean, this condition may be the source of my *duende,* the little fairy spirit of creativity that flies around inside me—"

"Don't dismiss that idea lightly. That may well be, and, in your case, is likely accurate. There's no question it can be an enhancement to creative, imaginative thought, as it embraces the fantastical. Fantasizers make for terrific artists, if they have the capacity to be organized and motivated. But many suffer from depression. Fortunately, you show no signs of bipolarity or depression."

"So how bad is my case?"

"That's the best news. The fMRI scans indicate your gray-matter loss is not extensive compared to that of patients with full-blown schizophrenia. You're not an advanced case. Perhaps it's the reason you've been able to be so productive, driven, and professionally successful."

"And so do I have an enhanced mind? Or a problem?"

"Both. Your artwork speaks for itself. Accelerated brain loss brings a rainbow of potential afflictions and disorders as well as other influences beyond the biological. Environment is a considerable factor in schizophrenia and its cousins."

Given all this fresh medical intel, imagery, and verbiage, I had a run of creative ideas for painting and poetry.

"But with proper treatment, the condition can be controlled and, in some cases, reversed," Dr. Wincott continued. "There are antipsychotic medications that suppress dopamine receptor activity and antibiotics that target the gene that regulates synaptic plasticity. These have been successful. There are others, too, risperidone and the like.

"Lastly, Rodrigo, I strongly urge you to stop any further recreational or prescription drug intake unrelated to your affliction. Amphetamines and cocaine can result in psychosis, and can bring on episodes and worsen symptoms. It's like fueling the fire."

Then the doctor told me I should remain in the hospital for a few more days. I lobbied for two weeks to give me more time to work, but he could grant me only one.

"If you feel you've hurt anyone, try to make amends. You've been under extreme pressures and coping with a lot. I'm sure they would understand."

And that's what I would do. Make amends. Eventually. But first I had a few more *Hospital* collages to complete.

43

SOHO 2.0

took the meds Dr. Wincott prescribed for my condition on a trial basis, to see how I would react and to assess their effectiveness. I did not want to be dumbed down or lobotomized. But the intake brought welcome results. I noticed I was less manic and hyperactive but just as focused. I considered that positive. My sleep was consistent and regular. Though I felt a fairly constant overall sadness, my moods were solid and did not show regression; I did not fall into snarky or sarcastic or bitter or caustic chasms, which was the type of negative mind-set I was trapped in when I left New York. I stayed optimistic and my creative juices were flowing, but they were more under control. I continued to write my poetry, which served as a novel, fresh outlet. Words meant more to me now, and I chose them carefully, whether written or spoken.

I was pretty much blockaded from the unified universe, however. I wasn't inviting dialogues from other dimensions. And whether my otherworldly interactions had been sleeping dreams or waking fantasies, now they were not coming through at all, at any time. And that meant one thing. I missed Carlotta. Immensely.

I invited my New York colleagues to see me individually. One by one. I spoke to Rafaela first. I was pretty sure Julia had informed her what I had said about her in Madrid, though I didn't know for sure; I didn't ask. But Rafaela was cool, she had taken everything in stride. It appeared she had a new boyfriend, which I considered a plus. She wouldn't have to monitor me as she had in the past; I needed to handle things on my own, and I was definitely getting better at it.

I saw Jean Paul, too. I apologized to him for my unprofessional behavior. Naturally, he inquired about my new works, but I was at best noncommittal. He had seen some digital images snapped and sent by Julia before she spotted me passed out beside my "poet-tree" in the grass. Jean Paul was pretty keen on the works—rather ecstatic—likening them to Francisco Goya during his dark period. He still had the show lined up in Paris that he had been pressing me about around the time of Art Basel—if I cared to be involved. The show was to be at the Centre Georges Pompidou, no less. But my contract with Jean Paul as my exclusive representative and dealer had run out—a fact he seemed to have forgotten—which meant that I didn't need to report to him on any new stuff. I was free. I didn't bring that up, however.

I also met with Alan Steinberg, my attorney. He was gentlemanly but no less strategic. I authorized him to cover any damages to the house in Ronda. I kept him on board. Legal was a necessary part of one's life and commerce (if there was to be any) in any metropolis, as lamentable a notion as it was.

ALMOST THREE WEEKS TO THE DAY after I was admitted to the hospital, I returned to my apartment. The first move to my new hands-on approach was organizing the delivery of *The Unified Universe* series from the Brooklyn warehouse to my studio in SoHo, and I oversaw its arrival and took inventory. As I X-Acto–knifed away the bubble wrap, I was proud of what I saw. Some of the canvases I'd even forgotten, as I had painted them while on a twenty-four-hour tear. Others I could never forget, nor the experiences that accompanied them.

If the truth be known, *The Universe* did talk to me. The individual portraits, the wheres and whens; I could hear the conversations as if they'd been yesterday. I wondered what Akira was up to. And how Heriberto was doing. And Desideria. And Ana Paola. And Dr. Abreu. And Sebastian and Salvatore and Giuliana. You see, I still believed in them. Whether friends, figments, phantoms, or fantasies—they lived. Perhaps in their own space and time. But definitely inside me. And they would forever. In this way, I was a believer.

And, of course, Carlotta.

Through my numerous sessions and interactions with Dr. Wincott and his team, it had been ingrained in me to let thoughts of this alternative nature pass, because they might not be healthy. Inviting the so-called otherworldly paracosm to inhabit my consciousness could be at the risk of my health. I didn't know if that was the case, but clearly, I didn't have all the answers. I had never been able to explain or validate my unified universe. It was like astrology, or religion, or ESP, or UFOs, or the paranormal: some inexplicable ethereal design from the cosmos that could not be scientifically proved. So I let those meditations come and go like memories from childhood. I gave them glances and half-smiles, and then I moved on. Because life for me was in the here and now, and I was operating in one gear—forward.

As for Carlotta, I couldn't *not* think about her, because my freshly reformed mind-set and overhauled psychologies—philosophical orientation; spiritual enlightenment; choosing to live with dignity, nobility, integrity, and generosity of spirit—had all been adopted and honed in partnership with her. Whatever she was. Wherever she was. Though there may not have been any scientific proof, there was proof for me.

I was my own proof. I had positively and unequivocally evolved. I was a better person due in no small measure to her.

But the mood swings were absent, as were the dream-world fantasies and hallucinations, recreational-intake binges, and other self-destructive habits.

And what did I replace this paracosm with?

My imagination. Which always was a constant in these two worlds, but was now refreshed and perhaps improved. And alone in my studio, I continued to charge hard.

As I unwrapped and upturned the last box from the warehouse, a curious thing took place. Something slipped from the box and onto the floor. It was a piece of white cloth. With a sheen. I lifted and inspected it. On the reverse side, I discovered the two fiery red lipstick smacks stacked one over the other. I spun the napkin a quarter-turn to arrange the stamps vertically. And then I saw the butterfly.

I decided against collaging the napkin into the *Butterfly Triptych* and quickly stuffed it back in the box. It was late, and I wouldn't let my wandering mind play unhealthy tricks on my refurbished, innocent, and wide-eyed new imagination.

But the episode was still on my mind the next day. So I called Dr. Wincott. He explained to me that I had without a doubt received the napkin somehow in my travels and fantasized about it, introducing and imposing it upon the detailed image systems of my paracosm while at the same time misconstruing its true origin. That seemed palatable to me. And that is pretty much how I related to all of those memories that had given birth to *The Unified Universe*: I had invented a world to create a world, and it had resulted in perhaps the greatest works of my career. Not even perhaps. They were the finest representations of what I could accomplish with paint and canvas. I had no outlet for them; I still wasn't putting them up for sale. I didn't need to. I remained content doing things for myself without any thought of a marketplace. That redrawn attitude had been liberating, and it had contributed to the enhanced qualitative aspects of my new life.

My personal renaissance wasn't all about the work. The creative rebirth was fulfilling, but it was more about making me a more aware, more evolved being. Therefore, I had no regrets about the messy, chaotic nature of how I'd undergone the reformation, but I considered it all a part of my evolution. Because this was the kind of psychological overhaul I'd needed.

My soul had been crying out for change, and I had listened to it at the biological, molecular level. Given my affliction, this was how my survivalist mind had made it happen for me, with fantasy and invented worlds, and poignant, life-altering dream-world interactions. This was my journey, and it had been necessary for me to get to the next level of understanding. I was proud of myself for having endured such a challenging albeit enlightening period, and coming out the other end relatively unscathed and undamaged. I saw my fresh orientation as a solid foundation upon which I could build. And for the first time in a very long time, I liked who I was once more.

44

THE NEW MASTER OF
ARTS AND LETTERS

developed a new routine in the studio. Not only did I continue to produce works from my refreshed and enlightened perspective, but I also kept a journal and continued to write poetry. In addition, I became somewhat of an academic. I began to read texts of all sorts, scientific as well as spiritual. I read Freud's *The Interpretation of Dreams.* I read Dr. Wincott's medical papers and those of other leading doctors in the field of neuroscience, not just on my disorder but on all related afflictions. I read the Bible and studied the tenets of other religions, including Buddhism, Hinduism, Islam, and Native American beliefs. I became a student of science and religion in my own self-designed master's program. With the advice and written recommendation of Dr. Wincott, I was allowed to attend—without a grade or class credit—three courses in Columbia University's General Studies program: one in psychology, one in philosophy, and another in religion. I enjoyed going to school again immensely. I was determined

to become a maestro of arts and letters, which would then comple-
ment and inspire my painting.

One afternoon after class, I slipped into the men's room and used
the facilities in the bathroom stall. I was amazed by all the intellectual
graffiti scrawled on the walls. Most of it was vulgar, but funny-vulgar,
as there were some great brains uptown who interpreted life from
an expressively tangential, evocative, at times existential angle; and
though predominantly racy in nature, the attitudes explored had their
own intimately sophisticated albeit crude element. But there was one
quote I read that stood out, that was purely philosophical and unrelated to the erudite bathroom humor. And it had a profound effect on
me. It was written in pencil, and it said:

We are not human beings having a spiritual experience.
We are spiritual beings having a human experience.

—Pierre Teilhard de Chardin

With my own hand, I sketched a flower on either side of the
quote as I conceived of a new *Bathroom Stall Walls* graffiti-art series.
I noted, however, the prized quotation in my journal and learned later
that Chardin was a Christian mystic of sorts. This led me to read
books on contemporary spirituality, and that brought me to an inde-
pendent study of those philosophers who preceded the moderns and
had given rise to their teachings.

My academic pursuits added a new dimension to my life, and I
found not only the educational value in them; I also found being aware
of these treatises of science and religion to be fundamentally empower-
ing. I had a much more enlightened but also functional grip on things,
on the planet we inhabit, and I felt myself to be grounded like never
before. Knowledge *was* power, and it was a tremendous epiphany. I
was standing tall and erect, and my feet were planted on the earth,
moving forward inch by inch, stride by stride, and I was consciously

feeling like I was in step with, and part of, what most consider the universe, and ready for whatever it held in store for me—and I it.

I had held off from engaging socially since my release from the hospital. But given my fresh orientation to the planet, one day I realized that I should not be living such an isolated life. I had needed time to strengthen myself and fill the shoes of the new me, but now I felt equipped and fortified, mentally and physically. When Rafaela asked me if she could have an engagement party at my apartment with her boyfriend, Tomas, and a group of friends, I gave her the overwhelming okay. The party was scheduled for the following weekend.

It made me consider previous friendships, and I began to seek out former social acquaintances. I asked them to lunch individually. I'm speaking of Tex and The Raven and Rachel, my PR gal. I even tracked down Akira and met her out in Brooklyn. To each of them I apologized for my behavior and let them know of my journey as I saw it and where it had taken me. I knew they were on their own journeys and not necessarily even interested in mine. But I felt it my duty to at least let them know of someone in their lives who had taken such a path and was experiencing its rewards. I invited them all to Rafaela's engagement party as well.

As with many Manhattan parties, and especially with someone of my previous reputation for revelry, about three times as many people attended the soiree as were invited. That was okay, as I felt it would be uplifting and more festive for Rafaela and Tomas. I had made life difficult for her in many ways for a very long time, and I hoped to be there for her now as she had been there for me.

As guests streamed in, I was greeted like a long-lost pal. To do my part, I tended bar, I took coats, I passed around hors d'oeuvres, and I dumped ashtrays. Not because I was cutting back on services but because I was finding delight in the codes of decorum. The simple pleasures were appealing to me, and I was all too happy to leave my celebrity status at the door. My own door. And I was allowing my dedicated Alfonso to enjoy himself more as a family member than a butler.

Though I'd given up habitual drinking, I enjoyed the occasional glass of champagne, and I shared one with the lovely Akira when she arrived. She was no longer working at the illicit subterranean den; nor was she still seeing its proprietor. She was hoping to create her own Asian-couture fashion line. I was trying to explain to her what I had been studying, and what I had learned about soulmates, and what I had found with Carlotta.

"Wouldn't you like to find that, a real soul that matches yours, that you could be with forever? That you could find and re-find, perhaps every earthly life cycle? Many years from now, when your terrestrial body passes, your soul will remain. And it will seek out your chosen one again and again and again. It won't be this same body; it will be housed in another, as your soulmate's will be, too. I've come to believe that. Maybe this is too trippy or too much to take in. But wouldn't we all like to find that type of millennial partner for eternity? A love that is transcendent. That transcends space and time and this very singular Planet Earth existence?"

Just then I peered into the dining room and saw about twenty people who were seated, laughing and carrying on. Most of them were wearing sunglasses. I saw The Raven and Tex, too, and when Tex spotted me angled their way, he piped, "Hey, Rodrigo! We're having a glass-off!" and the throng belched raucously. They were competing as to who had the most stylish sunglasses.

Akira asked me if she could see the *Asian Angel* portraits I'd made of her, and after careful consideration, I saw no reason why not. As an engagement gift to Rafaela, I made the completely spontaneous decision to open the previously locked and off-limits studio doors to everyone.

The fact is, I wasn't feeling exclusionary anymore. I no longer needed secrecy. I was listening to my inner voice again, and it was telling me to stop closing down, shutting off, even hiding; rather, it was telling me to move forward, open up, expand, and most important—

share. Sharing was a form of love. In the same way I'd tried to extend love to Akira with our recent conversation, I hoped to extend it to others. Sharing my work was one way to do this; given the humblest of intentions, it was an act of generosity of spirit—and love.

The art reflected my character, too, as that of someone who had endured innumerable challenges and come through them, a survivor. And that effort alone should be acknowledged. Therefore, the series, whatever its artistic merits might be, should be considered a triumph—of the human spirit and will. No doubt my inner voice was an amalgam of the spiritual ideas I'd absorbed, from my Eagle and Carlotta's Panther, to Desideria's Butterfly and Ana Paola's Hummingbird, right up to the recent academic studies and new teachings I'd been immersed in.

I contemplated my soulmate once again, as well as the process of leaping forth and embracing the unknown. Not because I was trying to engage in that other world but because the feelings were valid and significant—and they applied here. I was well aware that my inner voice reflected this fresh knowledge and awareness. And in that context, restriction, imperviousness, and restraint could no longer be tolerated.

45

THE UNVEILING

The Unified Universe, with all its ancillary installments, was received with gasps and "ahh's." There was not enough wall space for the entire series, but I received an overwhelmingly positive response to what was hanging. I was rather taken aback by it all, I guess because I'd been living with it all these months, and the novelty had somewhat dissipated. With art, you never know how any one person will respond, and hearing each person's favorable appraisals of my work was incredible. It appeared that my *duende,* reflected in the pieces, was—in the poet Lorca's terms—"corkscrewing" into the souls of the small audience.

Conversation was lively and animated and went on for a couple of hours. I recognized that the party titans Tex and The Raven, even Jean Paul, were disappearing sporadically to indulge in their secretive amphetamine intake. Tex babbled offers in my ears for any of the works, repeatedly trailed by "If you ever want to sell . . ."

I just smiled and thanked him for the support.

After everyone had been able to take in most of *The Unified Universe*, Akira asked me about the rectangular construction of four silver walls that stood in the corner of the room. I told her it was a new project, and once again I figured, *Why not?* So I allowed them all a glimpse of *Bathroom Stall Walls*. The interior of *Walls* was decorated graffiti-style in international handwritings and cursives with select phrases, poetry excerpts, quotations I enjoyed, nude drawings, semi-erotic designs, and choice erudite vulgarities. In the middle was a toilet seat with a standing urinal opposite, while collaged into the walls were urinal-cleaning cakes, rolls of tissue, hand soaps, and towelettes. There was even a hand dryer inset on one wall.

When the flock left the silver *Stall Walls,* I was left alone with Jean Paul. He embraced me fully with a warm hug and congratulated me once more on the new body of work.

"You want a bump?" he added, and apologized soon after.

I pondered it momentarily and declined. He was about to slip out of *The Stall,* and against my better judgment, I held him back. I asked him to close the door. And I gave him the nod.

I took a few whiffs off my hand and a few more.

I figured I'd been well behaved for so long and had been so true and dutiful to myself that I deserved a little dopamine rush as a reward.

I felt instantly energized and intake-inspired as we left *Stall Walls* and joined the others at the studio couches and chairs. Akira sat beside me, Jean Paul sat opposite, and Tex and The Raven came and went as we engaged in lively yeyo-fortified dialogues. We covered the history of art, modern art, the art business, other artists—the conversation went on and on. I even delineated in detail to Jean Paul what I had learned about my condition from Dr. Wincott. And then I showed him the new canvases based upon the Warholian brain-image scans, which were stacked and hidden in the corner. Jean Paul and I had more bumps while we were apart from the group, and I felt somewhat liberated to be able to have a solitary blowout after all this time.

"Just brilliant, Rodrigo, *totalement.* The range of your new work is extraordinary. And in that context, there is someone I would like to mention here. The great Francisco—"

"Goya?"

"Yes," he said. "And you, as a fellow Spaniard, probably know more on this subject—on every subject," he added self-deprecatingly, "than me. But Goya's illness lent itself to perhaps the freest, most significant, and enduring of his works. Ask Manet or Picasso. Or Bacon. For this reason, he is widely considered the father of modern art. There are many *hypothèses* as to his illness and consequent madness. But it has been best broken down to two causes. Syphilis treatments. And lead poisoning. *Les lettres* imply this. Syphilis was widespread, and the treatment for syphilis at the time was a mercury ointment. But with prolonged use, it caused lesions on the central nervous system that led to neurological disorders. Anxiety, tremors, dizziness, tinnitus, depression. Depression does not affect you, Rodrigo—"

"No, I'm a happy boy, happy, happy, happy—" I said on the bounce.

"In addition, the mercury intoxication was enhanced by the paints Goya used. There was mercury in the cinnabar used to make the color red. And the lead content in the white and yellow oils was substantial. It seeped into the skin through the hands and splattered clothes. This was seen in Goya's paint bills, all the whites, yellows, and reds he bought in great quantity. I am not a doctor but a student of art. However, I learned the metals would accumulate, causing changes in the circulation and enzyme systems, and this may have brought on the hallucinations, delirium, various psychopathological states, depression, and dementia. This chronic mercury and lead intoxication is likely the cause of his change from the realism of his early works to the morbid fascinations later—horrendous, fantastical images, nightmarish scenes, monstrous characters, ghoulish faces, the very dramatic."

I pulled from memory the exquisite vision of Carlotta wearing her *Damas Goyesca* dress. I let it go, like a memory of scoring a goal in a sandlot soccer game in my youth.

"If you compare the *Meadow of San Isidro*," I explained, "to the *Pilgrimage*, completed thirty years later—basically the same scene— you see the difference. One is festive and full of joy; the second is horrific, with mouths agape, white eye sockets or eyes spinning back, and faces like horror masks."

"Precisely. There were two distinct periods, before and after his illness. Before there is joy and light, and after it's horror, monsters, witches, and ghosts. This would explain the hauntingly magnificent quality of the *Black Paintings*. But basically, when he was free to paint outside the royal court, he was free of restrictions. And once he achieved his independence, he could delve into his nightmarish dreams, fantasies, and all the dark forms and themes. But it was the onset of these neurological conditions that helped produce his boldest, most imaginative work, just as it was for you, Rodrigo. His was due to metal intoxications, and yours was—"

"Just intoxication—drugs and alcohol."

"No, but as you said, your condition may have been with you since your teens. But we all can see the same fascination with dreams, nightmares, perhaps fantasies. And I say this to you, not disrespectfully—*félicitations*—you have seized our imaginations. The work is significant, bold, and visionary. *Un triomphe véritable. Magnifique.*"

The small group erupted in applause.

"Well, *merci, monsieur*. And *gracias*," I said. Then I added, "So— Jean Paul—when is that show in Paris?"

That incited the most rapturous applause and cheers of the night.

"As Gaël Monfils would say—*allez!*"

"And the great Carlos Nadal—*vamos!*"

More hoots and hollers.

My thoughts immediately conjured H. L. Mencken, who said, "No one ever went broke underestimating the intelligence of the American public." I quickly transposed that to "No one ever went broke overestimating the ego of an artist."

Paris. *À bientôt!*

My last maneuver of the evening, once everyone else had gone home, was to have Alfonso help me load one of the *Asian Angel* portraits into Akira's car. She was ecstatic: "Thank you, Rodrigo."

"No! Thank *you*, beautiful angel. Without what you did for me, there would be no show."

When I went to bed, I had a profound sense of relief. I no longer feared fantasizing about Carlotta in some sort of unhealthy paracosm. Because it wasn't fantasy.

I knew now she was always with me.

46

PARTNER OF INTIMACY / PARIS, *JE T'AIME*

For the next month, Rafaela and I prepared for the Paris show, and I oversaw everything from packing to loading to shipping. I was a little more outgoing and even invited numerous friends to go to Europe for the show. I indulged in a few evenings of revelry as well, with smatterings of alcohol and light intake. I was pretty much back to my same old self—without the same old self.

I flew over early with Rafaela and checked in to my room at the Hôtel Costes about a week before the event. I went to see the space allotted at the Centre Georges Pompidou and found it to be impressive. I chose to make the show decidedly Spanish-themed, including the drinks and food.

I wanted some Paris time for myself. I had fond memories of the time when I had an apartment on Rue Dauphine in the Sixth, close to the Pont Neuf. I took strolls in my former neighborhood, on Boulevard Saint-Germain, in the Luxembourg Gardens, and along the

Seine. Across the river, I paid a visit to my old friends the gargoyles atop Notre Dame. I walked along the river and up Avenue George V to the Champs. Reacquainting myself with Paris was like seeing an old girlfriend with whom you never broke up; you just floated along in each other's consciousness through the years and back, hoping for a reunion. Those days prior to the show were our reunion, and we held hands and kissed cheeks a lot.

I visited the Musée de l'Orangerie to say hi to some old friends. Monet's water lilies dominate l'Orangerie, but I remembered reading that the museum had once mounted a temporary exhibition of some of van Gogh's works. I am especially fond of Vincent's irises, the periwinkle of which I used often in my own paintings—and in the trim for the *Goyesca* dress I had designed for Carlotta. Did mercury and lead make him go mad-brilliant, too, like Goya? I wondered.

I checked out some newer galleries, too, but was disappointed by the show art. The wall art. The "I like what you did but I have this crazy-big wall to fill, so stretch it and supersize it, even if you have to make potato heads, and we have a deal, you know?" art-by-the-meter art.

Rafaela and I shared several meals together at Chez Dave, Chez l'Ami Louis, and La Coupole. We went over logistics of the show. She was inquiring again as to price points for the works, something I was unconcerned with and was happy to avoid. My participation was about sharing, not profiteering.

On the morning of the show, I was beset with annoyances. They came from Alan Steinberg, my attorney. First of all, Jean Paul had sent over a contract for representation weeks before, and I still hadn't signed it. Something—my inner voice, the gut feeling that you have to listen to—had told me not to do so. I was not trying to be duplicitous or dishonest with Jean Paul, but something did not sit right with the situation, and I couldn't quite put my finger on it.

Second, The Raven had contacted Alan; he'd been detained at Charles de Gaulle in possession of Molly and Adderall. He had claimed they were for me, and he wanted me to bail him out. I could not get wrapped up in other people's misguided paths, sufferings, or failures at this point. The Raven would have to learn to turn his life around the hard way. Or not. But I could not intervene in his arrest.

In the early afternoon when I was still in bed resting, the concierge buzzed to say that a package had been brought for me, and I needed to come down to sign for it. I threw on some sweats and headed down. I stepped into the lobby and was told to go on back to the small, dimly lit bar. When I walked in, I saw the package resting on the top of the bar; a messenger wearing a hoodie was standing next to it, facing away from me.

"Is that package for me?"

The messenger spun around. I thought I was seeing a ghost. Her smile was bright, the hood fell away from her hair, and I was looking at a figure I'd given so much thought to, in my life and in my art. The thick ocean-boosted tresses, the dolce vita exquisite face, the Mediterranean skin, and the smoldering Spanish eyes. With a name potent enough to support it all. *Desideria.*

Was I dreaming? Had I slipped into the paracosm once again? Had the recent intake inflamed my affliction? After all, I had been in bed, floating in and out all day.

"Hello, Rodrigo."

"Desideria," I said woodenly.

"You look shocked."

"I . . . am . . ."

"Don't be frightened. I tried to call you, but, well, when I could not reach you, I thought maybe it could be a nice surprise."

I hesitated again. "It is."

"Forgive me. I should have gotten ahold of you. Are you okay?"

"I must say, I'm . . . confused."

"How so? You've made progress, no?"

"I have? What—? I'm not really sure of . . ."

"Of what? . . . You're crying." She squeezed my hand. "It's okay."
"Is it really you?"

"*Sí.* It really is. Let's sit down and talk. Shall we?"

I invited her upstairs, and we sat next to each other on the couch in the living room of my suite. I explained to her all I'd been through personally, medically, and psychologically. I even confessed to her that I wasn't sure if I was dreaming now or not.

"No, Rodrigo. You're not dreaming. And Ana Paola sends her love."

"But the people in New York had convinced me that everything in Valldemossa—you, Ana Paola—were all a part of this detailed phony world that I had invented. I have a fantasy disorder and . . ."

"We know."

"You do?"

"We have been in contact with Dr. Wincott."

"Why didn't—?"

"We decided it would be better to wait. Because you were not well when we met, and you were making progress under his care, so we didn't want you to be set back psychologically in any way."

"You mean—it all really happened?"

She nodded. "Many times I wanted to communicate with you, as a friend who cared for you . . . but I also had a professional obligation, and that took precedence."

"But the photos—when I checked the camera, they weren't there."

"I know. I removed and replaced the memory card. Not because I feared you would do anything with them beyond your work, but you never know—if they got into the wrong hands—and these days, well . . . it could be embarrassing, professionally speaking."

"Okay. But after the photos disappeared, I wasn't even sure I went to Valldemossa at all." I was stunned. "*Dios mío* . . ." I struggled for words. "But if that all happened, and you are real, why did the fMRIs you took show no problems?"

She eyed me levelly. "They did. And Dr. Abreu did inform you about it. Apparently, you redesigned what he said to reflect what you wanted to hear, which is somewhat common in these cases."

"I rejected the real diagnosis and superimposed a false negative?"

"Yes, to support your fantasy. To further validate the world you had created and deny any science that challenged it."

"What about the image scans you gave me, then? I thought I had collaged them into the *Brain* series portraits—"

"I forgot to give them to you. I'm so sorry. And your creative inspiration blended it into the fantasy."

"What about the napkin with the lipstick butterfly?"

"Signed by me in Jungle Red, at dinner." She smiled, of course. "I wasn't sure if you got that."

"*Mariposa*—Butterfly—you're coming to the show, no?"

"I'm afraid I cannot, regretfully. I have to get back to Valldemossa, to the hospital."

Desideria rose then and asked me to open the box she had brought.

I tore away the flaps and found within, carefully encased in newspaper and bubble wrap, a sculpture. A beautiful rendition of an eighteenth-century ship.

"*Maestro,*" I said, and shivers released through my arms and up my spine.

"He's still with us, doing well enough. Working a lot. Alzheimer's is degenerative. But he has been able to impose his fantasy on his work. He asked me to give this to the 'sailor' whom he had 'sent to the brig.'"

"So he never knew it was me."

"We think he did. Otherwise he wouldn't have asked me to give it to you. He's never made such a request before. You were special to him."

"*Heriberto . . .*" I whispered aloud.

I extended my hand to clasp hers. I asked her how she was doing. She told me she was starting to take on another life. As a painter. She was working from sketches. Then using oils. She was going to have a little show in Deià. She even showed me a few accomplished images on her phone.

"Butterfly," I said.

"*Gracias,* Rodrigo. Your encouragement was all I needed. And you?"

"I'm not impatient. I'm developing me."

"A new cycle?"

"*Sí.* And that's enough for now."

I could have broken down right then. But I held down the rising emotions. "How much time do you have?" I asked.

"My flight is in three hours."

"*Vamos!* Let's go!"

"*Dónde?*"

We dashed down Rue de Rivoli, and within ten minutes, we were at the Pompidou Center. We passed through security and were given access to my designated show area of the huge space. The crew was setting up still, finalizing all preparations for food, beverages, and decor.

Desideria praised the work and marveled at the pieces dedicated to our day in Mallorca. We paused at length before one in particular called *Señorita Butterfly.* She avowed it was her favorite. I located some masking tape and wrote "Reserved" on each one of the Mallorca series; then I removed the *Señorita* from the wall. An attendant noticed and alerted one of Jean Paul's on-site employees, who questioned me with concern. I told him the piece's inclusion in the show was a mistake and that the Mallorca series was to be sent to the hospital in Valldemossa. In the back, away from the show area, I rewrapped the *Señorita* in plastic and encased it in one of the packing boxes. I sealed it and carried it out the back alley to the street. I instructed Desideria to give it to the airline for special handling. She was exultant.

Outside on the curb, we kissed each other's cheeks, genuine kisses that said everything about everything.

"Thank you for bringing Heriberto's ship."

"As much as anything, Rodrigo, I came to congratulate you. And to let you know there are people who care, even in the littlest corners of the planet. And I'm one of them."

We embraced again.

"Keep soaring, Rodrigo."

"Bye, Butterfly."

I put her in a cab along with the painting, and they were two butterflies in flight. I think I smiled, too.

47

SHOW, SHARE, AND TELL

There were still a couple of hours until the show. After I put Desideria and the painting in the taxi, I took a cab to La Défense to see Miró's enormous sculpture *Deux Personnages Fantastiques,* and I sat in the garden for a while to get a taste of home. Texts were flurrying in to my phone, the usual suspects with their usual concerns. But I had my own plan to follow. I cabbed back to the Place des Vosges, one of my favorite squares in the city. Victor Hugo's house was there, but I sat on the benches and let the antiquity seep into my senses. Last, I marched up to Montmartre to get a good view of the city, of the planet, from the steps and terraces of the Sacré-Coeur.

I decided to skip the show altogether, but then I received a text from Julia, who had flown in from California. I was touched that she had come, and I could not let her down. There was poetry and value in her appearance as well. I bought a spiral and began writing, first a poem called "Sailing," inspired by, once again, Heriberto. I looked up to him more than ever now.

I gave long and celebratory thought to my days as a young boy, clutching protectively his little red box of prized coins, hoping to become an artist. And the rawness of a small creative flame that had been ignited, yet remained undisciplined, undeveloped, idealist, and pure. I'd possessed a talent, perhaps, and Heriberto had fed me the nutrients to allow it to grow. He was an example to admire, and it had taken me such a long time, such a circuitous path through minefields of vanity, self-absorption, and ego, to realize it. What he stood for was—and had always been—a long way from Art Basel. But with all my misguided instant gratification, I had forgotten how lucky I was that he had been there to guide me in the early days.

Finally trimmed of all that excess, I had the conscious feeling of soaring high in the clouds with all the other birds in flight as I floated weightlessly from Montmartre to the Pompidou Center.

I ARRIVED AROUND SEVEN-THIRTY, forty-five minutes late for the show. Jean Paul, Alan, Rafaela, and Julia were already there, and I was besieged by the obsequious fawning of the Western art world and its minions.

"*Bravo!*"

"*We love your* Universe*!*"

"*Génial!*"

Rafaela helped fend off the crashing blandishments, but there was no ducking Jean Paul.

"Rodrigo? What are you doing? You removed one work and reserved another eighteen. If I counted correctly."

"You counted incorrectly. I've reserved all of them."

"*Comment?* For whom?"

"I have a list."

"Rodrigo, this is not our deal."

"We don't have a deal."

"All the effort I have put into this show and we have no deal?"

"This is not a Jean Paul show."

"Then what is it?"

"It's a Rodrigo Concepción sharing."

"I'm not involved in sharings. We have—"

"With respect to me, that's exactly what you have dedicated your time to. And you will be compensated for it."

"Je suis désolé, but that is not my business, time compensation."

"You're not in your business, you're in mine. Alternatively stated, your business is your business, not mine."

"We have a verbal commitment."

"Jean Paul, I may be a foolish artist, but I'm not a fool."

Just then Alan spoke up. "Rodrigo. You—"

"Alan—*por favor*—do not speak of issues bound by our attorney-client privilege. You are my attorney until you are not. I will permit you one answer for all to hear. Do I have a signed deal with Jean Paul or not?"

"No. Your contract ended two months ago." Alan turned to Jean Paul and shrugged. "You're entitled to a commission for the gallery rental, of course."

Jean Paul's face folded, his chest sank, and he recoiled to reassess. Soon enough he placed his paw on my shoulder to take me aside as the flock of fawners continued to look on. At that moment Julia approached us. Then Rafaela. I greeted them as warmly as possible.

"Excuse us one second—" Jean Paul barked at them.

"No, please remain," I countered. "They have as much right to this discussion as you do."

"Look, I know you've been through a lot," he said. "And this is a lot to take in. A lot of eyes. Rumors. A lot of press. The stakes are big . . ."

"This is nothing. I could do it in my sleep. And I have. Only it's a nightmare. Which I will not give credence to."

"What are you saying?"

I turned away to avoid the confrontation, but I just couldn't. I spun back around. "Do you know what art is?"

"I believe I do."

"What it means? What it represents? Do you?"

"Yes, I do. And I've been doing a great job representing your art for many years. How many millions of dollars have I made you in the last ten years? A hundred million? One-twenty?"

"Since when is art purely about our bank balances or luxury galleries on Twenty-fifth and Tenth, or Bond Street? And champagne bids in multimillion-dollar auction-house salons—buying, buying, buying—for people who don't have a clue about valuations?"

"Rodrigo, *s'il te plaît*—"

"Ridiculous numbers that only make sense to greedy dealers—as they select some buffoon, often without an artistic bone in his body, then coronate him as the chosen one, inventing a false market, manufacturing the market, cornering the market, pushing the market, manipulating the market. You're a stockbroker. With inside information. With the taste of a hot dog salesman. Add a little ketchup, some sauerkraut, some spicy brown, and shove it down some fat cat's throat. You think anyone who can boil a sausage has 'potential' and 'promise,' the golden buzzwords of greed. In a golden greedy world. *Potential* for *you*. *Promise* for *you* and *your* bank balance. You know derivative. You know imitative. Infertility. You're the Anti-Innovator. You make alliances. Corporate employees. Vehicles. Not artists. And cultivate a garden of weeds."

"Talk about biting the hand that feeds you—"

"You don't feed me. I feed myself. And I feed you! And your kids! And their college tuitions!"

"And how did that happen?"

"Because *I* allowed *you* to handle some things. As opposed to anyone in this room who could have made the same phone calls."

"Let's cool it, guys," Rafaela interjected. And I saw Julia pull her back.

"Heriberto was right all along—"

"Who's Heriberto?"

"Exactly! Someone who shunned your limelight. And stayed true to his faith, his art, and his principles. He may be lesser known, but he's a giant in neon to those who crossed his path. He could always look in the mirror and know he lived an honorable and dignified life."

"He's lost it, Rafaela. What are we going to do? We have a verbal agreement—"

"Listen to what he's saying!" cried Julia.

"Jean Paul, whatever happened to visionary creation? Bold expression? Artistic statements? Innovation? Originality? Imagination? Who decided it should be all about profit and showing off like some sort of human freak show? 'Ladies and gentlemen, here is the bearded lady dancing on a horse, or the Siamese Twin Hobbits shot from a human cannon!' You're a talentless, uninspired, fast-food, flash-in-the-pan marketer—entertainer—in the unimaginative circus, the Cirque de Merde, that is the art world in the twenty-first century! *Vive le* Cirque de Merde*!*"

And then I stood up on a chair and raised my voice. "Welcome to the sharing—I am your host—but I'm afraid I can offer you only shame. And please share with me the same embarrassment and self-reproach. For our perversity. For our crude and tasteless intervention into something so transcendent and pure. A sacred profession that has forty thousand years of history, and we've treated it like an electro-rave party of dollars and euros while we all dance to our desperation, insecurity, lack of knowledge, understanding, love, and respect!

"Whatever happened to true art? And what happened to the true artist? Not some unimaginative slob body-snatched and trained like a dancing bear to line everyone else's pockets because he's shown 'promise' drawing stick figures and vomiting sidewalk pizzas against the wall!

"What happened to noble patrons? Worthy, dignified, and educated collectors? And curators with integrity? People who actually care about the work and its legacy and influence on future generations? Worthy of our children and history books? *Where the fuck* did all that pure sense of purpose, artistic merit, creative credibility, and *duende* go? Where's the outrage? *Let us pray—*

"Today, as you know, I am rich, I have fame. But in the quietest of moments, when I'm alone with myself and listen to the silent beating of my heart, I cannot conceive of having the audacity to call myself *an artist* in any meaningful historical context. Michelangelo, Botticelli, Leonardo, Vincent, Goya, Renoir, Monet, Bacon, Picasso—they were artists. I am only a marmite. A goldfish. A rhesus monkey. With a paintbrush. A cog in a corrupt system. A game manager. A technician. Which all means an artist, yes, but *con artist*—no better than the defrauding dealers, collectors, and curators. We are *all* con artists.

"I have processed the morally impoverished times and used them to my advantage to the best of my opportunistic, pastel-deceptive abilities, given the idiocy, soullessness, narcissism, self-aggrandizement, servility, perversion, and avarice of everyone around. I am a twenty-first-century artist in the twenty-first-century art world. And what does that mean, *en fin—*? Let me show you!"

I then dashed over to the *pata negra* table, where the thin ham slices were being carved off the black hoof, and I snatched the carving knife from the server and charged down the row of paintings and stabbed each one in the center, all the while proclaiming: "That means this is *shit! Shit! Shit! Shit! Shit! Shit! Shit! Shit!*"

One canvas after another I appraised in four letters and then physically attacked.

I heard the bootlickers gasping at my show, the real show, the authentic confession, as well as the most genuine expression of truth that my compromised nervous system could formulate at the time.

I was eight slashed canvases into my expression when the security guards wrestled the knife from my hands and me to the ground.

Everyone huddled over me, and when the guards finally turned me loose enough that I could stand up, I saw the imposing face of Tex, with his canary-yellow sunglasses, glaring stupefied at me.

"I never liked you, Tex, I just want you to know that. I despise everything you stand for!" It was rude, perhaps, to greet a transatlantic voyager this way, but it also had the intention and, I believe, the merit of being sincere. "But I'm liable, and I share the blame and the shame with you! *All of you!*"

As I heard mumblings that the *policiers* were on their way, I released my wrists from the security guards' anonymous clutches, and I turned to Rafaela.

"Rafaela *amor, muchas gracias* for your time and patience. Follow Julia's lead. Because when the lawyers start circling, she won't run. And you're not in any position to hold my ground. *Bueno?*"

"*Bueno.*"

I withdrew a sheet of paper from my jacket and turned back and handed it to Julia. She looked at me pitifully, her brow pinched, her expression etched with concern bordering on terror. So I whispered to her, "All is good, love. Perfect."

And I meant it. I could feel the sense of peace within and the smoothness of my face and firmness of my convictions. I was nonnegotiable.

As I spiraled around to flee, I caught the tears welled in her eyes, and I turned back. "Don't worry."

"I'm scared for you."

"Don't be. I'm the happiest I've ever been in my life." I kissed the tears from both her violet eyes.

"I love you," she said.

"I know. I've felt it all the way. *Gracias,* and may heaven's choicest blessings be showered upon you for that and the elevated soul you are—"

Then I sidestepped quickly and away toward the back. Instead of running, I made my departure seem controlled—in case the police arrived before I could escape, I didn't want to call attention to myself. But as soon as I was out of sight, I tore down the corridor, out the back, and through the alley door. It was the same path I'd taken with the Mallorcan Butterfly earlier, before I watched her nobly flutter off for all the world to see. In that way, my stage exit was well rehearsed.

48

LE JARDIN D'ÉDEN

When I was blocks away from the Pompidou Center, I slowed my gait. I decided against any type of hired car and took a relaxed promenade through the Tuileries Garden. It had gotten dark, so the colors of the flowers had faded to a muted gray, but the bouquets were still fragrant and, combined with the crisp early-evening air, made for delightful passage. I could depend on *les fleurs*. I knew by morning they would reclaim their resplendence, and their colors would be popping for all to see. It was one of the better nature walks I could remember.

I arrived at the Hôtel Costes and passed by the bar. I ordered a bottle of rioja and took flight up the elevator. I was packing my bags when room service arrived with my Spanish red. When I opened the bottle, I contemplated the "corkscrew" and Lorca and *duende* fairies. I poured a generous amount into a wineglass and took intermittent sips while I finished packing.

I gave thought to my spiritual reawakenings and felt nothing but gratitude to the gods of all religions for guiding me on an ascendant path. I was Eagle, flying close to the heavens like never before, and in touch with the divine.

I wrapped myself in a robe from the garment closet and slipped into the bathroom to turn on the brass tap in the bathtub. As a searcher and seeker, I had been not only saved; I had also found what I was looking for. I'd met my millennium soulmate, and I knew she was always there. There was nothing holding me from her any longer. I had love for all those who had shown me love and even for those who hadn't. I hoped for a similar transcendence for them, that they would be able to find the same completeness in their chosen terrestrial or spiritual lives. But there was nothing keeping me there, nothing left for me there, only the quotidian, more of the same. So why delay a superb and rejoicing reunion in the infinite?

I checked the water temperature, and at the appropriate blend of hot with cold, I slipped out of the robe and settled into the tub. I sipped on my wine from time to time and closed my eyes and let the warmth envelop me like a soothing blanket by a fire.

The cut was quick and sharp and painless. This was my plaza. This was my ring. I watched the fluid of noble bulls stream from my wound, and in it I saw all the colors, swirling, twirling, spreading, it was one color every color, the entire chromatic index reflected in it, in this most beautiful pool, the most amazing palette I'd ever witnessed. It was authentic and pure and good; it was everything and anything my commonplace and limited sensibilities could ever ask for.

And it was then I recited from memory the bit of the poem my friend Sebastian had read to us at dinner, the one his grandfather the matador had always carried folded in his pocket into the arena, and I saw my countryman Lorca's words come to life in white across the blazing pool: "'I want to sleep for half a second, a second, a minute, a century, but I want everyone to know that I'm still alive . . .'"

Respectfully, I wanted to add to that: *I am more than alive.*

As lights began to dim and sounds began to quiet, I felt all the mundane tensions pass from me and disappear.

I was transfixed by the swirling pool, my last canvas, as it were, but it was better than that, better than two dimensions, it had depth and promise, and it had all the dimensions, maybe four. I'd heard of a fourth dimension, perhaps my unified universe, but neither mattered. They were semantics at this point, and there was no time for petty earthly thoughts. I was on to bigger and better things.

Because I was coming. Coming back. To the world that had so gloriously presented itself to me. In my dreams, where everything was possible, as my mother had informed me in her own way so long ago. But my sleep had constituted my waking hours. And my world with Carlotta was as valid as any world ever proposed. It had come to me organically, from the firing of biological synapses, the functioning basis of all animal forms. It was alive because I was alive. Because in that vital and vivid world, I'd met my matching spirit, my cherished *amore,* who challenged me to be a better being and guided me on the path to enlightenment. I had evolved into my own living proof, and I was merely leaving behind a shell containing a thousand *gracias.*

As my body faded and its functions waned, I still absorbed the warmth. I was bathed in it and embraced by it, and I could feel the love all around me, and all the faces and all the places, and then they diminished, too, and dissolved before my eyes into a whiteness, a wide canvas spread out before me, a canvas without borders, a canvas to infinity.

But it was not long before the whiteness became filled with the colors and shapes and exquisite forms that I knew well, a Garden of Eden with lush blooms, flowers, jungle vines, sacred mountains and groves, waterfalls, creeks and streams, foliage forever, and all the animals of the kingdom trekking to splendiferous water holes—a paradise.

I could hear the crooner music, and smell the alberese soil, and taste the Sangiovese grape, and hear the rising voices of a Ballerini *pranzo* at noon in the distance, and touch her flesh, and we walked hand in hand to the far end of the vineyard, past corridors of denuded, harvested vines. And I was filled with such joy and unity and humility and harmony. She had taken her Panther leap and soared, and I had soared and leaped to meet her. And we came together in embrace and melted into each other.

I'd found my soulmate for all eternity.

It was more than any world could ever provide. More love than any universe could ever contain.

And I felt the love all the way home.

EPILOGUE

There are sounds. Slight traces of activity. I hear the faintest spike of laughter. A dog barks. I can hear the creaks of the floor softened by the carpet. Someone comes into the suite. Their steps are light and polite, seemingly so far off and yet so close. The smells are familiar, like those of old wood and plaster. I'm coming out of a slumber and see the high tin ceiling, and sunlight glimmering at the edges of the window shades. Death is so warm and inviting. You can actually still see things, too.

"Your paper, sir."

"Wha—?" I attempt to speak and am shocked that words are coming out.

"Crispy, as you like it."

"Alfonso?"

"Yes, Rodrigo."

I see him. He is there above me, holding the tray, the morning tray.

"But—"

"Everything okay?"

"No!"

I leap forward and up. I am not in any suite. It would appear I am in bed in the SoHo apartment. But how could that be?

"You have a visitor."

"What? Where am I?"

Alfonso laughs. "You are home, sir."

"It cannot be! What about my plans?"

"I don't know what you're referring to. But your visitor is waiting."

"Visitor?"

"A very special visitor," he says with a warm smile.

"Not now, no. I'm going back to sleep."

Clearly, I have passed through another channel, or portal, and I've got to go back. Alfonso exits the room, a room I want to get out of. I close my eyes and pray. For sleep. I have to find my way *back*. Moments later, there is a knock on the hellish door. Why is there a room and a door, even? I am still in the wrong dimension.

"Rodrigo?" I hear the voice say on the other side of the damn door.

It's the cruelest of jokes. I have been made a fool of.

But that can't be.

I rise from the bed and stumble to my feet. I walk over to the door. I'm going to step right through it and into the *proper* dimension, the one I have planned for, exactly where I am meant to be.

I open the door wide, and I think I gasp, but I'm not really sure. I'm overpowered with relief, and icy chills climb my spine.

She is standing there with sparkles in her emerald eyes, and she unleashes what could only be considered poetry from her Tuscan lips.

"*Sì*, Rodrigo."

"*Sí?*"

"Yes, I will marry you."

My chin shudders. I smile through the confusion. I am reminded now. Carlotta kisses the tears from my face. The gods of all religions have helped me achieve my dreams, and I am a very grateful man.

I did my best. I am home. *Bueno.* All is good.